PRAISE FOR
FARRAH NOORZAD
— AND THE —
RING OF FATE

"**Ingenious plot twists and astonishing action scenes.** I can't wait for readers to meet Farrah and her friends."

—A. F. STEADMAN, *NEW YORK TIMES* BESTSELLING AUTHOR OF
SKANDAR AND THE UNICORN THIEF

"A fast-paced dance among the spirits and creatures of Persian and Middle Eastern mythology, led by the curiosity and grit of a bright, brave girl. **You've never seen jinn like this, and you've never met a girl quite like Farrah Noorzad.**"

—KIYASH MONSEF, *NEW YORK TIMES* BESTSELLING AUTHOR OF
ONCE THERE WAS

"With **page-turning mysteries** you desperately want answered, and full of **wondrous magic** from the jinn world."

—GRACI KIM, *NEW YORK TIMES* BESTSELLING AUTHOR OF
THE LAST FALLEN STAR

"**Oh, how I've wanted this story for . . . maybe my whole life?** Deeba brings the fabled jinn crashing (on a cloud) straight into the modern world with blazing lightning bolts and sinister shadow monsters. Full of real heart and—at times—painful honesty. **So hang on to your cloud. You're in for a ride!**"

—SARWAT CHADDA, *NEW YORK TIMES* BESTSELLING AUTHOR OF
CITY OF THE PLAGUE GOD

"**A heartwarming story about the messiness of family [and] growing up.**"

—M. T. KHAN, AUTHOR OF *NURA AND THE IMMORTAL PALACE*

"Zargarpur highlights Persian mythology and Islamic lore via sharp narration and lively characters to cultivate **an epic adventure about family, identity, and self-discovery.**"

—*PUBLISHERS WEEKLY*

"Unfolds through fast-paced action with unexpected plot twists. . . . **An engaging read with an original and courageous young hero.**"

—*KIRKUS REVIEWS*

ALSO BY DEEBA ZARGARPUR

MIDDLE GRADE

Farrah Noorzad and the Ring of Fate

YOUNG ADULT

House of Yesterday

FARRAH NOORZAD

AND THE
REALM OF NIGHTMARES

BOOK 2

DEEBA ZARGARPUR

LABYRINTH ROAD | NEW YORK

Labyrinth Road
An imprint of Random House Children's Books
A division of Penguin Random House LLC
1745 Broadway, New York, NY 10019
penguinrandomhouse.com
rhcbooks.com

Editor: Liesa Abrams and Emily Shapiro
Cover Designer: Katrina Damkoehler
Interior Designer: Michelle Canoni
Copy Editor: Clare Perret
Managing Editor: Rebecca Vitkus
Production Manager: Natalia Dextre

Library of Congress Cataloging-in-Publication Data is available upon request.
ISBN 978-0-593-56445-5 (trade)—ISBN 978-0-593-56447-9 (ebook)

The text of this book is set in 11-point Scala Pro.

Manufactured in the United States of America
1st Printing

The authorized representative in the EU for product safety and compliance is
Penguin Random House Ireland, Morrison Chambers, 32 Nassau Street,
Dublin D02 YH68, Ireland, https://eu-contact.penguin.ie.

TO MY MADAR JAN FOR ALWAYS CHOOSING ME.

And to Arzu—always.

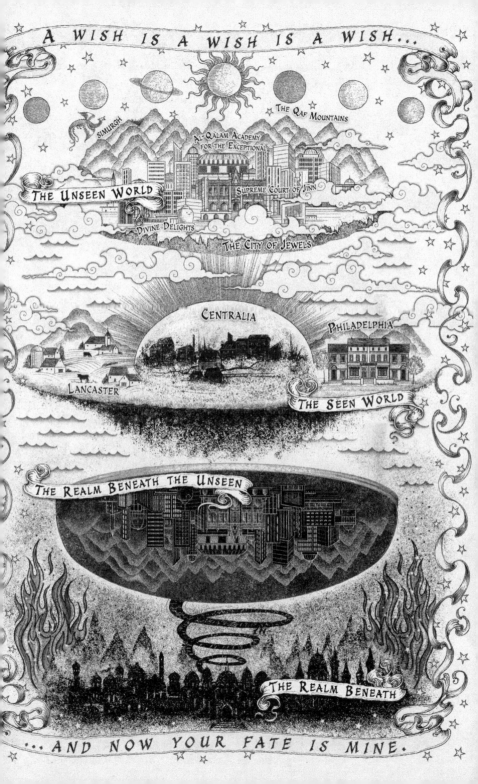

CHAPTER ONE

THE BEGINNING OF WHAT?

Every night, I fall into a nightmare.

We are back in the Realm Beneath the Unseen, and we are running out of time. The shadow jinn watch with their blinking ruby-red eyes while my half brother, Yaseen, and my friend Idris sprint through the golden gates and down a long, winding jeweled staircase.

It's the final-boss moment—the pause in time and space—where I will finally do the impossible: undo my wish on the cursed ring of fate and free my dad from within it.

Except . . .

I stop running when Idris yells "Now!" and Yaseen's spear slashes through the air, unleashing a huge bolt of lightning right at the army of shadow jinn in front of us.

They scatter like bowling pins.

"Take that, shadow puppets!" Yaseen laughs.

"Wait. Haven't we . . . ?" *Been here before?* I watch Yaseen charge ahead, going farther into the Realm Beneath. "Haven't we . . . ?" *Already done this?*

"Something wrong, Noorzad?" Idris jogs back when he notices I've stopped. His white hair is stuck to his cheeks and neck.

"I just . . ." Everything feels so fuzzy. "Need a sec."

"You've got to take it easy," Idris warns. "You're not indestructible anymore, remember?" Sweat drips from his chin.

"Remember . . ." I rub my face. What do I remember? A wish on a ring during a dark and stormy night. A ghostly boy with a cloud in a pen who flies to magical, floating jinn cities in the sky. Seven thrones and a ticking clock. A journey with my brother and my best friend across farms and realms unseen. A broken elephant pin and a power that glows from my palms . . .

. . . It slips like sand from my thoughts, but I hold on as tight as I can.

"I can see the bottom," Yaseen shouts from below. A glittering throne roars to life through the bright red flames. A small, worn ring glints atop it. Five gems glow.

"Get down, Yaseen," I yell just as the ground rumbles. "The sixth gem is about to glow!" We *have* been here before. I remember it now.

"Wait, what?" Yaseen hesitates, but it's too late.

The entire staircase shakes. I jump and roll out of the way, dodging a huge chunk of molten rubies before it crashes on my head.

Six jinn kings down, the exiled jinn king Azar's voice roars, *one to go.*

"No!" I slap the floor of the shaking staircase. "This isn't supposed to happen again!" I watch in horror as Yaseen stumbles and trips. His fingers wave through the air as he falls backward, plummeting to the ground. "We've already defeated you!"

We traveled through realms, both seen and unseen, fought countless shadow jinn, solved all Azar's riddles, and broke through every illusion. I made a deal with the forbidden fire jinn king, and I won. I undid my wish.

I saved my dad and the other jinn kings from the curse of the ring of fate. I saved everyone. And most importantly, I saved myself from disappearing into nothingness . . .

. . . Didn't I?

Did you? Azar's question slithers around me. *It's a shame you don't recall.*

"Not another riddle. My brain can't handle another!" I clutch my forehead because everything *hurts.* From my elbows to my knees to my bruised heart to my fingers and toes.

"Noorzad, you can't keep fighting like this." Idris kneels and holds my hands in his. His wide eyes stare into mine. They're so clear, I can see the fire around us reflect through them. "You've got to catch him."

"But we did catch him," I shout.

So why is Yaseen still falling?

Why is the ring still glowing?

Why are we still *here?*

You mean, why are you still here. Azar's voice buzzes in my ears.

I blink. Idris is gone. So are the staircase and the shadow jinn and Yaseen.

Somehow, I'm in front of Azar's golden throne. The cursed ring of fate is floating in the center. All seven gems glow, but there are seven chains now holding the ring to the throne.

"That's weird, I don't remember this happening," I mumble while taking a step closer to touch one chain that has an imperfect link. Little wisps of dark energy float around the chain until it covers my hand in a cold fog.

An endless age, the fog rumbles in my chest. *A fate defied.*

"Huh?" I try to wrestle away from the clouds that curl around my wrist, moving up my arm, but I can't. My eyes get heavy. The Realm Beneath goes blurry.

Without its roots. It trails up my elbow. *All things shall die.*

There's a loud crack as an impossible thing happens. A whirlwind of golden fire shoots out of the ring, along with Azar's gleeful laugh. He zips and zooms into the air. I can barely keep track of him. Everything in my head is so sludgy.

But should the end come rear its head. It trails up my neck and whispers in my ear. *There will be more than kingdoms dead.*

The cold fog is everywhere. It dances in front of me until it takes the shape of a shadow puppet. *My* shadow puppet.

"Help me," I try to say, but my mouth doesn't move.

My shadow jinn's red eyes never blink. Behind her, a

hazy mountain looms, engulfed in fire. She leans closer to me, places her cold hand on my cheek, and mouths, *Don't you know?* "*They will be—the beginning of the end.*"

"The end of what?" I want to say.

She dissolves back to fog without answering. The dark wraps its way up my chin, past my nose and eyes. Azar's mismatched gold and red eyes smile at me. They are the last thing I see before the light winks out.

It's time to wake up and find out, little one.

CHAPTER TWO

BACK TO REALITY

I wake up with a wad of gum and packing tape stuck to my face.

"Ugh, gross." I immediately rip it off—along with the little baby hairs on my cheek. "Argh, that hurts," I yelp, and hold my throbbing cheek. My reflection on my tablet shows a big red mark, the same spot where my cheek got slashed in Centralia.

I can't believe it's been three months since I traveled to the exiled jinn king Azar's realm to save my dad and the six other jinn kings from being stuck in a ring of fate for eternity (after I *accidentally* wished them there). I never thought saving my dad would mean giving up my invincibility to protect my best friend in the entire world, Arzu Ahmadi, leaving me completely normal and powerless . . . but that's okay. I tap the pink scar on my face and swivel around in my desk chair. Sometimes being a good friend means giving up awesome power. I know Arzu would do the same for me. I do miss being indestructible, though.

Especially on days like today, when I'm facing a sea of open moving boxes. Being superstrong would totally make packing up my room a lot easier. The afternoon sun splashes rays of gold and pink against my crumpled bedsheets and comforter, where I'm sure I've lost an empty bowl or two of ice cream somewhere. In my defense, in a couple of days I am uprooting my entire life and saying goodbye to the only home I've ever known (and I only threw *one* tantrum when my mom spilled the beans).

Because, spoiler alert, saving my dad and the rest of the jinn kings three months ago still wasn't enough to convince my mom to stay in Philly.

"I'm so glad we can be honest with each other now," she had said when she'd tucked me into bed for the first time since I was spirited away to the Qaf Mountains and learned the truth about my identity—that I'm a half-jinn ("princess," Arzu would add later) and that my father is King Shamhurish, one of seven jinn kings that rule over the unseen world. "Because I never want you to think I don't choose you, janem. *I will always choose you.* But this only works if you choose me too."

"Of course I do, Madar." We hugged under the neon-blue ocean lights in my room. In that moment, I knew choosing my mom meant leaving home, because Philadelphia made her sad. And even though leaving everything I've ever known is scary, facing down Azar and his shadow jinn taught me to face my fears.

So here I am, facing my fears . . . in the shape of organized chaos becoming *actual* chaos. Seeing the toppled-over boxes shakes loose the overflowing boxes in my head—the ones filled with memories and feelings I pushed away for the last twelve years. I don't know where to start. This might be more chaos than I can handle. If only I had Yaseen's self-cleaning chest, that'd make my life a whole lot easier (or cleaner, at least).

Suddenly, my bedroom door swings open. Well, attempts to swing open. "What the—" a muffled voice grumbles. The door thwacks against a stack of heavy boxes filled with my most treasured possessions, my books and climbing gear. "Farrah, are you alive in there?" Arzu calls out while pushing against the door. "Scream once for yes, twice for no."

"AAAAAAH," I shout, officially giving up on any more packing. I dive underneath my comforter. My foot hits a sticky bowl that still has ice cream in it. "AAAAAAAAAAH GROSS."

"You better not be actually dying." Arzu finally pushes the door wide enough to wiggle through. I can see the tips of her curly brown hair as she contorts through the maze of chaos. "Not when I have *excellent* news to share with you."

"Well, in that case." I pop out of the blanket, wrapping it around my head. "I take back exactly one scream."

"That's great, because then there wouldn't be any excellent

news if you were dead." Arzu's hazel eyes twinkle as she sits in my chair and spins herself round and round before letting the chair slow down on its own.

"Which is?"

"This deserves a little fanfare." Arzu drums her hands on my desk, shaking my pens and colored pencils onto the floor. I laugh and crawl over to my headboard and join her drumming. "That's better! It's official, my parents said I could spend spring break in New York with you." She says it all in one big breath, her cheeks flushed.

"No way!" I scream.

"I told you it was excellent."

I rush out of my tangled sheets and pummel her in a hug. We both go spinning and laughing in the chair. "The most excellent!" Mostly because it's a well-known fact that our Afghan families *never* allow friend sleepovers, so I can't believe her parents are letting her go away for that long. But mainly because I was already worrying about missing my best friend, and I haven't even left yet. "How did you convince them?"

"I mean, after the whole explaining-why-I-disappeared-after-*you*-disappeared fiasco . . . I thought it was going to be impossible." Arzu nods sagely. We came up with a cover story—that we went in search of my dad (which was technically true), camped out in the woods, got lost, and had to rely on a local Mennonite family to guide us back to civilization, where I finally got in contact with my mom. So, a big Operation Failure on our part, but safe and sound (without any mention of what *actually* happened). "I was on house arrest for two whole months, but after talking to your mom, and promising my parents we won't run off again, they agreed . . . with a catch."

"Don't tell me . . ."

"I've got to bring one of my brothers to keep an eye on us."

"That is not ideal." I groan while Arzu notices a sparkly piece of paper on my desk.

"Speaking of brothers." She waves the shimmering paper around. The apples of her cheeks glow a soft pink. "Will a certain handsome jinn prince be crashing our spring break too?"

"Don't be gross." I snatch the invitation out of her hands and lay it gently back on my desk. "You know Yaseen can't visit the human world. It's against the rules."

"How could I forget the *rules*." Arzu gasps dramatically. "But then how do they expect you to, you know, respond to that?" She raises her eyebrows at the glittering paper. The purple insignia of the Supreme Court of Jinn dances across the page as big, bright letters blink like fairy lights.

YOUR PRESENCE IS REQUESTED, FARRAH NOORZAD.

"No clue. It didn't come with any instructions on how or when I'm supposed to get back to the Qaf Mountains." For weeks, I slept with one eye open, keeping an eye out for shadows with blinking red eyes or wisps of enchanted clouds. I waited for something, anything. A sign that the jinn world was real and I didn't make the whole thing up in my head. I waited while sitting through class and movie marathons with my mom and grandparents and afternoon strolls around Center City with Arzu. I knew the jinn kings would reach out to me eventually—they wouldn't forget the near destruction of their careful order so easily—so when the letter showed up two weeks ago, lying neatly on my windowsill, I wasn't surprised, but . . .

It was a little bit disappointing.

"You sure it didn't come with another note?" asks Arzu. "Or maybe it's got supersecret ink and we just haven't cracked the code yet?"

"We've already tried every trick in the book." Like holding the paper over a lit candle (which did nothing but singe the corner) and sticking it inside a UV tanning bed at my mom's gym (which got us banned from the facility) and spraying a mixture of baking soda and water onto the paper (which just made it smell clean). "And since we don't have access to any jinn essence or magic . . . this might be a code even I can't crack."

"Well, there's one thing you haven't tried yet. . . ." Arzu trails off. She gives me a look, and I grip my hands into fists. "Technically, *you're* magic. . . ."

"Don't remind me," I groan, tapping away at the paper with my finger. That's the worst part. If there were a message hiding in plain sight, the jinn side of me should be able to feel it. The buzzing, swirling energy that burst out of me when we finally defeated Azar in the Realm Beneath the Unseen—it was awesome. I wondered every night what true power lay in store for me, but since then, there's been nothing. Not a whisper or a pulse of energy. "I'm completely . . . normal again." I shudder while kicking at a box on the floor.

"Farrah, you are many things—brave, stubborn, a total snack hog—" Arzu swiftly ducks the eraser I chuck at her and twirls closer to my window. The sunshine cuts across her curls. "But you've never been normal." She cups her hand under her chin and tilts her head to the side. "And one day your dad and the rest of the jinn world will discover what I've known all along."

"Which is?"

"That you're the best person I know." She gives a little shrug, like it's obvious. "Actually, I take it back. I hope your dad thinks you're completely normal."

"Some friend you are." I roll my eyes and resist throwing another eraser at her.

But Arzu turns quiet and serious while scrolling through her phone. "If your dad ever realizes how great you are, then they'd take you away to that royal school you were telling me about. What is it called again?"

"Al-Qalam Academy for the Exceptional," I say. My stomach flips a little when I mention it.

"Yeah, so actually, this is way better. Maybe they'll forget they sent you that message." Arzu keeps scrolling. A little *v* forms between her eyebrows. "The only thing worse than you moving to a new state is moving to a new *realm*."

Her bright eyes blink up at me. "That would be the absolute worst, wouldn't it?"

"The worst." My voice cracks the tiniest bit.

"At least I can visit you in New York," Arzu continues, leaning back on my bed and typing out a message on her phone. "And honestly, I think I've seen enough of the unseen realm to last me a lifetime."

"Yeah . . ."

What Arzu doesn't know is, I've been itching to go back for months now. I spent so much time learning about the jinn kings and their world (well, as much as my local library and online searching allowed) to prepare me for when I'd see them again. Some nights, I'd stay up late and stare at the stars through my window, imagining I wasn't in my room in Philadelphia but in a dorm at the academy, swishing about in my fancy uniform, being exceptional. Imagining I had the chance to finally prove to Padar, and the rest of the jinn, that I belong in a world of magic and wonder and adventure.

But I'm not sure how to tell Arzu that, much less Madar. . . .

So I don't say anything at all.

"Though I wouldn't mind a certain someone popping through the window on an enchanted cloud for a romantic weekend adventure across the sea." She sighs, staring out the window. "Oh, speaking of." She brightens at the thought. "No word from our favorite quarter-human?"

"Idris is the only quarter-human we know," I correct her.

Arzu waves her hand, like *So what?*

"And he's definitely not my favorite," I mutter.

"So still no word, then?" Arzu frowns.

"Nope." And I really don't want to talk about that either.

"That's weird—"

"Farrah jan, Arzu jan, I need your tasting expertise on something!" my grandmother calls from the kitchen.

"Coming!" Saved by Grandma! I bounce up and out of my room, happy for the subject change.

"Guess it's still a touchy subject," Arzu mutters while chasing after me. We bound down the stairs, taking them two at a time until we're crowding the small kitchen island, where my grandma is adding vinegar to a concoction of sliced potatoes, chickpeas, kidney beans, chutney, and jalapeños all mixed up in a bowl. Her phone is propped up so she can watch some news channel in Farsi while cooking. *Unusual weather patterns making this a record year in environmental fires . . .*

"Is this too sour?" She dips a spoon into the bowl and holds it out for Arzu to taste. "Or not sour enough?"

Arzu takes a slurp and chokes. "Uh—I think it's great. Only a *little* too sour." Her eyes water as she coughs. "Maybe a little less jalapeño while you're at it."

"Hmm." My grandmother's brow furrows as she takes another taste. She winks at me. "Maybe I need a second opinion?"

"No can do. Arzu's taste buds are superior to mine." I wave my hands and laugh nervously. The dish—*kacholu shoor nakhod*—is literally called *potatoes and salty chickpeas*, which is an auto no for me.

"Well, it'll be nice to have more enthusiastic taste testers when we get to your khala Fazilat's house," my grandma harrumphs while adding another dash of vinegar. Arzu goes a little bit green at the sight.

"Yeah. It'll be great." I chew on my lip and watch my grandma wash freshly peeled carrots under the sink, listening to the soft drone of the news channel. *Smog is forecasted to cover eastern North America if forest fires continue . . . and now a song break from Aryana Sayeed!*

"Ah, finally, a little music to brighten the day," my grandma says, humming along to the tune. "Can't wait to have more space at your aunt's house. She tells me they recently renovated their kitchen. A chef's dream. It's going to be wonderful."

"Wonderful," I mumble. A brand-new kitchen sounds nice. I'm sure my aunt's kitchen won't have scuffs on the spice cabinet, like mine does. And it won't have a crooked handle on the fridge because it wasn't installed properly. It definitely won't have the same personality as the slightly chipped countertops my kitchen has from years of arts-and-crafts projects with my grandparents. No, my aunt's kitchen will be way nicer—with a lot less love and memories. *A chef's dream.* I get that prickly feeling in my throat and immediately try to put it away in a box, but Arzu grabs my hand.

"You've got this." She squeezes encouragingly. "Because you've got me. And I won't let you feel so alone like last time."

"Promise?"

"I am the invincible one now," she laughs while throwing an arm over my shoulder. "Well, when I'm wearing the protection charm, at least."

"Eat another bite of that, and I'll believe you." I roll my eyes and chase her around the kitchen with a spoon. ("Girls, *please*, not again," Bibi jan laments when she nearly slips on a potato slice.)

So instead of putting tough feelings and worries into boxes in my head, I laugh it out with Arzu.

And you know what?

I think she might be onto something.

CHAPTER THREE

MOVING ON

———— ❖ ————

There are a few worries I can't laugh out, though.
Especially when bedtime rolls around and I don't
have Arzu to distract me.

"Ready for one last bedtime tuck-in?" Madar's soft voice
peeks through my bedroom door. "Or is that too embarrassing?"

"I mean, if *you* need it, I can allow it." I look up from my
tablet on my mattress. After Arzu left, the adults took charge
of the rest of the packing, so now mostly everything is taped
up and ready to go. Except for my bed (for reasons that don't
have anything to do with *me* needing a bedtime tuck-in).

"How generous of you to *allow* a bedtime tuck-in." My
mom laughs while waltzing past the moving supplies, show-
ering me with hugs and tickles.

"Not fair!" I wheeze.

"Just had to make sure my daughter came back and not a

robot or a changeling." Madar giggles and lays one big kiss on the top of my head. "You never know with those tricky jinn."

"What if they did trade me out?" I duck my head under the covers and roll to face the wall.

"Then I'd fight to get you back, janem." Madar frowns and snuggles next to me so she's Big Spoon and I'm Little Spoon. "What's with the hiding?"

"I'm not hiding," I mumble, and hide more under the blanket.

"Okay, Miss Not Hiding." She rests her head right next to mine and says, "I know the past few months have been a lot for you. And I know how much you're giving up to make me happy, but can I tell you a secret?"

I shrug.

"Can I tell the secret to you and not a blanket worm?" she jokes.

"Fine." But only because it was getting hard to breathe. The cool night air through my open window chills my face when I push my comforter down under my armpits.

"I'm a little afraid to leave too." She whispers her secret into my hair.

"But moving was *your* idea." I roll around so we're face to face. "How can you be afraid of something you want to do?" The shadows from my window make a funny pattern on my mom. Since coming back from the jinn world, my mom looks different. There are new hollows around her eyes that weren't there before. New worries. New sadness.

"Because it's scary," she says. "Because I grew up here too. So much of my story is in these four walls. The best moments"—she nudges me—"and the worst." Her eyes drift, and I know she's thinking about Padar and the deal she made to protect me. "This city is as much your world as it was mine."

"Was?"

"Was." Madar's soft brown eyes go shiny when she looks at me. A wet drop hits my nose after a blink. "Your adventure made me realize how long I allowed myself to stand still, how afraid I've been to allow myself my own adventure. How much I felt I didn't deserve it after everything with your father."

"Don't cry, Madar jan." More tears splash down my mom's cheeks, and I sit up next to her and wipe them away one by one. "You're going to have your adventure soon." Before all this jinn business, my mom *never* talked about my dad. Even though they'd agreed I'd get to see him once a year on my birthday, she always pretended the visits never happened. Seeing my mom now, I get why. I know what it feels like when someone you love doesn't choose you.

It can make it hard to choose yourself.

"Ugh, look at me. I'm such a mess." Madar laughs and rubs her face. "But what I'm trying to say is that sometimes the scariest moments can lead to the best moments in our lives. And that's what I'm holding on to when we go tomorrow. I want you to hold on to that too, okay?"

"But what if—" I want to tell Madar that sometimes scary

moments can just be scary moments, like when I almost disappeared in the Realm Beneath when my wish nearly went through. I want to ask her: What if there isn't always a best moment that comes after the scary part? Because if that were true, then after undoing my wish, my dad would have kept his promise that things would be different.

But after three months, it feels the same.

No letters, no surprise visits. Just a stupid summons that he's probably already forgotten about.

"What were you saying?" She yawns and buries her face in my pillow.

"You're right," I say, and snuggle next to her. "I'll hold on to it."

"That's my brave girl," Madar whispers.

I count sheep in my head until my mom enters dreamland. Soon her breathing gets even and slow. The sound takes me away to when I was really little, back to when my mom used to drive me to the beach for the weekend—*just to get away*, my mom would say. We'd shove fried Oreos into our mouths, ride every roller coaster twice, and get caught up in the waves. I'd pretend I was a mermaid washed ashore, looking for a way back home.

But what I remember the most were the nights I'd wake up and see my mom alone on the beach, staring at the starry night sky, searching for . . . something. Or someone. I'd always run out and sit next to her. Listen to her breathing and the crash of the waves. And take in the feeling of her sadness. An emptiness I couldn't understand but tried to fix with good grades. Fill with extra hugs and endless video-game marathons. I thought being perfect—the fastest, strongest, smartest—could be enough to fill the hole in her heart.

As I watch the smile on my mom's sleeping face, I decide I don't want to bother her with my silly worries. Not if it'll make her sad again. So I'll hold it in. For now.

The problem with bottling worries up is that it makes it hard to sleep.

When I'm sure my mom is solidly snoozing, I carefully extricate myself from her and crawl over to my window. I might not be superstrong anymore, but it's like muscle memory at this point, the way I jump out and climb the fire escape to the roof. My fuzzy pajamas flutter in the wind, with the hood of my shirt tangling into my hair. I sit on the ledge, right above the twinkling fairy lights that are still blinking, even though they've been outside in the rain and snow for months. I breathe in deep and kick my legs out, staring at the sparkling night sky, and wait.

For a flash of white hair.

Or glinting red eyes in shadows.

Or the static of a voice whispering in my head.

Or for my true power to emerge.

I look at my hands again—my soft, normal, human hands—and sigh. "I'm not sure if you know this," I say to the night sky, "but I'm not the patient type." A slight breeze carries my words up, up, up into the clouds, where I imagine they tumble and toss through my realm to my father's. The scent of smoke lingers in the air. "Once a year doesn't cut it anymore." It never did, but now more than ever. "I wish . . ." *You'd show up. Finally be a dad. Stop keeping secrets. Let me into your world.* I shake my head, though.

I've had my fair share of wishes. And look how that turned out. I almost caused the destruction of the jinn world.

So instead of wishing, I wait. "C'mon," I whisper. "One of you has to show up. I know you're out there." I scan the glittering skyline for Idris. It's been my routine for the past three months since our group defeated Azar and we all scattered— with me and Arzu in Philadelphia, Yaseen and my dad back in the Qaf Mountains, and Idris . . . somewhere else.

I was expecting him to be snooping in my room (or my head) after he dropped Arzu off, but instead he left her with a message.

"He said he wanted time to think," Arzu had explained to me when we were back at school.

"Think about what?" I'd slammed my locker door a little harder than necessary.

"How should I know what goes on in the mind of a teenage boy?" Arzu had shuddered. "But if I had to make a scientific guess, he probably needs some time to process everything that happened."

Idris was trapped in the ring of fate for a hundred years before I accidentally freed him (and, as a result, trapped my dad instead). He thought he could wish on the ring to change his fate and save his family from the treaty the seven jinn kings signed to ban all jinn with mixed blood from existing. But as with all cursed magical objects, things hadn't gone to plan, and Idris had lost more than time—he lost his memories too. He became a stranger in his hometown, the City of Jewels. He was lost in every way a person (or jinn) could be lost. And worst of all, he was alone.

"I guess that makes sense," I'd told Arzu. But I'd be lying if I said I wasn't hurt. I thought we'd made a deal. After traveling across the seen and unseen realms, and solving all of Azar's tricky riddles and sneaky turns of phrase, we freed my dad and the rest of the jinn kings from the ring. And because Idris helped me save my dad, I promised I'd help him do the same—find his family too.

"He'll show up, don't worry." Arzu had pulled on the straps of her backpack and walked me to class. "And if he doesn't, he'll have to answer to *me*." She'd flexed her thin arm, and we'd both burst out in laughter.

That was *months* ago. And tomorrow, we're moving.

"I can't wait forever, you know!" I stand up, face scrunched, and hold my hands in tight fists. "If you're backing out of our deal, you could at least say it to my face!" I shout into the night. "Last chance!" I stay frozen, trying to listen for the rustle of paper, and a pen scribbling furiously against a page, followed by a quiet *Sorry to keep you waiting, Noorzad.* My shoulders slump as the minutes tick by. "Were you ever my friend, Idris?" I whisper to the wind. "Or was it all a lie?"

When there's no answer, I rub my eyes and stare as hard as I can at City Hall.

I stare until everything goes fuzzy.

And instead of packing my disappointment in a box where a certain recollector can find it, I throw it away.

"Goodbye, Idris." I turn away from the tower and head back inside. "Whatever it is you're off looking for, I hope you find it."

It's time to move on.

BEING CURSED

Idris had a problem.

Well, in theory, Idris had *many* problems, including, but not limited to, half his butt going numb from sitting outside in the cold, being stranded in the human realm with an empty cloud pen, and not being able to remember his last name. No matter how hard he tried to puzzle his memories together (of which there were many holes, and not many pieces), when he could recall a piece—like the flutter of a woman's laugh or the clink of glowing vials brushing against each other—it would eventually warp and slither away as quickly as it came.

While the not-remembering and the butt-numbing were problems, they were not *the* problem.

The problem was this—Idris was cursed. He was sure of it. And to make sure he didn't forget that major detail, he pulled out his worn leather-bound notebook and wrote down three other things he was sure of:

- Being three-quarters jinn (therefore one-fourth human)
- Unusual knowledge of the planets and their powers (and other miscellaneous trivia)
- A deep fear of the rulers of those planets (which feels the most obvious, considering . . .)

And then, beneath all he knew, he traced over and over again in big, bold letters:

WHO AM I?

The answer, Idris decided, was somewhere in the City of Jewels. There was just one small, teensy snag, and he was staring at her.

From his hiding spot at the very top of the clock tower in the center of Philadelphia, Idris could see Farrah sitting on her roof. She glittered under the open night sky in the human world. For weeks—when he wasn't wandering in alleyways or museums or parks—Idris would watch her enjoy barbecues with her grandparents, skip down the street arm in arm with Arzu to school, and stargaze with her mother for nights on end, getting answers to all her questions.

Each night that Idris watched, an ugly jealousy grew in his heart.

He was jealous when he peered through her window and saw the invitation back to the jinn world sitting on her desk.

He was jealous now, even as she paced back and forth on her roof, yelling questions at the sky, like *Where are you, Idris?* in the same way he did when there weren't clear answers.

A small part of him felt good that she was hurting.

It made him feel less alone.

"Which is why you cannot be her friend," he muttered to himself as he kicked his legs from the ledge of the tower. "It will be easier to break your curse if you're not."

Because the crucial part of his plan meant breaking his promise to not use his power on her and those around her, and that would make him the very worst type of friend.

"It's the only way to control the collateral damage," Idris reminded himself as he jumped from the ledge and silently flickered in and out of view until he landed on solid ground. It was a handy new power that had manifested—he couldn't explain how or why, but he couldn't explain most things when it came to himself—so he just accepted the disappearing-in-one-spot-and-then-appearing-in-another. Made jumping from great heights a lot easier.

It also made appearing on top of tall moving trucks a breeze.

No need for exhausting climbing.

So that is where Idris sat, on top of a cold moving truck, watching the lights finally go out in Farrah's bedroom window. He knew, hidden somewhere in her room, was a summons.

And that was exactly what he needed to fix *the* problem. He was sure of it.

CHAPTER FOUR

FOREVER BRACELETS

"**R**eady?" Madar grunts while slamming the back of the moving truck shut.

"My dear, let me help you with the lock." Baba Haji takes the lever and pushes a big metal lock through the holes. It clicks shut with a clang. "God willing, we'll make it to Long Island in a few hours."

"More like four hours with the traffic on the LIE," my grandmother retorts, referring to the infamously busy highway. She adjusts the front of her cardigan before hurrying past me up the stoop stairs. "Everyone, either use the bathroom now or forever hold your pee because I *refuse* to use public restrooms."

My mom giggles just as my grandfather shakes his head. He takes a deep breath and wraps an arm around Madar's shoulder. They both give our house one last good look. The morning sun is bright around them. A little rainbow shines above my mom's right ear. I duck my head and curl my hands around my knees. I can't believe moving day is here.

"This is it." Her voice shakes a little bit. "We're really doing this."

"Yes," Baba Haji agrees. "We really are."

Madar pulls out her phone. "Farrah, why don't you stand with Baba Haji so I can take one last picture. Doesn't that sound nice?"

"Um, I'm okay." I duck and dodge away from my grandfather's embrace and run down the sidewalk for a bit. "I already took my photos." I smile through my excuse.

My grandma reemerges, and she poses with her hand on Baba Haji's chest. Everyone looks so happy to go. It makes my stomach hurt.

"Do my eyes deceive me!" Arzu screeches from down the street. Her bright, puffy jacket billows against the wind at the crosswalk, making her look like a giant, fluffy croissant. Beside her are her parents and her three younger brothers. She shakes her fist when the light stays red. "I will break the law and jaywalk if I miss out on these pictures!"

"Jaywalk, jaywalk!" her brothers chant as they tear across the street.

"Hey, that was my idea, you little heathens," she shouts while racing against them.

"Oof!" Three sets of arms knock me flat on my back. Little stars dazzle in my eyes.

"We're gonna miss you," chirps Arun, the youngest brother.

"And the mountain of snacks you normally hide under the stairs," laments Adam, the middle brother.

"And the extra controllers you always leave behind," admits Amir, the eldest brother.

"Thanks," I wheeze under their weight.

"Enough with spreading your germs everywhere." Arzu shoos her brothers away and almost knocks me over again with her hug. "Nothing is sacred with those kids running amok."

"I am not a kid," Amir corrects her. "I am only fifteen months, twenty days, and thirty-three minutes younger than *you*."

"And a million times more annoying." Arzu sticks out her tongue before quickly smiling serenely when her parents walk into earshot.

"Today's the big day," her mother says while embracing first my grandparents and then my mom.

"We brought you a little something for the road." Arzu's father hands my mom a plastic bag filled with lumpy shapes covered in aluminum foil. I can tell from the smell it's boloni—a stuffed flatbread, usually fried and filled with potatoes or leeks.

"That is so kind of you—"

"We caught you at the right time. At golden hour!" Arzu fiddles with her phone, leaning it against a light pole before running into the shot. The zipper on her jacket lowers just a little. Her protection pin shines against the sunlight, making her sparkle even brighter. "Come on, lighting like this doesn't happen every day!"

"I mean, technically, golden hour happens twice a day," I mumble. Once after sunrise and once before sunset. I shrink back and watch her on the sidewalk, trying my best not to focus on her sparkling pin or the way magic pulses ever so slightly around the tips of her curly hair. "Plus, you look great without me. Invincible, even."

"What?" Arzu's face falls when she notices her pin showing. She immediately zips her jacket up. The magic winks away. "Sorry, I didn't mean to make you feel ba—"

"I know," I say.

"It's just, when I wear it, I think of you and how lucky I am to have you as my very best friend in the world. I know it bothers you when you see it." Arzu runs up to me and grabs my hands. Her eyes are big and wide. "And I know the odds are stacked against us." She pauses for dramatic effect. "New state, new school, new friends. It's only a matter of time before someone replaces me—"

"That's not going to happen."

"I know, but—"

"There are no buts." I plant my hands on Arzu's shoulders and shake her. "You only get one best friend, and you're mine. Nothing is going to change that. Okay?"

"Well, I'm glad you said that, because I would have been really mad if you didn't, especially after getting you this," she replies while taking something out of her jacket pocket. "Ta-da!"

"What is it?"

"Well, since someone won't teach me how to make my own protection charm—*how rude*—I had to think of the next best thing." Arzu puffs out her chest proudly, handing over her gift. It's a delicate golden chain with a tiny, jeweled butterfly charm in the center. "It's a forever bracelet! I only saved enough money to get it last night before the shop closed, so you'll need to get it melted on, but once you do, it'll be stuck on you forever, and you'll never get rid of me." She grins evilly and laughs.

"It's perfect, thank you." I hug Arzu close. "You're the best."

"Now wherever you go, you'll have a piece of me with you too." She taps the butterfly as I lay the bracelet on my wrist. "For every new beginning. Just like you'll be with me." She rests her hand where her protection pin is hiding. "Best friends forever."

"Forever."

Arzu has been my truest, best friend for my entire life. She's more like family than my cousins, and probably, when we grow up, we'll buy a house together and never let anything tear us apart again.

Except . . .

There might be one thing that could, that small wish I've kept hidden.

"Um, there's something I need to tell you. . . ." I fiddle with the chain.

"What is it?" Golden hour lights up Arzu's hopeful face.

"About the invitation from the jinn world. I—" Can't do it. I can't tell her there's a bigger reason why I want to go back to the Qaf Mountains (besides answering the invitation). A reason that involves emerald uniforms with silver stripes that remind me of shooting stars on the airways. A reason that involves being exceptional.

A reason that requires moving farther than a hundred and fifty miles away.

"In case it doesn't go well with the jinn kings. Be careful with your protection pin." I say a half-truth instead. "Try to wear it as much as possible. Just in case."

"If any jinn dare mess with me *or* you"—Arzu looks around shiftily—"it'll be their funeral." She laughs, throwing an arm around my shoulder. "Loosen up, everything is going to be fine. Your dad'll be there. He'll fix everything. That's what dads do, after all."

That's what dads do.

"And then you'll be back to tell me all about it," she says.

"Right."

"Time to rock and roll!" My mom honks the horn in the moving truck. "Let's go, Farrah. Adventure waits for no one!"

I give Arzu one last quick hug before climbing into the

moving truck. I am squashed between a mountain of bags and blankets. In the side mirrors, I can see Baba Haji driving diligently behind us. Bibi jan is already knocked out and snoring in the passenger seat next to him.

The sun is at peak golden hour, glaring against the towers in Center City.

"New York, here we come!" whoops Madar.

"Here we come," I whisper, and watch my hometown get smaller and smaller, until I can pinch it with my fingers. The farther away we drive, the heavier I feel. I hold on tight to my new forever bracelet.

"You're going to love our new home—well, your new home, my old one." My mom talks to herself. She's practically buzzing with excitement. In fact, she looks radiant—like she's *glowing*. "I feel as light as a feather, like I'm finally shedding all that baggage."

"I'm happy for you," I say, and curl in on myself. I mean it, I really do. I'm happy for my mom, but I'm sad for myself too. That's the thing about dreams and grand adventures. Even if you want to explore uncharted lands, you can't help but miss what you're leaving behind too. I scroll through my phone and watch Arzu's stories, liking the photos she took of herself in front of my house. The butterfly on my bracelet throws little rainbows across the screen.

"We won't stay at your aunt's house forever, though. Only long enough for us to find our own place. Just me and you. The possibilities are *endless*." The words pour out of Madar like a waterfall. "We'll find the perfect apartment, maybe by the water. Or maybe in New York City. Oh, or Hoboken! I'll get the best job, and you can go to the best school. We can be free to be whoever we want to be. Do whatever we want to do." And then, softer, "I can finally be me. I can finally start over."

Start over swirls in my head.

Because I don't want my mom's happiness bubble to burst, I pretend my starting over and her starting over are one and the same.

"YOU'RE GOING TO LOVE IT HERE," MY MOM SAYS FOR THE fifty-seventh time when we arrive.

Spoiler alert: I do not love (and have not loved) the three total times I've visited Khala Fazilat's house. But after one non-stop Taylor Swift playlist, two rest-stop breaks, and three hours of traffic on the George Washington Bridge alone, I practically leap out of the truck and kiss the grass.

"Farrah, please, you don't know what's touched that grass," Bibi groans, exiting the car behind us.

"Can't be any worse than enduring 'I Can Do It with a Broken Heart' on repeat for the past three hours."

"Excuse me, that is music gold," my mom sniffs while appraising me. "And I'm sure your aunt and cousins will be very impressed with your pop music education." She brushes crumbs off my shoulders and licks her fingers to tame my flyaways. "We want to make a good impression, after all."

"That is disgusting." I peel away and shake my head to get any offending spit off me.

Madar rolls her eyes. "You were just kissing grass."

"Grass is natural!"

"So is spit," Madar laughs. "Also, I birthed you, so really, if you want to hear about natural—"

"I can't hear you!" I stuff my fingers in my ears, my eyes wide in horror.

"Now you're both acting like children," Baba Haji scolds with a grin. "Come, let's hurry inside before it gets too dark." He hobbles ahead, leaning on his cane to guide him up the winding driveway. A sliver of light stretches across the porch when Khala Fazilat welcomes Baba Haji in a big hug.

"Help an old woman keep her balance, my dear?" Bibi jan wraps her arm in mine as we make our way toward the house. Madar lags behind, the screen of her phone illuminating her face. Bringing her head close to mine, Bibi jan whispers, "Now, I know you don't need me to tell you this, but I think it's for the best to not disclose any of your recent travels to the jinn world."

"Why not?"

"Because some truths, my darling girl, are best kept close at heart." My grandmother sighs. "And your safety will always be my top priority."

"What's safer than family?" I ask.

"Trust me, my dear. The fewer people who know, the better," says Bibi. "In time, you'll understand."

"But—"

"And there she is, Fazilat jan," my grandma interrupts. "Is that a new haircut?"

"Salaam, Madar jan, it's so good to see you." My aunt Fazilat, with her perfect teeth, hair, and complexion, embraces Bibi jan. Her sweet floral perfume twirls under my nose. It makes me sneeze. "Oh, Farrah jan, is that really you? You've gotten so big." I'm next in the hug parade. I hold my breath and wiggle my way out of my aunt's arms and into her brightly lit home.

"That's what happens when people get older," I say. "They grow." Not like she really cares. It's been four years since the last time I visited . . . and uncomfortable doesn't begin to describe how seeing my family in their own domain makes me feel. If there was a model for the Perfect Afghan American Family, it would be my aunt's. A pretty house with the latest and greatest interior decoration and electronics—it's hard not to be a little jealous.

"Your place is lovelier than the last time we were here," my mom says politely. She curiously looks around when she notices the house is unusually quiet. "Where are the kids? And my brother-in-law?"

"Oh, there was a gathering at their father's side, so they'll be there all weekend." Khala Fazilat waves it off like it isn't a big deal. "Plus, I thought it'd be better to get settled privately, you know?"

"Right." A little of the light dims in Madar's face. "Privately."

"How thoughtful," my grandmother says.

More like *rude*, but I keep that to myself. Even though my mom and grandparents try their best to pretend like our little family is fine, the larger community of relatives (my aunt and her husband included) are still weird when it comes to associating with the out-of-wedlock kid. That's the big reason why we rarely visit in the first place. There's only so many *it's her* whispers I can take.

Maybe my grandma is right to keep the jinn world a secret. They barely understand me now; imagine how they'd react if they knew the *truth*.

"Come, come. Let me show you where to put your things." My aunt is already waltzing up her elaborate staircase to the second floor. "I'm sure you're exhausted after all that driving."

My room is conveniently all the way at the end of the hall. When my family turns right from the stairs to reach their rooms, I'm the only one who turns left.

"For your privacy," my aunt says without looking back when she opens another door for my grandparents.

"Right, *my* privacy," I mumble. But once I shut the door, I'm a little glad for it. Without a second thought, I throw my backpack on the floor, belly flop onto the bed, and take a picture to send to Arzu.

welcome to my latest jail cell

looks pretty comfy to me

comfy with PASSIVE-AGGRESSIVE politeness

lolol you're so dramatic

there's always a spot for you here

My eyes get a little teary when a picture of Arzu's bedroom pops up in our messages. Where my room was organized chaos, Arzu's room is pristine perfection. From her impeccably made four-poster bed to her color-coded bookshelf and desk, chaos and Arzu would never cross paths if it weren't for me. I heart her message and throw my phone across the bed. Even though I'd rather step on hot coals sans indestructibleness than spend another minute at my aunt's house, this is where my mom wants to be, so I've got to suck it up. And who knows, if she sees me supporting her, then maybe she'll be happy enough to hear the little whisper that's been growing in my heart. I crawl to the edge of my bed and grab my bag from where I threw it on the floor, then rummage through it until I find my summons—with its promise of adventure in swooping, glittery letters.

Letters that are slowly peeling away from the page and re-forming to shape a brand-new message.

YOUR PRESENCE IS REQUESTED.
AT MIDNIGHT, A CLOUD WILL BE WAITING.
DO NOT MISS IT.

CHAPTER FIVE

YOUR PRESENCE IS REQUESTED

I should have known the jinn kings had horrible timing.

"Midnight tonight?!" I hiss at the page. "You couldn't have picked a worse time!" We just got here, and now I've got to go? My heart flutters when I imagine telling Madar. *I know we said no more secrets but I've sorta been keeping one and now I've got to go back to the jinn world but don't worry I'll be back before breakfast.*

Yeah, somehow I doubt that will work.

Unless . . . I go without telling her. Again.

There's a knock at the door. My guilty conscience jumps as I quickly hide the letter behind my back.

"Wanted to double-check on you." My mom's head peeks in. "We're going to unload our stuff into a storage unit. I figured I'd give you a break from that since I've got some extra hands."

"Sounds good." I smile so hard, my eyes start to water.

"You sure you'll be okay if we go?" Madar looks worried. "Or maybe we can wait until tomorrow. New place, maybe we—"

"I'll be fine, it's late anyway. I'll probably pass out soon," I lie through my smile. Well, it's not entirely a lie. I *am* tired and it *is* late. Plus, if Madar keeps staring at me like she can read my mind, I might actually pass out.

But then Madar smiles, a magical megawatt smile that makes the sun look dim. "We are going to be so *happy*, I just know it." She gives me one last shining look, like she can't believe this new life of hers exists. "Away from those pesky jinn and their rules. We're going to start over and live happily ever after."

"Happily . . . ever after." The words stick like peanut butter in my mouth. *You've gotta tell her,* I scream in my head, but the letter gets heavier in my hands. I'm afraid if I give my mom this weight, she'll break. Especially after the last time. When I got back from the Realm Beneath the Unseen, I promised myself I'd never let Madar be that sad again.

I can't be the one to take the light from her a second time.

"See you soon." She quickly strides into the room and ruffles my hair. "We're going to have to get this mess trimmed. Don't forget to brush your hair *and* teeth before you pass out."

"Aye, aye, Captain." I mock-salute with my right hand. With a last wave, my mom is off.

"Come, come, these boxes won't unload themselves." My aunt Fazilat's muffled voice floats from the driveway. I hear cars turn on, doors slam open, then shut. "The boys are already at the storage place."

"Patience, Fazilat jan," my bibi jan's soft response whirls out. "They can wait a bit longer."

After a few minutes, I peek through the open curtained window to make sure all the cars left. When I'm sure I'm alone, I check the time on my phone. It's already ten-thirty p.m. That doesn't leave me much time.

Do I pack? Technically, I would have to *unpack* first. No, that's not the point. I won't be staying too long. Just in and out before Madar knows I'm missing.

You promised you wouldn't do this again, my guilty conscience scolds.

The stars wink on and off as they look on, listening to the battle inside my head. In a few hours, I could be back out there, on the airways, feeling the breeze in my hair, the magic wrapped around my shoulders, feeling like anything is possible.

My heart soars with hope. I would be heading . . . to a new normal, with a foot in both worlds—I'm sure my parents could work out a schedule where I could come back and forth. Maybe.

That's if the meeting with the kings is in my favor. I shiver when I remember the first time I stood in front of them and learned what happened to forbidden mixed jinn. Death or exile. I gulp. *Be strong. If you can defeat Azar, you can face the seven jinn kings.* Plus, I saved their lives, so that's got to count for something. Right?

You need not be afraid when it's they who should be afraid of you. I remember Azar's old warnings when he used to talk in my head. *Don't you want to know why the jinn kings fear you?*

"They fear *you*, not me." I drag a chair next to the window and sit. Bubbles fizz and pop in my stomach, making me queasy. "I'll show you and the rest of the kings that mixed jinn can have a place in the clouds too." With my eyes to the sky, I await my destiny.

I hope this isn't a big mistake.

THE CLOUD ARRIVES AT EXACTLY 11:59. IT KNOCKS GENTLY ON the window, waking me up from a horrible dream.

"I DON'T WANT TO EAT FRIED SPIDERS!" Drool sticks to the window from my cheek. I'm so glad dreams fade away to nothingness after waking up—'cause I don't want to be remembering *that* unpleasant image. "Oh gross." I wipe the drool away and slide the window open. My heart flutters when the cloud slowly floats into the room toward the summons. Tendrils of wispy air curl around the paper on the desk. The moment it touches the summons, it disappears. A glowing golden vial appears in its place.

"An Ever-Place solution," I whisper.

Of course! Traveling this way is so much faster. I'll be back in no time, before my mom worries. That makes me feel a little better. I grab the vial and embrace the slight buzzing in my fingers. It blooms into a warmth that encircles my entire body. *Picture the space you wish to face,* the vial hums and whispers in my ears, *and I shall deliver you there.* I shiver at the magic, and for a fleeting second, I feel complete.

I guiltily look around the room, making sure no one can hear me when I whisper, "I want to go to the Qaf Mountains. . . ." I open the vial and splash it against the door. Nothing happens. "Please," I add. The door bursts into bright light, humming with energy so familiar, my heart almost stops. I picture the grand mountains floating in the sky. I imagine the starry halls of Al-Qalam Academy for the Exceptional. And in my mind I see my dad and my brother on the other side, waiting for me to come back to the City of Jewels.

Entranced by the pull of the light, I reach for the door. But before my fingers touch the cool metal, I remember the first time I used an Ever-Place solution and portaled back to the roof of our rowhome. I remember my mom's teary face. But most of all, I remember the way Madar *chose* me. I hesitate and gulp. As much as I don't want to tell her, I can't disappear on her again.

"Argh, why are promises so hard to break?" I grumble, and quickly video-call my mom. She picks up immediately.

"I'm so sorry, it's taking longer than I thought to empty

the truck. There's this weird smog making it a little hard to breathe. And your grandfather threw his back out because he refused to listen to me when I told him that chair was too heavy." Madar rolls her eyes.

"I merely needed a rest, that's all." Baba Haji pops onto the screen. His bushy black eyebrows curl together. "Don't believe a word your mother says. You know I can handle it. I'm not an old man yet!"

In the background, muffled coughs and laughter float gently through the speaker of my phone.

"We'll call it a night in twenty minutes, okay?" Madar's forehead wrinkles. "What's that light behind you?"

"Um. That's why I called. I, um." I look quickly from the glowing portal door to Madar's increasingly worried face and take a deep breath. Time to rip the Band-Aid off, Farrah. "I . . . got a letter. . . ." I lower my voice when I say, "From the jinn kings."

My mom freezes. "A letter," she breathes. "Show me the glow."

"I—"

"*Now*, Farrah," Madar orders. She gasps when I flip the camera and show her the portal. "No, they can't take you. . . . Not again."

"They're not taking me," I reason. "They summoned me. To determine my future. It could be a good thing."

"Nothing good ever comes from the unseen." Madar

moves quickly away from the rest of my family and speaks even faster. "Do not go through that portal, do you hear me? I forbid it."

"How do you even know it's a portal?"

"That doesn't matter."

"But—"

"No buts, Farrah." My mom, while strict sometimes, never orders me to do anything. That's how I know this is bad. Her face is stern, but her eyes shine like storm clouds, ready to flood everything in their path. "I promised you I would keep you safe, and that means you staying put."

"But what if I want to go?" I whisper in the dark. The portal's glow starts to dim and shrink. Inch by inch, it begins closing.

"You . . . want to go?" The words feel like a thousand electric shocks to my heart.

I nod.

Madar goes quiet. Then she whispers, "You won't make it out of there alive."

"Padar is there," I say. "He'll protect me. I know it."

My mom doesn't look so sure.

"What if . . . I'm meant to go?" I admit my darkest secret to Madar. "What if I could be great in Dad's world? I could be exceptional. Shouldn't I get to choose where I start over too?"

The portal continues to shrink. *The kings wait for no mortal,* the doorway warns. *Once the gate expires, so does your fate.*

If I don't go now, I'll miss my chance to find out. Once and for all.

The spark of happiness vanishes from my mom's face. She recoils in on herself. "You don't know what you're asking me to do, janem," she says. "You don't know what danger lies waiting for you if I let you go."

"I'm used to it," I joke. My mom blanches. "Hiding me in the human realm won't keep me safe. You know that and I know that. But I need to know more, Madar. I need to know who I am. I need . . ." So many unanswered questions crowd my head. In the Realm Beneath, Azar mentioned my true power, but ever since I returned to the human world, I haven't been able to figure it out. I'm just plain, normal, human Farrah. But I know there's something my dad isn't telling me. His response, *Who told you that?*, when I let it slip that there might be more to me than invincibility proves there are answers out there. Answers I'll never get here. Not if the adults won't tell me.

"I'll let you go on one condition. Just . . . promise you'll come straight home after the summons so we can further discuss this, okay?" Tears trail down my mom's cheeks, and I almost say, *Don't be sad, Mom, I'll stay.* But the hum of the unseen realm is calling, and like a moth to a flame, I can't pull away.

"I'll be back before you know it," I whisper, and wipe away a tear of my own. "I'll always choose you, Madar."

My mom's shining eyes stare at me for five long seconds, like she's putting away tough feelings into boxes in her head. "I'll see you soon. Love you." She hangs up the call.

"Love you too," I mumble to the dark screen.

The butterfly on my forever bracelet glints on the desk where I left it. *New beginnings.* I grab the bracelet, hold it tight, and hope. *Let this be a beginning and not an end.* Taking a huge breath, I stare down the portal.

"Ready or not, here I come!" I pull the doorknob open and walk through the door.

To my future.

CHAPTER SIX

THE SCALE OF DEEDS

T he cold sting of metal is the first thing I feel when I pass through the Ever-Place portal. I'm so surprised, I almost drop my forever bracelet.

"What the . . . ?" The golden light of the portal turned solid and snapped around my wrists. It looks a lot like . . . "Handcuffs? Am I . . . a prisoner?"

"It was either that or an essence-draining bodysuit," a familiar voice answers. "Though I wish they didn't have to give you essence-blocking shackles to begin with, but you know how the jinn kings are."

"Yaseen?" He comes into focus as the portal vanishes. It returns to a normal, jeweled archway. I'm back at the Supreme Court of Jinn. In front of my brother, who I haven't seen in months. His bright green eyes are clouded in apology when we finally get a chance to really look at each other.

"The one and only," he half jokes while awkwardly

scratching his arm. "I would hug you, but it seems even the walls have eyes these days."

"Let me guess, they've sent you to babysit me again." I tug at the cuffs, trying to get some space between my hands.

"Actually, they don't know I'm here." Yaseen attempts to pick at his eyebrow but quickly shoves his hands down into fists. He takes a small step closer and lowers his voice. "I tried to get word to you sooner, but—"

"Our dad blocked you?" I guess. That would explain the radio silence.

"It's more than that. The jinn kings are angry. It's been tense here since Baba got back. Finding out you exist has made them paranoid. He tried to delay this meeting for as long as poss—" Yaseen is cut off by the sound of stomping boots. He mutters under his breath, "Darn, they weren't supposed to come for at least another five minutes." He looks up at me, his eyes big and guilty. "I meant to warn you."

"Warn me about what?" I ask.

Yaseen doesn't get a chance to answer.

"By order of the great jinn kings, I order you both to take five large steps away from each other," a guard commands as he reaches us. His companion stares menacingly down at me when Yaseen refuses to move.

"That means you, Prince Yaseen, son of Shamhurish, heir to the realm of Jupiter," the other guard says, a bit softer. "For your safety."

"She is my sister," Yaseen whispers, and moves even closer

to grab my wrist to make his point clear. "Where she goes, I go." He stares defiantly at the guards, who hem and haw. I can't help but grin inside. This is how I imagined having a brother would be—having a protector, ally, and, most importantly, friend.

"I guess he goes with the half-human," says the first guard.

"If the jinn kings complain, this was one hundred percent your idea. I'm not looking to get on their bad side today," retorts the second.

"Every side is their bad side. . . ." The first guard rolls his eyes and grunts, "This way."

"Thanks for that," I whisper while we follow the first guard. The second guard walks suspiciously behind us. "I don't remember the welcoming committee being this . . . pleasant last time. Wanna fill me in on what I missed?"

"A few days after we got back to the City of Jewels, there was a reckoning," Yaseen mutters quickly. "No one in the city knows what happened around the winter solstice, but there's unspoken tension between the seven realms. I mean, there's always been some tension with the kings, but it's never been this bad." His eyes dart around as we turn away from the corridor that would take us to the main court, where I first faced the kings. Instead, the hallway grows darker and smaller the deeper we go. Marble stairs wind us down, down, down. Glowing bubbles of lightning float by our feet when we reach the bottom floor.

"Where are they taking us?" I scan the eerie corridor and

try not to squeak as something fuzzy scurries across my feet. Wherever we're going, it can't possibly be good. Was my mom right? Did I just walk into a trap? My stomach twists and turns faster than we do.

"To the place where sentences are served." Yaseen gulps once we reach a set of obsidian stone doors. The guard stomps his foot three times, making the ground rumble and growl. Dust chases our ankles, rising into my throat, making me cough. "To the Court of Punishment and Exile for Dangerous Beings."

Punishment and exile? Dangerous? Me?

"B-but why?" My feet stay glued to the floor, even as Yaseen gently pulls on my arm. "I haven't done anything wrong." I should be thanked, not judged! I did everything right—was the strongest, the fastest, the best. I *saved* my dad and the kings from Azar's schemes. Shouldn't it be my dad's turn to save me?

"I know," Yaseen whispers, "but that doesn't matter to the kings."

"But our dad has to—"

"Baba doesn't exist here." Yaseen shakes his head. "Only King Shamhurish. You'll . . . get used to it."

When the dust clears, I finally see the seven imposing thrones lined up neatly in a row with all the jinn kings facing me. My eyes go straight to my dad.

My dad, who used to spin me in the air, who taught me how to lead-climb all on my own, and wrapped me up in blankets and stories of impossible things—like phoenixes and faeries and dragons and jinn.

My dad, who showed up with a smile bigger than the sun.

My dad, who sits on a cold throne, who isn't smiling at all now, who I barely recognize with his shimmering blue skin and pointed ears. His eyes harden at the sight of me.

"Bring the girl in," his voice booms in the chamber. "You two may leave us now." My teeth rattle at the energy that pulses off the kings. At their *power.* The two guards nod curtly and quickly scamper away.

"Good luck, girl," the first guard mutters in my ear. "You'll need it."

A lifetime of birthdays flash in my mind, of Padar's warm smile, his belly laughs. Never in a million years did I think I'd ever be afraid of my dad.

"Step away from the half-human, Yaseen." My dad glares at Yaseen and tilts his head just a bit, his crown glittering darkly. "It is not your place to be here."

"Half-human?" I whisper.

"Yes, Baba," Yaseen mumbles quietly. I can feel him tremble when he lets go of my arm and quietly walks into the shadows. He throws me an apologetic look, but I get it. It's hard to stand up to your parents, especially when they're all-powerful beings.

I wish I could tell him I'm afraid too.

"We meet again, Farrah Noorzad," King Barqan says. "How most unpleasant for you and for my nose."

I gulp. I knew I'd be in a little bit of trouble, but I've never been on trial. I don't even know how regular human court cases go, but shouldn't I have a lawyer or someone to defend me?

"I r-received a letter." My voice cracks and my fingers can't stop shaking. I hold on to my bracelet for support.

"So you have." King Barqan's golden eyes, too old for his youthful face, study me before glancing at my dad. "Since our judge has so graciously joined our court again, King Shamhurish will have the floor."

"Off with her head!" yells King Ahmar, the jinn king of Mars.

The jinn king of Venus, Zawba'ah, sighs. "How many times have we gone through this? Beheading is not the answer we agreed upon." His four heads shudder at the thought.

"You're lucky this trial falls on Thursday and not Tuesday; otherwise your fate would be mine." King Ahmar's horns gleam in the low light. He crushes his hand into a fist. "Don't think I've forgotten the last time this one came to our court and imprisoned me."

"Yes, I know, Ahmar. Painfully so, since we had to share a space in that accursed ring," my dad interjects. "But since it is the day of my ruling, the half-human's fate will be in my hands."

"Hey!" The twisting and worrying in my stomach bubbles at *half-human*, giving me the courage to finally stare my dad in the eye and say, "My name is Farrah Noorzad. I am the daughter of Shamhurish, the jinn king of Jupiter and the ruler of Thursday." I blink back angry tears. "Who I *saved* and traveled deep within the Realm Beneath the Unseen to do what none of the other jinn kings could. I broke the ring of fate and trapped the banished fire jinn king, Azar, in it. So my name is not *half-human*. And you know it."

"Seems this one picked up some insolence on her travels." The jinn king of Saturn, Maymun, *tsks*, leaning back in his chair. His wings are curled tight against his body, shimmering like the night sky. "Maybe she needs a reminder of her place." Wispy, cool clouds trace the edges of his robes. "To understand the nightmare of her situation."

"I'm not afraid of you," I say.

"Not yet." King Maymun's teeth gleam. "But you will be."

"Enough of that," King Mudhib, the shining ruler of the Sun, scolds. "That is not what we agreed upon."

"Agreed? More like coerc—"

"Enough of this bickering. There is much to do." My dad's voice rumbles and bounces against the chamber. "I am here to confirm in front of the entire court the truth to your allegations. It is true you are my child. . . ."

Half the jinn kings scoff and grumble at this.

"And I can confirm the validity of your quest to free us from an eternity in the ring of fate. For that, the jinn world owes you a great debt."

There's a pause.

"Why do I feel a *but* coming on?"

"But . . . your *crimes*, unfortunately, must be weighed on the scale for judgment."

"Crimes?" Like what? Being born? My face burns when King Mudhib snaps his fingers and a large golden set of scales appears right in front of me.

"And since it is my day of ruling . . ." My dad sighs, rubbing his forehead. His jeweled robes jingle against his throne. "Your future will be decided by the Scale of Deeds." I can't tell if he looks uncomfortable because he feels guilty for putting me on trial or if he's embarrassed about getting caught and having his little secret out in the open. Both reasons make me really sad. *Or maybe he's putting on an act for the other kings?*

Energy crackles from the scales as they grow larger. In the center is a dial that has four options: RELEASE. OBSERVE. EXILE. TERMINATE.

Only one of those options looks good. The rest . . . I clasp my hands together. This has got to be an act. My dad wouldn't let anything bad happen to me. Right?

"The Scale of Deeds will allow your actions to speak for you, both good and bad," explains King Mudhib. "All you have to do is . . ." He trails off while quickly glancing at something behind him. He blinks, then turns his attention back on me. "Place your hands in the receptacle there, and it will do the rest."

Right below the dial are two golden hands, their palms

facing up. The fingers twitch, and I shrink back. I do not like the idea of holding hands with . . . whatever that is.

"Go on, we don't have all day," huffs King Zawba'ah. "The sooner we settle this, the sooner we can go on with our day."

I turn to ask Yaseen, "Does it hurt?"

He mouths, *I have no idea.*

I walk up to the scale. "Here goes nothing," I whisper, dropping the bracelet into my pocket and placing my shaky hands on top of the receptacle. At first, nothing happens. "This doesn't seem so bad."

Then the fingers snap shut over my hands, and I scream. That's when the *burning* starts. Wind roars in my ears as shards of light and wisps of dark battle around me like a tornado.

"I take it back, this is really bad. Awful! Ow!" I struggle against the scale, but the fingers tighten their grip. "Let go of me!"

"She says it hurts!" Yaseen runs out from where he was watching. "Make it stop!"

I can barely hear King Mudhib respond, "It will hurt less if she stops trying to fight it."

"There's got to be a better way," shouts Yaseen. "Baba, do something!" He desperately tries to untangle my hands from the golden scale. The second his fingers touch the metal, a loud explosion throws him backward.

Judgment is for the judged, the scale whispers all around us. *Beware, the disruption of judgment is at the judged's peril.*

"Argh." I fall on my knees. "It's like—it's burning the

memories from my head." Stars burst in front of my eyes (and not the good kind). Little black spots follow, with scenes of my birthday, Padar chasing me through a winding trail, marching out to the forest that lies before us. I see myself wondering what secrets lurk in roots and leaves. The scale takes the moment and begins to weigh it. My wrists ache when I make my wish, when Padar collapses, and when I see Idris for the first time.

Or at least, it's the part where I'm *supposed* to see Idris.

In the clash of light and dark, there's a hole where Idris was meant to be. But I'm distracted by the pain. "My brain is on fire. Make it stop, *please*," I yowl. Little tears blur my vision, but I bite my lip and let the storm swirl around me.

My entire journey plays out in front of the jinn kings. Each moment, painfully ripped from my head and onto the scale. They all lean closer in their thrones, except for my dad. All he does is look at me. It makes me want to break the scale, destroy it until it can't hurt me anymore.

A small flicker of light pulses through my fingers before going away.

Padar leans even closer, his eyes narrowing.

"You've got this, sis." Yaseen kneels next to me, covering his ears with his hands. "You've faced worse! Just hold on!"

Back and forth, the scale tips. Deeds and crimes battle against each other, and super slowly, the dial moves. The silver arrow bobs between OBSERVE and EXILE. Back and forth, like it can't make up its mind.

"I can't take it anymore," I shout, and squeeze my eyes shut.

I imagine Arzu, hear her cheering me on. *You're the strongest person I know. But you don't have to do it alone.*

"How much longer?" Sweat drips from my bangs.

"It's still tipping," whispers Yaseen.

"Wait, what is that?" King Maymun asks.

A deed, bright and shiny, bursts out of my head and into the scale. I'm running between the barrier, once, twice, three times for Arzu. There's a bright light that shines from my chest, the same light that shined in Azar's kingdom. That just now flickered within my fingers. What I didn't notice before was how the barrier started to break and fade away when I collapsed . . . right before Arzu came back to help me.

"Curious . . . ," mutters King Mudhib. He and King Abyad share a look. "Very curious."

The memory lands on the deed's platform.

Everything goes fuzzy after that. The boxes in my head, filled so carefully with hard feelings, slip away, shatter, and fall. There are thousands of hands rummaging in my private space, and nothing I do can stop it.

"Everything's gonna be okay," a voice encourages. A voice I haven't heard in months.

I open my eyes. "Idris?" I whisper, but through the chaos, there's no sign of him.

The judged's crimes and deeds have been collected, roars the scale. **And now your judgment is ours.**

All at once, everything stops. The room is unbearably still as the scale glows and the last pieces of my memories settle in to determine the balance. My eyes are glued on the dial. It's right on the edge of OBSERVE and EXILE.

"No, no, no," Yaseen pleads. "Come on, tip over. A little more."

But the scale doesn't move. The black arrow reads EXILE. My heart sinks. That can't be right. I didn't fight all those shadow jinn, almost lose my soul, to be exiled from the jinn world.

Not like this.

My dad doesn't say a single word, but I notice his shoulders relax. It looks like he's holding back a smile. My heart sinks further.

"Well, all those theatrics for exile," sniffs King Ahmar. "Can't say I'm not disappointed."

"Wait, there's got to be something else." I try to rack my brain for something, anything that might help me out.

"The scale does not lie, half-human," says King Barqan. He scowls. "In fact, you should consider yourself luck—"

Yaseen gasps. "Look!"

Ever so slightly, the scale trembles, and something, a glimmer of light, floats like a feather onto the deed's platform . . . pushing the dial to OBSERVE.

On the longest day of the year, all will be made clear. A voice emanates from the scale as it releases me. I fall backward.
Until then, your judgment has been served, Farrah Noorzad.

BEING KIND

Idris hated promises.

He hated them more than broccoli dipped in milk chocolate. Because promises were more than words—they were a duty, an oath, a *responsibility*. In a way, a promise held power over a person's heart.

And that was what made promises dangerous, especially when they involved his own heart.

While Idris could not remember his birthday or the color of his mother's hair or the sound of his father's voice, or if he came from a family of three or three hundred, he knew this: he would do anything to get those details back, including sitting on the roof of a cold and windy moving truck, listening to horrible pop music for hours on end, sneaking through Farrah's aunt's house, and jumping through an open Ever-Place portal uninvited.

And now, standing in the Court of Punishment and Exile

for Dangerous Beings, Idris was closer to breaking his curse and getting his memories back. Under the cold light of the chamber, he scurried through the closed gates to where Farrah stood. She could not see him (nor could the kings or the guards or Farrah's insufferable brother), which made it easy for Idris to walk past Farrah and Yaseen toward the seven glittering thrones until he was behind the jinn kings. One of them had to know what was wrong with him.

All he needed to do was open their minds to find out. One by one until a key to the puzzle of his missing memories was found. Once he did that, he wouldn't have to involve Farrah in his troubles or break his promise to her. It was the least he could do—the last act of friendship in his darkening heart. He'd slip away like a forgotten thought—a blip in the stories of their lives.

Seven ornate thrones glittered in front of him, each made of a distinct metal—but there was one he instantly disliked. The gold throne. Something flashed in his mind—*falling through a dark ocean, screaming as he went down, down, down, weighed in gold chains—*

"What was that?" Idris whispered, his heart racing.

Was that a memory?

With his hands poised over his trusted notebook, Idris shuffled closer to the sun king's throne and decided to start with him.

"The Scale of Deeds will allow your actions to speak for you, both good and bad. . . ."

Idris tuned out the sun king's voice and unleashed his power. He let his mind go and waded through the golden haze of what was, what is, and what will be. Entering the pool of recollection was always unpleasant, but Idris gritted his teeth, pushed through the cold expanse of *what was*, and concentrated his energy on opening the sun king's mind.

Show me what you know. What was that I just saw?

Unfortunately, Idris's questions were met with a golden wall slamming right in front of him, followed by six other walls blocking his further attempts.

"Blocked?" Idris grew frustrated. "Fine, I'll just try another—"

Then Farrah began to scream.

"What is happening—" Idris looked up in horror at the cyclone pouring from Farrah, spilling their past adventure for all the kings to see . . . without him in it. "That's . . . not possible." Idris watched a story unfold without him, but how? *Why am I not there?* He walked toward the scale, feeling more ghost than boy, more imagined than real, more forgotten than ever.

Watching Farrah's memories was his living nightmare.

"What does this mean?" he asked the scale.

Trials are for the waking, the scale whispered back, *not for those who slumber still.*

"But I'm right here," he shouted. "I'm here!"

And yet you are not here nor there, the scale rumbled in his head. *You are not anywhere in anyone's minds, not even your own.*

"You're wrong," Idris shouted back. "That doesn't make any sense."

There is no right or wrong. Simply the truth. The scale glowed one final time, its dial set on EXILE.

"We'll see about that." Without thinking, Idris plunged his hands into the scale, holding on to Farrah's hands so the scale could see *him* too. "You can't tell the truth without the whole story." For a moment, the scale connected them—the twister of light coiled around them both, tangling the weight of her heart's truest wish with his.

There were so many questions running through Idris's head, but he couldn't let his curse ruin Farrah's future too. Whatever curse destiny had in store for him, he would rise to meet it.

Whatever it was. Just not at the expense of his friend's happiness. Not even his own jealousy could want that. "Everything's gonna be okay," he mumbled to her.

What a curious kindness, the scale rumbled. *For that, I will grant you a singular kindness as well. Do with it what you will.*

So from Idris's own heart fluttered one feather of light.

And tipped the scale.

CHAPTER SEVEN

WHAT'S IT GONNA TAKE?

"There has to be a mistake," shouts King Ahmar. "She's tampered with the scale. I know it!"

"Regrettably, while this is a rare moment where I find myself in agreement with Ahmar, we must allow the half-human to be permitted in our city." If King Barqan's glare could kill, I'd already be long gone. "The scale has determined she is to be our *guest* for the next few months."

"So I can stay?" I try to rub my wrists, but the golden cuff gets tighter. "Is that what it means?"

"Technically, yes . . ." My dad sighs. "Though specifically"—he swallows and sighs again—"it means you are to remain in the City of Jewels."

Yes!

"Under *close* observation," he adds.

Oh.

"What does that mean?" I ask.

"It means you aren't allowed to *leave*," King Mudhib explains, "until we come to understand exactly what the scale wants us to observe. There can be many outcomes, but we just don't know yet what those may be." He pauses. "But given your half-human status, we will need to watch if you are a threat to our careful order. At least until the summer solstice."

"And if I'm not a threat?"

"Then . . . that will warrant another discussion." King Mudhib hesitates while eyeing my dad. "On your potential . . . *residence* here."

Yaseen and I exchange a surprised glance.

"So you get to stay!" Yaseen's face brightens at the idea.

"For now," my dad corrects him. "For now," he repeats, even quieter.

"Well, on that unfortunate note, I must depart." King Maymun gets up, his fierce wings expanding and blowing a gust of wind my way. "There is much to do. I've left my realm unattended for too long."

"We'll be watching you," King Ahmar growls right before he disappears into a cloud of smoke. The rest of the jinn kings shoot wary looks at Padar before they vanish too. Only King Mudhib gives my dad a sympathetic nod.

"Could cut that tension with a knife," I say to Yaseen.

"Yeah . . . the kings haven't been in a great place since we returned."

"*That* is the understatement of the century," Padar says

while rubbing his face. "Though I'm not sure we've ever been in a great place, but this current situation is a real problem for me, Farrah."

I'm quiet when my dad says my name. It brings me back to the Realm Beneath and Azar's final riddle. *Why is your father worth saving?* This moment pokes the bruise that formed on my heart, making it a little bigger. I shift from foot to foot, causing the chain on the cuffs locking my wrists together to clank.

"Ah, the shackles. Let's get them off." Finally, my dad looks apologetic. "There's just a lot on my mind, and certain pretenses must be made in front of the others. I'm sure you understand." He strides over from his throne, looking every bit a regal king if I ever saw one. Jewels drip from his robes, and I notice the many rings on his fingers, each glittering and humming with some sort of power. There's even one made out of tree bark that glows a bright green. I shiver when he hovers his clawed hand over the cuffs. The ring on his pinkie finger glows aquamarine and neutralizes the golden chain on my wrists.

"You didn't have to call me *half-human*," I mumble, rubbing my sore wrists with my hands. Even if it was an act in front of the other jinn kings, it hurt to hear. The moment the chain disappears, energy comes rushing into my fingers and toes, crashing like waves into my chest. Finally, I can *feel* the essence of the jinn world.

"You look better already," agrees Yaseen. "Though it'll

take some time to get the cabbage smell out. But lucky for you, I've built up a tolerance to stink." He smiles proudly. "Oh, those bruises don't look good." He frowns when he sees my wrists. "We could head to Al-Qalam's infirmary. They should have something to fix you up—"

"There will be no visits anywhere I can't keep an eye on your . . . sister," my dad says, hesitating. He keeps glancing at me with his eyebrows furrowed. Once, I thought his big bushy eyebrows made him look like a burly ant. But that was when he was in his human form. Now, in his true form, it's hard to accept the all-powerful jinn king standing in front of me is the same dad.

A big part of me feels like he isn't the same at all.

"But why?" Yaseen throws his arms out. "They've got the best healers, and since she's got to be here anyway, why not stay at the academy?"

"Because Farrah is not normal. She cannot attend the academy in her current state," my dad replies. "How could I explain it? And more than that, her existence is *forbidden*. It puts us all in greater danger." He kneels, looking both Yaseen and me in the eyes. "It isn't safe for you here, Farrah. Not now, and not in the future."

All the little daydreams back home of wearing an academy uniform and being exceptional shatter into a million pieces.

"I don't understand. You made the rule." I remember Idris saying there was a time when mixed jinn and humans were welcome in the Qaf Mountains. "Can't you undo it?"

"It's not that easy," he replies.

"Why not? Because of that prophecy?"

A hundred years ago, there was prophecy that warned of the end of the jinn world by a mixed jinn, which is why the treaty was created keeping all mixed jinn out. But that was so long ago. My dad can't think I'm dangerous . . . not after everything I did to save him.

"What if . . . we hid that Farrah is a half-human?" suggests Yaseen. "Temporarily." He runs his fingers through his topknot while he thinks. "Since she has to be observed anyway, the academy is the best place she could be. There are eyes and ears everywhere. Plus, the jinn kings already know who she really is. No one else has to."

"Hide?" I frown. I don't like the idea that I have to hide again. That doesn't sound like belonging to me. That sounds like what I've already been doing my whole life. "I don't wanna go if I can't be me."

"After the observation period, maybe you could stay, without the disguise," reasons Yaseen. "You heard King Mudhib. What better way to prove you aren't a threat to our world than to show you can blend in?"

"I mean, when you put it that way . . ." But I wonder if staying means leaving my mom for good. I don't want to be forced into another either-or situation.

Padar doesn't look happy to hear that. "Let's not get ahead of ourselves." He pauses. "Though there is some wisdom to learning our ways. The only thing more dangerous than a mixed jinn is an untrained one with nothing to do. . . . But it's just a Band-Aid. You wouldn't be a *real* student."

"Why not?"

"The academy is an incredibly ancient institution meant to guide young royal jinn into the roles they were born into. Each student comes from an important family within a jinn king's realm. There are important functions that are passed down to heirs to keep our realms in order. Yaseen, for example, will follow in my footsteps should anything ever happen to me when I can no longer rule as a king," he explains. "You do not have a role at the academy, nor could I reveal that you are my daughter. It would not do."

Ouch. That stings more than the Scale of Deeds. The bubbles start to rise in my gut, making me want to run very far away from this conversation.

"Then take me home," I demand. My mom was right. I shouldn't have answered the summons. I was silly to think my dad would be any different. "That'll solve all your problems. You can have your perfect order in your perfect jinn world." This magical place will never be my home. Not when my own dad won't fight for me. "At least in the human world, I've got people who actually want me there."

"You don't have that choice anymore." My dad gets up, wipes his knees, and turns away from us. His hands are behind his back as he stares up at the stone ceiling. "You physically cannot return to your mother until the longest day of the year arrives. In June."

"That's months away!" I shake my head. "You have to let me go back home. I promised her I'd come back. I—"

"Promises hold no weight when magic is involved. Consider this one of many lessons in our world." He walks toward his throne, where an ornate piece of parchment materializes. "You say you want to be part of this realm, but I'm not sure you have what it takes to survive among us." He pulls a jeweled pen from inside his robe and signs the bottom. "It's not your fault—human hearts are flawed in that way. Soft. But since there's no way around our current situation . . ." He turns around and holds out the paper for me to grab. "I suppose you'll see for yourself."

"What's this?" I snatch the paper from his grip. AL-QALAM ACADEMY FOR THE EXCEPTIONAL—ENROLLMENT FORM. The words glitter and leap off the page. My dad's signature is bold and messy. "What about my mom?" I look between Yaseen and my dad. "Doesn't she need to sign too?"

"She's not a jinn, so . . . no." Yaseen shrugs. "But this is great, right? You're going to the academy! Just like you wanted."

Is it just like I wanted?

"Listen carefully to my instructions," my dad warns. "There are three things you must do. The first—do not lose that enrollment form. You will need it to gain admittance to the academy. Second, you will make one stop to the top floor of the courthouse to King Abyad's court to gather an illusion enchantment to conceal your true nature. No one"—he stares intently at Yaseen and me—"must learn about Farrah's true identity. *No one.* Is that understood?"

"Yes, Baba." Yaseen clasps his hands in front of his belly.

"Farrah?" Padar doesn't move until I've nodded too.

"What's the third thing?" I ask instead.

"You will meet with me every Thursday, in my court, on the fifth floor," Padar orders. "To continue with your observation. Whatever that scale wants us to observe, I must be the first one to discover it."

"But—"

"Disregard these instructions, Farrah, and breaking your promise to your mother will be the least of your worries," he says. "Now go. I'm late for another appointment."

"No. Not until you promise you'll let my mom know I'm okay." My blood runs cold when my dad shoots me a withering glare.

"What did I just say about promises?"

"Please," I add, imagining the ocean of sadness already looming around my mom, and how I'm going to make that hole bigger. "She gets sad. You don't understand. Without me there, she . . ." What I don't say is, my mom is going to be sad *because* of me. And I'm afraid of what will happen if I'm not there to patch the hole.

"You are not responsible for your mother's emotions." My dad is quiet for a long moment after that. "I never understood that about your mother. Not then, and not now, but if that is your one and only request to follow my instructions, then it

shall be done. Your mother will be informed of the situation."
He moves his long robe to turn away, calling upon thunder
to portal out of this room. "She will see you returned in three
months' time. Or at least, that is what she will believe."

"Has this happened before with the scale?" I throw out
one last question and ignore Yaseen's pleading *stop interrupting and let him leave* stare. "The observation period *has* happened before, right?"

"Once, yes," he responds.

"And everything turned out okay?" I hold my breath and
hope.

My dad doesn't answer. Instead he glances over his shoulder and says, "Every Thursday, Farrah."

Without another word, he disappears in a crack of thunder.

My dad's lack of answer only makes me more nervous
when we trek to the top of the courthouse into King Abyad's
court.

"Ah, right on time." King Abyad smiles.

Here, silver shines *everywhere*. It makes it hard to see the
white jinn king as he shimmers toward us like a mirage. Yaseen loops his arm through mine as the heavy silver doors
slam shut, leaving us all alone.

"H-how did you know we were coming?" I ask.

"I've already seen through the shimmer and peeked at the"

Eternal Tablet." King Abyad waves his hands. "I know why you're here. Come along, this way, but watch your step. Don't accidentally fall into a shimmerfield. Can't have you scaring the mortals too badly now."

"A shimmer *what*?"

"Don't worry, I've got you." Yaseen tightens his grip around my arm and leads us forward in the long hallway, making a quick beeline behind King Abyad. The end of the king's long gray robe dusts the top of our shoes. All around us, there are glimmers of deserts, forests, cities, appearing in the distance. One second I see the edges of a palm tree in an oasis; then I blink, and it's gone. "King Abyad is the jinn king of the moon. He has lots of nicknames, but the most common one is the White King," Yaseen whispers. "In his realm, he channels the power of the moon, which gives motion to the universe—including seen and unseen realms."

"No, no—that's not right—no, it's not there either," King Abyad mutters to himself as he darts left, right, zigzagging, peeking into different shimmerfields. "I know I placed it in this century—I think. . . ."

"What are these?" I reach out to touch a shimmerfield, and my fingers pass through, trying to catch the horn of—is that a triceratops? "Are those dinosaurs?"

"Farrah, don't touch!" yells Yaseen.

It's too late.

The second I touch the horn, I am ripped from Yaseen's

grip, and I fall headfirst toward a swampy-looking pond filled with stampeding legs of dinosaurs with big scary teeth and—

"Up and out you go." A cool mist swirls around me as King Abyad's cold grip pulls me out right before I hit the water. "Never a good thing to tumble into an extinction event." I fall flat on my butt, bumping into Yaseen. My heart is racing a mile a minute.

"W-where was I?"

"Mortals, always too curious for their own good." King Abyad ignores my question and continues his search. He spins a ring made of bark on his finger. "Tell them not to do something and they do it."

"Shimmerfields are dangerous. Don't be fooled by how pretty they look." Yaseen helps me up. "They're pockets of liminal spaces—a thinning of the barriers between realms. You don't want to get lost in one of them. Fall in and you might never come out."

"So they're like portals?" I ask. Or maybe mirages.

"Not exactly."

"HERE IT IS!" King Abyad reaches into a shimmerfield and pulls out a delicate brushed-silver perfume bottle. "A classic—my Eau de Illusion. A powerful trinket made from the finest metals in my realm that casts a formidable illusion on its wearer. Guaranteed to conceal all unwanted appearances and stenches for six hours in a single spray. Ah, but we will need a new formula for you. . . ." He unscrews the bottle, dumps out the liquid, and holds it out to me. "I will need a sample of your essence."

"Like what?" I grab the chilled bottle. The tips of my fingers go numb.

"Skin, bone, blood, hair, spit—it does not matter, so long as you give it freely," explains King Abyad.

"Oh right." I look nervously at Yaseen. His gaze goes steely. "Guess hair is easiest?"

Yaseen shakes his head. "Spit is your best option."

"But that's so gross."

"Trust me" is all he says.

"Mortals are just so curious," King Abyad mutters while plucking three items from different shimmerfields. "Curious and trusting."

"If you say so." I hand the bottle back after I spit in it three times. ("Illusions require an auspicious number," said King Abyad.) At least it's not a clear bottle—now, that would be gross.

"A handful of moonstone, five teardrops from a sightless salamander, and a sprinkle of vanilla—unless you prefer lavender?" asks King Abyad when he drops everything into the bottle.

"Vanilla is fine," I say nervously.

"And last—a drop of my essence to complete the formula." He pricks his finger with one of his claws. A small drop of shimmering blood falls into the potion. He twists the top back onto the perfume bottle, gives it a shake, and hands it back to me. "So long as you use this, your identity will be concealed."

"Thank you." I fumble with the bottle as it heats up in my hands. "For giving this to me." Maybe I was wrong. Maybe there can be kind jinn kings. I've always thought of the moon as calm and peaceful and transparent. Maybe the White King is like that too.

"Mortals are such curious things." He waves his hand and walks away. "Can't see through the illusions they make in their minds. Thinks an item is a gift." He laughs and disappears into a beam of shimmering light. "Can't see what they've really done is a trade. Such silly, trusting, curious mortals."

CHAPTER EIGHT

WORRIES OR WISHES?

"A trade?"

There's a deep pit in my stomach when Yaseen and I exit the White King's court.

What did he mean by that?

"Jinn never *give* things," explains Yaseen as we wind down a huge stone staircase. "I thought you knew that from dealing with *you-know-who*." A kaleidoscope of stained-glass light sparkles against us. "There's always a cost in some way. Even if it seems free . . . our realm is always taking something."

"Why didn't you remind me?" I shake the perfume bottle, angry that it slipped my mind. "I wouldn't have done it if I'd known that!"

"And interrupt a king? Are you out of your mind? Our dad told us to pick up your illusion, not question whether you should take the trade or not." Yaseen whirls on me. "And I did help you. You wanted to offer *hair*—do you know what a jinn can do with a sliver of human hair? You could have been turned into a puppet." He rolls his eyes. "I gave you the safest option. No one really cares for spit."

"Next time," I grit through my teeth, "tell me beforehand." Angry bubbles pile up in my fingers and toes. I press on the perfume button, spraying his whole face with the solution.

"THOSE ARE YOUR GERMS!" yelps Yaseen. He races down the stairs, wiping frantically at his hair. "DISGUST-ING! IT REEKS!"

"Does it?" I tentatively spray over my head and let the mist fall down around me. Since I've already made the trade, I might as well use it. "Smells just like vanilla. I kinda like it." But I notice a problem. I still look the same. I shake the bottle suspiciously. "Isn't it supposed to do something?"

Yaseen crosses his arms and stomps down the final stair, heading toward the long hallway. High archways glitter in never-ending rows. The exit feels like a speck at the end of the hall. "Look down at the floor," he says.

"Why am I *blue*?" I shriek. My reflection in the shiny tile jumps back, equally horrified. "And my ears—why are they like that?" Two pointy tips stick out of my hair, but when I touch my ears, they're normal and round.

"Your undertone is more blue." Yaseen rolls his eyes again. "It's not like you look like a blueberry."

"My teeth aren't sharp and pointy either." I tap my tongue against my canines. In the reflection, they match Yaseen's— sharp and dangerous.

"It's an illusion, remember?"

"So I'm still me." In a really high-tech disguise.

"Yeah, but we'll need to work on your backstory."

"Backstory?"

"For your secret identity." Yaseen keeps walking. "You heard our dad. If we want this observation period to go smoothly, no one can find out who you really are."

"Right." I stop short and watch my brother stride across the great hall like he owns the place. Like he *belongs*. Will I ever get to walk like that? Is that what the observation period is going to reveal? That mixed jinn aren't a threat? That I can belong too?

So then why does your father want to be the first to find out? A familiar voice whispers so softly in my head, I almost don't hear it. *Maybe he fears that you are . . . a threat.*

"Hey, why'd you stop?" Yaseen yells from down the hall. "We've got to get to the academy!"

"Y-you're not supposed to be able to talk to me," I whisper to the floor. "We locked you away. We—" Imagined shadows whisk and whirl around my jinn reflection on the ground, where I can see Azar's bright mismatched eyes staring right into my heart and reading into my deepest worries.

Worries or wishes? Azar's reflection mouths.

"You okay?" Yaseen's shoe breaks the reflection, and Azar's image disappears. "It'll take some getting used to, but I think you look way more normal—more like us now!"

"I—" My eyes shift around the hall, searching for a shadow

that doesn't belong. Blinking red eyes. Glimmering multi-colored gems pulse up and down the walls and domed ceiling. It makes it hard to spot one of Azar's puppets. "I heard him, Yaseen. . . . He's back."

"*Him* him?" Yaseen's eyes go wide. "In your head?"

"Yeah, he—"

"Walk and talk, Farrah. The walls have ears around here, especially on our dad's day." Yaseen grabs my arm, and we hurry out of the Supreme Court of Jinn and into the glittering main square.

The Qaf Mountains loom high over the skyscrapers of the city, casting it in a light green glow. Little clouds filter into the street, making it all seem like a beautiful dream . . . that Azar is ruining.

"Didn't we get rid of him and his pesky puppets . . . ?" Yaseen starts fidgeting with his sweater, his eyes shifting up, down, left, right.

"Yep." Right before we busted out of the Realm Beneath the Unseen, I trapped Azar in the ring of fate as a trade for my last wish, for the ring to not be able to make any more wishes. One fate for another—his *should* have been sealed. "Unless he got out. Somehow."

"Which feels like really . . . inconvenient timing on his part," Yaseen mumbles, "or very convenient, depending on how you look at it."

"It's really *in*convenient," I snap. "I'm being watched by the kings, and I can't make it one day without something suspicious happening." I cross the street without looking and bump into a group of grumbly jinn. "What if"—I swat at low-hanging ribbons and streamers strung along trees lining the path—"this is exactly what the scale wants the kings to observe? What if *you-know-who* has something else up his sleeve?"

"That's not going to happen," Yaseen jumps in. "Whatever that old fart throws our way, we can handle it."

"Easy for you to say. You're not the one under observation." Worries blast all around me. A deep weight presses against my chest. "The kings already look at me like I'm a threat. Finding out he still talks to me is all the proof they need." I don't want to be exiled, but being *terminated* would be even worse. "You heard our dad when I asked him about the last time this happened. We all know what a nonanswer means." I can read between the lines. The last time this happened, it didn't go well. Not at all.

"Message received, loud and clear." Yaseen throws his hands up. "I'm one hundred percent in the *don't want to face that old fart* boat. We just won't tell anyone that he's out of the ring. Plus, even if he's out, so what? He's still chained to his realm. It's not like he can actually do anything here."

"That's true. . . ." I rub my forehead, trying to think it all through. "All I have to do is ignore him. What's he going to do from all the way in the Realm Beneath? He can't reach me here." My shoulders loosen, and I let out a sigh of relief.

"Get the nerves out before we get to the academy," says

Yaseen. "Focus on the end goal, and don't let his chaos get to you. No one knows what the observation period means, so all we are going to do is prove to the kings that you are *good*. And after the solstice, they'll make you—the *real* you—a full-time student. That's the plan. I'll be right there with you to make sure you blend in."

"Thanks, that makes me feel better." I let out a laugh. "And you know what? *Old fart*'s got a ring to it. Definitely a better code name than *you-know-who*."

"What can I say? I'm a genius."

We reach the end of the path and pass by a long, dark obsidian gate. Little wisps of darkness spill out of the bottom, whirling and winding their way around our ankles. Goose bumps run up my legs.

"Oh, forgot to tell you, don't walk too close to the gate." Yaseen hops on his left foot away from the mist.

"Where is this coming from?" A part of me wants to touch it, but the smarter part of me follows Yaseen.

"It's the gateway to King Maymun's Realm of Nightmares," explains Yaseen. He points at the gated entrance rising into the sky. The iron twists and unfurls menacingly. Above are two pointed spires with two clear gems bursting with light beams.

"A gateway?"

"All the jinn kings have their own portals," replies Yaseen. "If we were to walk around the whole city in a big loop, we'd see all seven gateways. It's how you know you're on the outskirts of the city. Baba's realm is all the way on the other side over there. Maybe one day, I can show you my house." He picks at his eyebrow. "My real house. Not that weird upside-down purgatory you saw in the Realm Beneath."

"I doubt our dad will be happy with that idea."

"Who says we have to tell him?" He laughs nervously as we turn the corner away from King Maymun's gate. A giant winged jinn flies overhead right before the portal winks out of view. Once he soars past the two gems, he vanishes in a burst of bright light. Yaseen shivers at the sight. "I wonder what it's like in that realm."

"You've never been?"

"Nope." Yaseen shakes his head. "Our realms don't really get along—you'd never see a nightmare resident in my baba's realm. We're practically enemies."

"Why's it called the Realm of *Nightmares*?"

"King Maymun's nickname is *the Winged Nightmare*. Mostly because he rules over the unconscious world, and I've heard stories about jinn being snapped up and kidnapped, just to be tortured in their dreams there. . . ."

"I wouldn't want to go in there either." I always thought the Realm Beneath was the worst realm in the jinn world, but King Maymun's realm could be in the running. "Uncon-scious realm . . . The last thing I need is for someone else to be poking around in my dreams."

"If you think that's bad, wait until you learn about King Ahmar's realm. I hear it's built like a fortress, and all the jinn there are conscripted into deadly combat service." Yaseen claps his hands together in relief when the academy comes into view. Students flurry in and out of the entrance, laughing and banding together in their shimmering uniforms. "Ready for a new beginning?" He glances over his shoulder, looking nervous and hopeful. "I know it's not the start you wanted, but—"

"A new beginning." I grip my fists tight and immediately think of Arzu. I go to touch our forever bracelet in my pocket—and promise that I'll find a way to let her know every detail of this new school—when I gasp in shock. "Oh no! My bracelet is gone!"

"Your what?"

"My forever bracelet!" I roll up my sleeves, check all my pockets—nothing. "It must have fallen back in the Court of Punishment and Exile," I whisper in horror. "I've got to get it."

"You heard what Baba said." Yaseen grabs my wrist. "Straight to the academy—we can't deviate—"

"*I don't care*," I practically shout. "This is Arzu's bracelet. It's the only thing I have of home. What if it were your protection charm? You wouldn't leave it there!" So many angry bubbles make me rip my arm away from Yaseen. "I've got to—"

"Missing something?" someone says from behind Yaseen and me.

"You!" I say, wheeling around. I don't mean to, but my fist hits Idris square in the jaw.

"That's a weird way to say hello," Yaseen says, shocked.

"*Did you just see that girl sucker punch that guy?*"

"*Wouldn't want to get on her bad side!*"

"I . . . deserve that." Idris stumbles back a little, rubbing his cheek. "I should have learned the first time to never startle you."

Say something, my brain tells me. There are a hundred normal responses I could give.

What are you doing here? Where were you these past three months? Why are you holding Arzu's bracelet? Why did I hear your voice in the court?

But my heart is short-circuiting.

Instead, I grab the bracelet from Idris's outstretched hand and flee into the academy, leaving a very confused Yaseen behind.

CHAPTER NINE

WELCOME TO THE ACADEMY

The entrance hall is inky black, dazzling with starry curtains and midnight-stained windows. I quickly slam the door shut and press my back flat against it. "Anything else you'd like to throw at me, universe?" My hand throbs, which is a great distraction from the one-eighty my life has taken in less than twelve hours. "No more surprises, okay?"

"Well, I caution students from asking for promises that cannot be kept." A faerie half my height pops up in front of me. I scream in surprise. "Oh dear, not another screamer. You see, delicate ears, I've got." She rubs the side of her head and massages her pointy ears. Her shiny blue dress sways as she places her hands on her hips. Her wings flutter in protest. "Now then, up you go. Off the floor, can't you see you're ruining the carpet sliding your feet around like that." The faerie shoos me up until I'm on my feet. "In this institution, we learn to greet the building properly. Not wander around making a mess of the carpet and breaking children's noses with our fists."

"Technically, he's not a child," I mumble under my breath. If you count the time Idris spent in the ring, he's closer to one hundred thirteen years old than thirteen. . . .

"What was that?" asks the faerie.

"It's my first day, and my parents weren't very . . . informative." My ears go red. I pull out my rumpled admittance paper and hand it to her.

"If it's any indication of what to expect for the rest of the term . . ." Wide-rimmed glasses appear on her nose as she evaluates my father's signature. "I see I will have my hands full with you, Miss—" She looks up expectantly at me.

"Um. It should say Farrah."

"Yes, that's clear." She brings her voice lower, careful of the curious glances from passing-by students. "I meant family name."

"N-Noorzad," I stutter.

"Daughter of . . . which realm?" The faerie looks at me again.

"Um."

"MARS!" Yaseen bursts through the doors, causing more of a scene as more eyes are glued on us. His bangs are stuck to the sides of his cheeks. He quickly wipes them away. "I— I mean, after such a violent display, I'd guess you're from King Ahmar's realm?"

"Oh yep. Totally violent. Yep," I babble sheepishly. "Unleashed a plague of locusts once, um, to prove a point."

"What an interesting combination you two are." The faerie's delicate eyebrows rise. "Well, Miss Noorzad, given these most curious circumstances, I welcome you to the academy." Her fingers wave around the paper, making it glow. The words slowly light up one by one, burning my dad's signature to be replaced with another name, changing the emblem from Jupiter to Mars. "You've arrived a bit late. The term has already started. The girls' dormitories are always to the right. Boys to the left. The starry staircase will take you to the second floor, where your room has already been assigned. There will be a packet with rules and expectations, along with your schedule for your first day tomorrow." She frowns, still looking between Yaseen and me. "Where is her protection charm?"

"Oh . . . it's—"

"Broken," I interject. "It was an accident."

"An accident," she repeats.

"Yes, um. It's a long story and really boring, so I'll get out of your hair and get to my room and not cause any trouble! Thank you!" I walk quickly toward the right, carefully dodging more curious stares.

"Did you hear that, a Mars girl . . . ?" a student says to her friends from across the hall. "Haven't had someone from the Red King's realm in a looong time."

"I'd steer clear. She admitted to *unleashing locusts,*" another girl sneers. "Who does that?"

"Was just once!" I shout, and wave cheerfully. "Nice to meet you!" I hear the faerie sigh in exasperation.

"Trust the unexpected students to cause a ruckus," she huffs as she flits away.

"Have you ever heard of lying low?" Yaseen speed-walks until he's right next to me. "Somehow I don't think nearly breaking Idris's jaw is the best way to prove you're *non-threatening,* Farrah." We make it to the foot of the staircase.

"It's not like I planned for him to be there," I hiss.

"Well, whatever's going on in friendship land needs to get resolved, because I can't have two mixed-jinn loose cannons running around the—"

"Hey, you okay down there?" A girl's voice floats from the third floor. Her head pokes out over the spiral railing. Soft brown hair flows over her shoulders. "I thought I heard Miss Cerulean grumbling more than usual."

"Everything's fine, Sufia," Yaseen calls out. "No need to—"

"Oh, Yaseen, there you are!" Sufia jumps on the railing and slides all the way down, her hair and academy uniform sparkling behind her. "I was wondering where you were all day."

I recognized her instantly. She's Yaseen's friend—the girl I talked to in the second-year library when Idris and I snuck out of Yaseen's dorm room.

"Yeah, it's Thursday, my baba's day, so I decided to visit

him at the court," Yaseen hedges. "And ended up running into Farrah—who got into it with the building spirit."

"She's not a faerie?"

"A faerie?" Sufia laughs. "Could you imagine Miss Cerulean, a faerie? Though with those wings she likes to add on, I could see how you'd think that. She's the building *spirit*. She protects the academy."

"We don't have them where I'm from." If there were spirits in the human realm, I hadn't seen any.

"Strange." Sufia's brown eyes blink curiously at me. "I've never seen clothes like yours before. They're so . . . vintage."

"It's . . . my parents. They're into antiquing."

"I was about to say, the material looks primitive." She nudges my sweatshirt. "There's no essence infused in these. Do you need any help getting to your room?" She looks around for luggage. "No bags?"

"They were already sent up." Yaseen uncomfortably scratches the back of his neck. "Is what I overheard earlier."

"Oh yep. Yep. Already in my room." I nod a little too enthusiastically.

"All right." Sufia looks curiously between Yaseen and me. "You know, you look awfully familiar." She tilts her head to the side, her silver skirt swaying. Her dainty fingers tap against her cheek. "Those eyes . . ."

"I must have one of those faces, I suppose!" I rush up the starry staircase.

"Totally average, forgettable face," agrees Yaseen nervously.

"Wait, this isn't a proper welcome!" Sufia loops her arm around Yaseen's and drags him up the stairs. "We don't get new students often—least we can do is walk you to your room."

"Can we not and say we did?" Yaseen grits his teeth.

"I'm just one floor above you." Sufia ignores Yaseen and pushes through the glass doors, leading the way down the winding hall. "After you." She holds Yaseen back and lets me pass. There are only a couple of doors in the hall.

"But I don't know which door is mine."

"No one ever does the first time," Sufia says encouragingly. "You'll see."

"Okay . . ." I hold on to my bracelet and continue taking steps forward. There are doors made of lead, gold, copper, and then finally tin. Something in my chest buzzes and burns when I stare at the door. "Wait, this one feels . . ." *Right.* I place my palm on the center, and it erupts into molten lava. "IT'S ON FIRE!" I jump away and watch the door transform from tin to iron, bubbling and bursting with hot magma. The symbol of Mars is burned into the door. Hundreds of tiny red gems—garnet, hematite, ruby, and jasper—are embedded to look like stars.

"No one can say Mars doesn't know how to create an entrance." Sufia tucks her perfect hair behind her ears. Her eyes glitter in welcome, and I can't help but grin nervously. She seems to pick up on the tense energy, because suddenly she announces, "How rude of us. You must be exhausted. It was so nice to meet you, which isn't something I'd ever think I'd say to a patron of the Red King's realm, but"—she clears her throat—"I mean, I'm sure you know about all that, but what I'm trying to say is, I like being surprised, so thank you. For surprising me."

"Suf, I think she gets it." Yaseen rubs his hands over his face.

"Right. Well. See you later!" Sufia flashes a peace sign and turns on her heel, dragging Yaseen along with her. "Just wanted to be extra welcoming," she says in a low voice in Yaseen's ear, "in case the rest of the academy isn't . . . You know how the other realms can be—"

The rest of her sentence is cut off by the slam of the glass doors.

I am so dead tired and drained from this whirlwind of a day, all I want to do is pass out on my bed and sleep away all my worries for the next three months. Instead, I slowly shut my dorm door, sink down to the cold lead floor, and slip out my phone.

> does the offer still stand

> id like to take my spot at ur place please

I know there's no way Arzu will ever get these messages, but I still send them. Knowing she's out there, on the other end of the line, makes me feel less alone.

how am i gonna do this

im in way over my head

wish u were here, magic sucks without u

This is not how I imagined my new adventure in the City of Jewels would begin. The pressure in my chest starts back up when I think of Arzu waiting by her phone, wondering why I haven't answered her calls, or when I picture my mom having to explain to my aunt and grandparents where I went, or replaying my so-called friend popping up out of nowhere like he wasn't gone for months, pretending like everything is all right when everything is all *wrong*.

In the quiet of my room, the worries and questions pile up again—*why did you disappear, why am I so easy to leave, why are promises so hard to keep*—poking the bruised spots in my heart, and paired with the kings watching me, I feel like I've got the weight of the world on my shoulders.

I'm afraid if I make one wrong step, it's all going to topple down and fall.

Which means there's only one option.

I can't let it.

IDRIS

BEING GIFTED

I dris was in a memory.

Or a vision. Or a nightmare. He wasn't entirely sure, but he knew it was his, and that it was important. And for the twelfth time that day since the scale revealed it to him, he lived it, searching for answers.

A kindness for a kindness, the scale had rumbled as Idris was thrown backward in time and plunged into an endless, icy, dark abyss.

You won't get away with this. The words flashed in Idris's mind as boundless anger coursed through him. Anger, followed by a dull pain that radiated in his head and wouldn't let go. Idris couldn't understand where the words or emotion came from, but he knew the more he struggled against the gold chains dragging him farther into the water, the quicker he was headed to an icy grave. *You can't stop destiny no matter how much power you amass.*

A million questions ran through Idris's head.

How had he gotten here? Why was he so angry? What did destiny have in store for him?

Was this his past, his present, or his future?

That is a mystery that even transcends my power, the scale had answered the first time he'd asked. *That you will have to figure out on your own.*

"How is this a gift?" asked Idris aloud. But as the vision came to an end, he felt the last of his energy drain as the words were ripped from his throat. *This was it for him—just as was predicted—the end.* That, and a loop of words repeating in his mind that stayed with him long after he lost consciousness. *But with all magic comes a price. In pieces, chained through mist as cold as ice.*

When Idris opened his eyes, he was no longer in the grip of the vision. Instead, he was hidden away in a secluded tower in the academy. The moonlight filtered through the spires and cast long shadows on him and another boy—Farrah's brother, Yaseen ibn Shamhurish.

"So, ready to tell me what the heck is going on?" demanded Yaseen, gripping his hands into fists.

And so Idris did.

CHAPTER TEN

ANOTHER DAY, ANOTHER SUMMONS

The lofted twin bed in my dorm is supersoft (and I think my pillow might actually be made out of a cloud?), but no matter how hard I try to get comfy, I still sleep uneasily.

I fall into a nightmare.

Idris, Yaseen, and I are back in the Realm Beneath the Unseen, walking through the gates of the snow-globe purgatory world. The upside-down version of the Qaf Mountains looms before us. Little bits of pebbles and grass fall from the sky—the only hint that we fell from the human realm into this new one.

"Oh, I'm going to be sick!" Idris wails, running into Yaseen's house. "Where are the trash receptacles so a jinn can vomit in peace!"

Yaseen gives me the look. "That isn't suspicious to you?"

I pause. Wait a second. "You've said that before. . . ." My

shoes are crunching against the rocky ground. The air is still and hot. I squint up at the dark dome. I remember again. We've been here before. "I don't understand why I keep coming back here."

"Back where?" asks Yaseen.

"To this night." I rub my arms (purposely *not* looking at the frozen fountain of blood) and head into the house to chase after Idris. The great room unwinds and whirls, full of so many artifacts and historical pieces. "It's like I can't wake up from it."

"You're acting like that's a bad thing." A new voice comes from behind me.

It's *her*.

My shadow puppet.

Now *that's* different. "What are you doing here?" I jump away, knocking a vase off its stand. It tumbles forward but doesn't fall. That's right, time doesn't work normally here.

"I could ask you the same thing," my shadow puppet says, walking around me. Her red eyes glow like hot coals. Smoke twirls around her fingers and toes. In the center of her right palm is a speck of bright light. "But what's the fun in asking a question when you already know the answer?"

"You know why I'm here?"

"No, *you* know why you're here." She walks up to a row of decorative plates displayed on a shelf and tips one over. They domino but don't shatter and fall. My confused face frustrates her. "It's because you want to be." She flicks another plate. "Here."

"Why would I want to come back here?" This place is a nightmare.

"It's your truth, not mine." She smiles wryly. "After all, I'm just a puppet, so what do I know?"

My truth? I frown.

"That's so funny," she continues, tipping plates, vases, lamps, and swords. Creating small ripples of chaos wherever she goes. "Even here, in a place where you've got only yourself, you still don't want to see it."

"See what?"

The girl laughs, ignoring me. Why are jinn like this? Why can't she just tell me the answer?!

"Hello, Earth to—" The ground rumbles and shakes. Something roars in the distance. "W-what's that?"

"Dunno," the girl says. Her red eyes glance up and around. "It's not coming from here."

"Then where—" More shaking. The floor cracks every which way beneath my feet. "Well, whatever it is, we've gotta get out of here. Hey!" She doesn't listen to me. She just stands where larger pieces of debris fall from the sky. Little shadowy wisps curl around the pieces, coating the ground in a soft mist. "Did you hear me? Hey!" This is so frustrating. "What's your name?" There's only so many times I can say *hey* or *you* or *girl* or *shadow puppet*.

"My name?" Her face—my face—blinks in surprise.

"Yeah, I need to know who I can yell at when we get crushed like pancakes if someone doesn't start moving!"

"If I had a name . . ." She glances sidelong at me, totally unfazed by the screeching and crumbling of the upside-down world, and says, "I think I'd like to be called Hura."

"Great. Now let's get out of here before this whole thing turns us into breakfast."

"Don't worry. It never does, not since the last few times you've been here." Hura smiles sadly.

"You're saying I've dreamed this before?"

"Don't feel bad. The waking never remember the other world." Hura merely shrugs. "Until next time, Farrah Noorzad." She waves the second the glass dome shatters. "Maybe then you'll finally be able to face your truth."

"What truth?!"

Hura doesn't get a chance to answer. Huge chunks of glass are about to crush us in three, two, one . . .

I WAKE UP RIGHT WHEN I FALL OFF MY BED.

The ground keeps shaking, like a huge train is roaring by.

"Now, that hurts. . . ." I groan, rolling onto my stomach. "Who makes lofted beds without rails?" The jinn world, apparently, because that's where I am, in my dorm room, as a student at the academy.

A *fake student*, my dad's voice echoes in my head.

"Thanks for the reminder, brain," I grumble. At least the ground stops shaking, so that's a plus. I take two deep breaths to calm my racing heart—it happens often, stirring from unpleasant dreams that slip from my head when I wake—then I get up.

Time to face the day.

The sun is blazing through the windows. I can hear the morning sounds of the city awakening. Clouds filled with jinn zip by. Flying birds and other creatures screech and roar through the skyscrapers. Some fly straight into round green buildings, disappearing instantly. The floor shakes a little more when something huge and blue shimmers up and into a giant nest at the tallest peak of the Qaf Mountains.

"Oh, so *you're* responsible for that unpleasant wake-up call." I rush over to the window and slide it open to lean out and catch a glimpse of the simurgh. "I wouldn't mind you being my alarm clock, but warn a girl next time you want to shake the city, okay?" I shout out, and wave. My heart thrills at the sight. The emerald mountains glint, sending rainbows of light against the glass floor of the city. The Supreme Court shines solid and white against it all.

Even though I'm stuck here against my will, this city is *marvelous.*

Maybe Yaseen was right. Maybe this could be good. Maybe *I* could be good.

It's like he said—no one knows what the observation

period means, so why stress myself out about it? As long as I stick to the plan and blend in, I'll survive long enough to laugh about it with my mom and Arzu someday. Plus, how hard could jinn school be?

I spin around and take in my new room with a fresh perspective. Yesterday sucked, but today is gonna be better. My room is small and simple, with a twin bed, a desk, a chest, and one wardrobe for clothes I don't have . . . until I open up the doors and gasp in surprise. It's filled with sparkly silver uniforms. Three pairs of shoes are tucked underneath. "Are these all mine?" I whisper, touching the smooth and silky material. It feels like water slipping between my fingers. I immediately try the skirt on—it's even better than the swishy uniform pants. Energy buzzes in each thread and gently tap, tap, taps against my skin, waking me up faster than a large iced coffee. I put on the rest of the uniform—shirt, sweater-vest, socks, and shoes—and the buzzing intensifies. I could run a marathon, swim across the Atlantic Ocean, and climb Mount Everest and still not be tired.

I never want this feeling to go away. I need to see myself in this uniform, stat.

"There's gotta be a mirror in here somewhere. . . ." My skirt swishes against my legs as I march over to the bathroom. Above the sink are three shimmering buttons on the wall. Which one activates a mirror? I press the first one—soapy perfumed water immediately falls from the ceiling. "No, no, no!" I smash the second button—hot air blasts from the walls, spraying soapy water pellets all over me. "I already hate jinn bathrooms!" I jam both buttons at the same time, hoping it turns everything off—it just makes the water freezing cold. "FORGET IT." I run out of the bathroom, shivering. "Why doesn't anything have labels or a manual . . . ?"

You know what doesn't need a manual or dangerous button-pushing?

A mirror . . . which I just remembered jinn don't use. They use reflectors. Something I don't have at the moment—oh wait, there's one right here on my desk.

"Still got to get used to the no-mirror thing." I tap the top of the triangular device. It emits a rectangle of light. Within it, I see myself—sopping wet and shivery cold—but I'm still me in my silver uniform, with green stripes running down the sides of my skirt and sleeves like shooting stars. I imagine my mom walking into the room, gasping as she twirls me. *You look amazing,* she'd say. *Perfect and almost grown-up.*

Well, nearly perfect.

I spray the Eau de Illusion and let it fall over me. The transformation in the reflector is instant. My hair—all wet and tangled—turns sleek and shiny, while my skin shifts to the lightest periwinkle blue. Little shimmery freckles scatter across my nose and cheeks like constellations. "Unreal," I whisper. My brown eyes sparkle to match my freckles. My teeth get a little sharper, my ears a little pointier. I stare at the girl I could have been, if I'd had a different mom— a jinn mom.

My fingers touch my holo-reflection, and I stare in the quiet space where it's just me and my thoughts. *If I had a different mom . . .*

"Would you be happier, Madar?" I remember my mom lying on my pillow, tears slipping down her cheeks. "Would you have already gone on your grand adventure?" I ask. "Would both of our lives have been easier if things were different?"

Guilt rears its head, and I quickly shut off the reflector. Of course I'd never want a different mom—why would I think that? This perfume's gone to my head. That's gotta be it. I pocket it and hurry out of my room, slamming the door on that uncomfortable thought.

"NEW GIRL!" SUFIA WAVES FROM THE BOTTOM OF THE NO-longer-starry staircase. Now it looks like a garden in bloom, bursting with pinks, violets, and greens. Heavy gems grow out of the flowers, just waiting to be picked. A few students do pick them, filling their pockets. "I was worried when I didn't see you at breakfast!"

"Oh, I didn't know it was so early." My schedule that was on my desk said Fridays were free study days—so no formal classes—but I didn't think students would wake up early on their *own*. My feet trip over the petal stairs, which swing and bounce on every step. "What happened to the starry staircase?

Why is it full of flowers now?" I cling to the railing to avoid a massive belly flop down the rest of the flower staircase.

"Want some advice?" an amused voice calls out. There's another girl standing next to Sufia.

"Sure!"

"The trick is to not look down. Look forward, and you won't trip," the second girl recommends.

"Oh, no fun," a third girl whines. "No one helped me my first time down the spring staircase. I nearly lost my nose falling down those stairs!"

The second girl giggles. "Not the nose! What would you do without it?"

"Besides not smell you?"

I stare right ahead and make it down the stairs. The girls were right. It worked.

"Thanks for the tip," I say. "I would have lost more than my nose if it weren't for—"

"The name's Tamira Talvyr," the second girl says. Her curly hair is piled up high on her head with her tiny ears sticking out in a way that looks really cute. Her amethyst eyes sparkle, especially when a little burst of blue energy springs from my chest and transforms into a small blue bead. The girl grabs it and adds it to the small chain around her neck (where a rainbow of beads already lies). "And you owe me for that tip."

"What just happened?" I ask.

"Already racking up debts, huh?" The third girl throws

one end of her scarf over her shoulder. A little bit of lavender hair peeks up from the top. Her dark skin twinkles against her silver scarf. She glances at me. "Nothing ever comes for free around here—you should remember that. That's the only advice I'll give ya free of charge, but next time." She shakes her finger and points at the bracelet around her wrist, also full of beads.

"I wouldn't try to intimidate the newbie, Laila." Sufia throws her arm around my shoulder and immediately absorbs me into the group. "She's a Mars girl, after all." Sufia winks at me as we walk into the great hall.

"MARS?" Tamira and Laila yelp.

"It could be worse," I say nonchalantly, trying to keep up the lie. "I could be from the nightmare realm."

"Don't Mars and Saturn get along, though?" Laila squints her eyes at me. "Aren't the Red King and the Winged Nightmare buddies?"

"Uhh—"

"King Ahmar is always flipping sides—depending on his mood." Sufia turns thoughtful. "Especially lately."

"Suppose you're right." Laila shudders but agrees.

"So tell me, new girl, what's your story?" Tamira pulls out a chewy stick that looks a lot like licorice. She bites a piece off and points at me. "We never get new students halfway through the year. Must be pretty special for the academy to make an exception like that."

"Oh, um, well." My mind draws a blank. Having that

backstory Yaseen mentioned would have come in handy right about now—there goes the blending-in plan. "My parents had a huge fight"—technically the truth—"and I got in big trouble with my old school, so"—if you swap *school* with the jinn kings—"I'm kinda stuck here now."

"What got you in trouble?" asks Laila. Her eyes light up, turning all gold, and I feel like she's staring straight into my soul. "A secret?"

"Uhhh . . ." I can't look away. Why can't I—

"You don't have to talk about it if you don't want to." Sufia sends a glare in Laila's direction.

"What?" Laila blinks, and the connection is broken. "Was just trying to get a read on her."

"First day of spring and already causing trouble, Laila?" Yaseen calls out, his arms full of books. His hair is sticking up every which way. "You know it's against academy rules to use your power on other students."

"Like anyone follows the rules." Laila rolls her eyes. "Can count on rule boy here to ruin all the fun. Case in point." She plucks a book from his stack. "*Treaties Through the Ages: A Complete History.* Professor Jade got you studying all that boring stuff on your track?"

"New independent study class," Yaseen mumbles.

"I didn't know you had a new class?" Sufia tilts her head to the side. "Why didn't you tell me—"

"Can't talk," Yaseen abruptly cuts in, making Sufia frown. "Just on my way to deliver a message to the new girl." He lowers the stack and reveals a golden sheet of paper sticking slightly out. "Summons from King Mudhib."

"A *summons* from the Golden King?" Laila's eyes widen in interest. "Now I've really got to know your secret."

The three girls crowd around me as I pluck the paper from the stack. Glittering letters curl on the page:

YOUR PRESENCE IS REQUESTED IN
THE ROOM OF REVELATIONS
BY THE HONORED KING MUDHIB, THE SHINING KING,
THE GOLDEN KING OF THE SUN.
IMMEDIATELY.

"Who are you, new girl?" wonders Tamira, her nose crinkling. "And why do you wear so much perfume?"

Sufia just looks between Yaseen and me, still frowning. "Well, can't keep a king waiting, I suppose." She watches Laila put Yaseen's book back at the top of the stack. "Assuming all goes well, can I count you both in for Sunday night?"

"What's on Sunday night?" I ask.

"During the first week of spring we like to stargaze in the academy gardens," says Sufia. "See if we can read the future of this year in the sky." She smiles. "It's a tradition."

I blink. "That sounds—" *So awesome.*

"Sounds like we're going to be late if you keep talking. Come on." Yaseen grabs my hand and drags me out of the hall. "You can socialize later."

"I'll take that as a yes!" shouts Sufia. "See you then! And don't let Yaseen's grumpy act fool you. He's as sweet as sugar under that tough exterior!"

"This way," Yaseen huffs, and turns on his heel, looking redder than ever.

"Am I in trouble?" We walk through winding halls and more flower staircases, bumping past nosy students with their curious eyes on us. "And why is everyone staring?"

"You're new," says Yaseen. "And new around here usually means . . ."

"Awesome?" I joke.

"Gossip," he corrects me. "Something we're trying to avoid."

"Right." Blending in, that's the goal. Which means avoiding anything that would make me the talk of the school, like if it ever got out that a certain someone could remember seeing me, a very *human* me, once before. . . . "I have to tell you something that happened last time I was here. With Sufia."

"What happened with Sufia?" Yaseen pauses before two gleaming doors, his hand halting in midair.

"She, um, *saw* me. In the library when I escaped from your dorm," I confess. "I might have . . . talked to her. Told her my name."

"Why would you do that?" he hisses.

"It was an accident!" I hiss back. "It's not like I thought I'd ever return. Do you think . . . she remembers me?"

"It doesn't seem like it. Farrah is a pretty common name." Yaseen sighs heavily. "And you do look different, so let's just hope it stays that way." With that, he pushes open two gleaming doors, and we enter a chamber, empty except for a large stone arch in the center.

Clear glass gleams from where the skylight hits. But even stranger are the walls—little glowing orbs shimmer in orderly rows, from floor to ceiling (and it's a really tall ceiling). Off to the side of the arch, a very golden jinn king waits. The doors shut behind us all on their own.

"Finally," King Mudhib says. "We can begin."

CHAPTER ELEVEN

DESTINY CALLS . . . AGAIN

"I see you've paid a visit to King Abyad." King Mudhib appraises my disguise. "A most pleasant scent. Now, while your inner self is concealed, I'm here to provide you with the external self while you are here."

"The external what?"

"Instructions from your father on how to behave," he says. "And yes, I am well aware of this *new situation* at the academy. I cannot speak for the other kings, but I agree with your father. An uneducated jinn is a dangerous jinn, and so I have agreed to this little charade for now."

King Mudhib adjusts the fluffy golden halo wrapped around his neck. His robes trail behind him as he approaches the back wall of the chamber, which is filled with rows of glowing orbs.

"Now, listen very carefully. This academy is unlike any school you've attended before." He puts on silver spectacles lined with diamonds, magnifying his eyes. "The mission of the academy and its students is simple—it is a purpose-driven school with an extremely spare student body. Royal jinn births are *rare*." His long fingers trail along the rows of orbs, tapping each one. "Each student has a highly personalized and unique track to empower our students to do great things while also remembering where they come from. Which means every student who attends plays a very important role in our society." His eyebrows rise at *very important*.

"Except I don't have one," I say. "Not yet."

"Hopefully not ever." The jinn king sighs. "But that is precisely why we are here, to see what the future has in store for you. As your trial decided, we are to observe you, and observe we shall." His golden gaze freezes me in place.

"Right, I'm being watched. Got it." I inch back, feeling very nervous.

"And should there be a discovery of Miss Noorzad's true identity during this observation period," King Mudhib continues, "consequences will fall on you as well, little prince." The Golden King blinks at Yaseen, baring a threateningly calm smile.

"What kind of consequences?" Yaseen gulps.

"The most severe," answers the king. "So let's not have one single slip. Is that understood?"

"But—"

"Is that *understood*?"

"Yes, King Mudhib." Yaseen keeps his hands fisted by his

sides. Proving himself to our dad has been all Yaseen ever wanted—to be seen as a successful heir, but mostly as a son. A fear Azar uncovered when we fell into the Realm Beneath. But I don't think he anticipated putting everything he's ever cared about on the line to have me be here. So if I slip up, Yaseen is gonna hate me. As if I weren't already stressed out enough. Now I really hope Sufia doesn't recognize me.

"Until we can understand what your destiny holds, there are rules you need to abide by while in our world. Make no mistake, while you are posing as a student, you are not a true member of this academy. We will provide you with a proper education on our world to protect our careful order, but you are not of noble birth. You will never be referred to as an heir or princess, and should anything happen to King Shamhurish's true heir, there will be severe consequences for you and your family. Is that understood?"

I nod, hating the way my knees shake under the sun king's gaze.

"Though your attendance bears no real-world impact, there is one matter we need to settle. You have Shamhurish's blood running through your veins. And it is known that each child with a royal bloodline will exhibit a prophecy once in their life. Big or small, it does not matter what it is—only that it exists and will happen."

No wonder the jinn kings are on edge. They already have a problematic prophecy regarding a mixed jinn. Imagine *me* getting one.

"I would not worry. They rarely manifest at this age." King Mudhib adjusts a glowing ring made of bark on his finger. "But rarely is not the same as never, so I personally check every student to track for such prophetic activation." He waves at Yaseen, who steps forward and stands in front of the arch.

"It's super easy," he says, glancing backward at me with a strained smile. "We do it all the time. That's what all the orbs are on the walls. Past prophecies."

So that's what they are. My mind starts to wander. Is the prophecy that spurred the treaty one hundred years ago hidden somewhere in this room? Am I meant to find it . . . ? Maybe if I look hard enough, I could—

"Eyes forward, Miss Noorzad." King Mudhib clears his throat. He moves like rays of sunshine on a hot beach day. Heat rolls off his rings. Little letters on each ring light up when he presses his right hand on the arch. The bark ring pulses green. "Center yourself, little prince." Golden light threads its way around the stone arch, filling the engraved designs with piercing vibrations.

Yaseen takes a big breath, shakes his shoulders, and shuts his eyes. The light flares in front of him. I'm not sure what King Mudhib is looking for, but he clicks his tongue.

"Your time hasn't arrived yet," says the king. "Miss Noorzad, if you would."

"See? Piece of cake," Yaseen says cheerfully, but his

shoulders droop a little in disappointment. "It'll be the same for you. You've got this."

"Yeah. Okay." I walk toward the arch. *I do not need a prophecy. Please let me fly under the radar.* One step, then another. The closer I get, the hotter the light becomes. Each step ripples in the glass. I can feel it shake around my feet. I squint. There's something . . . there. What is it?

Once I'm inches away from the glass, I realize the figure within the arch is me. Okay, nothing weird there. Probably just my reflection, but then . . . why is there a huge tree looming with dark shadows swirling around it? My nose is nearly touching the glass as I get closer to see it better. Feathers shrivel and fall from its branches like dying, burning leaves.

That might be a little weird.

"What is that?" I lean closer to the glass.

"You've got to be kidding me," says Yaseen. "You actually *see* something?"

The sun king doesn't say a word. He just watches, his golden eyes serious.

"Wait, it's saying something." Words bloom from the shadows, twirling around the branches of the tree. The lines float to the front of the glass so it reads:

An endless age, a fate defied
Without its roots, all things shall die

But should the end come rear its head,
There will be more than kingdoms dead
They will be—

"*The beginning of the end.*" I finish reading the words out loud. Something about it feels familiar. . . . "This sounds like—"

"A prophecy." The sun king's eyes are haloed in sunshine as he holds an empty orb in his hands. Light and shadow pour out of the arch's glass and into the orb until it's full.

"I mean, what are the odds that wasn't a prophecy"—I look nervously at Yaseen, who is tugging aggressively at his right eyebrow—"and more like a glitch in the matrix or something?"

"The Arch of Oracles works directly from the Eternal Tablet; it can never *glitch.*" The figure in the glass reaches out her hand toward the sun king. He cradles the orb—a dark, swirling gray mass—and reluctantly hands it to her. She looks at me, winks, and disappears. The arch loses its shine, and all is normal again.

Well, as normal as can be with *that* weird message.

"What did she mean by the beginning of the end?" asks Yaseen. "The end of what?"

"That is not for prying ears to discuss." King Mudhib bows his fingers together, never taking his eyes off me. "It appears this is what the Scale of Deeds was cautioning about." He frowns. He doesn't look surprised by the prophecy. In fact, he looks like—

"You've heard this before," I realize out loud. Is that why it feels familiar?

"What!" Yaseen's jaw drops. "B-but how? Prophecies don't recycle; that defeats the purpose. Right, King Mudhib?"

"It seems there is much to observe indeed." He avoids my question by walking swiftly through the arch, the glass now gone, to stare upon the rows of glowing orbs. "You may leave, Miss Noorzad."

"But . . ." I hesitate. "Is this prophecy . . . dangerous?"

"It is too soon to jump to conclusions; we don't yet know what this means," the king says quietly, "but once a prophecy is active, no one can interfere. It is a sacred rule even jinn kings must obey." Strangely, the sun king's flaming halo dims as he gazes at the orbs, apparently in deep thought. He clears his throat and concludes, "It seems destiny has called upon you again, and our future may lie in the balance."

"THAT'S GOT TO BE A RECORD," GRUMBLES YASEEN AS WE WALK out of the prophecy room. "You can't help making everything about you."

"I don't want it to be all about me," I shoot back. "All I want is to blend in and be normal, like everyone else. You want my prophecy so bad? Then take it."

"I'm not the one *destiny* has called upon." He mimics

King Mudhib, taking a sharp turn up the stairs. "I'm just the sidekick tagging along," he says, just for himself.

"I'm not doing it on purpose," I argue. "And for all we know, this could be a *bad* thing." I stop halfway up the flower stairs. "In fact, the more I think about it, it is bad. I can't see how *kingdoms dead* and *all things shall die* is good, do you?"

Big waves of destiny and fate crash in my head, fighting with each other. All I wanted was a shot at an adventure in the City of Jewels—to maybe even get my dad to understand me better. But not this. *The beginning of the end*—that doesn't sound like an adventure. More like a warning. A warning about . . . me? Maybe I *should* be exiled. "It's not like I wanted this to happen."

"I know, that's what makes it hard." Yaseen sighs, big and heavy, before gesturing for me to keep moving. "Prophecy-solving wasn't on my schedule for this term, but I suppose I'll have to make room for it." He trudges up the stairs. "At least it happened on a free study day. Not sure my brain can handle a day of classes after that."

"Do we have to solve it?" I tug at my sleeves, popping an emerald button off. Just because something calls you doesn't mean you have to answer. "What happens if we maybe . . . pretend it doesn't exist?"

"Farrah, you can't ignore a prophecy."

"I'm sure someone's done it before."

"I'm sure they haven't, and if you don't mind, I don't want to be the first one to find out, so now would be a great time to stop being a pain in the butt and listen to me." Yaseen turns around, his protection charm glittering in the stream of daylight filtering through the windows. "King Mudhib said I'm the one responsible for keeping you out of trouble. So we're going to get through the observation period and figure out this prophecy, okay?"

"If you say so . . ."

"Good." He shakes his head while walking. "Plus, I've got our first lead."

"Already? How?" I rush up the stairs, following him as we go up, up, up the tower until he wedges open a window and slips out onto the roof.

"It doesn't take a genius to figure out if something strange and unusual is going on." Yaseen reties his hair into a high bun. "Probably best to have the strangest of them all on your team . . ." He clears his throat the second I get a good look at who is already here. "Can you guys squash your drama so we can get this prophecy over with?"

Sitting amid a pile of books in his black shirt, with his snow-white hair standing on end, is Idris.

Idris looks up. "Hey, Noorzad. Wondered when you'd finally get up here. Ready to talk now?"

CHAPTER TWELVE

WHAT HAPPENS WHEN YOU IGNORE A PROPHECY

"This isn't a lead. It's an ambush!"

"Don't blame me," Idris says sheepishly. "I told your brother it was a bad idea."

I whirl on Yaseen. "You've been conspiring with Idris behind my back?"

"*Conspiring* is a strong word." Yaseen dumps out the books from his pockets onto Idris's chaos pile. "And I wouldn't have *conspired* with him if you hadn't punched him in the face yesterday and run away."

"I thought you hate Idris," I grit through my teeth, wishing I could jump right back through the window and down the tower.

"Dislike. That's true." Yaseen sits next to the chaos pile and thumbs through some of the books. "But you don't, at least last time I checked." He opens up *Khwaja's Guide to the Celestial Treaties* and flips through the pages. "Plus, he had some good points. So duke out whatever you need to so we can get to the important stuff."

"I—" My brain is short-circuiting. Am I standing in an alternate dimension where Yaseen, my brother, wants to work with Idris? Has the world turned completely upside down?

"Nice disguise. You kinda smell like a pastry." Idris picks at his wristbands, scratching slightly under them. "Though I prefer how you really look, if that—"

"Why are you here, Idris?" Seeing him makes my stomach flutter, and I can't tell if I want to yell at him for disappearing or throw him over the tower. Both options sound awesome, if I'm being honest.

"Well, because we had a deal." He hesitates when I glare at him. "Okay, fine. The truth is . . . I'm cursed."

I cross my arms over my chest. "You've got five seconds to explain before I push you over the ledge." I glance over—it's a pretty steep drop to the bottom. "Time starts now."

"I already knew I was cursed because"—he taps his head—"missing memories and all, so I thought after breaking *you-know-who*'s ring, my curse should have broken too."

"Spoiler, it didn't," I say. "So?"

"No, it didn't." Idris winces. "I thought, *Maybe it needs time*, so I waited"—he tilts his head so his moon-white hair falls into his pale eyes—"but nothing. I was still cursed, and alone."

"You *chose* to be alone! I offered to help you find your family, and instead you just . . . disappeared."

"I was . . . jealous."

"Jealous of what?"

"Well, you. And your insufferable brother, I suppose."

"Hey!" Yaseen glances up from an old edition of *Untold Prophecies: A Collection*. He has a wry smile. "I am pretty insufferable, aren't I?"

"You see?" Idris rolls his eyes. "You got everything you ever wanted—your parents, your brother, even an academy uniform—all because your journey gave you answers. Which is great, for you." He uncomfortably folds his arms across his chest. "You found your family, but I didn't. And that made me feel . . . something I'm not proud of, okay? So I stayed away because I figured everyone was better off without me." He glances at me. "Are my five seconds up? Should I prepare to be shoved to my demise?"

"I'm still thinking about it." Going missing in action because he felt jealous sounds like a big excuse. It doesn't sound like the *whole* truth (and it never is with Idris). "You were jealous, okay. But that doesn't explain how you found *this*." I hold up my wrist that has my forever bracelet on it (that I conveniently fused together, thanks to my fiery dorm door, so now I'll never lose it again). "I know where I lost it. I just don't know how *you* got it."

"I . . ." He sighs and gives me that *guilty as charged* look. "May have seen what happened with the scale."

"I knew I heard your voice in that room." I reach over and

twist his arm so it's behind his back. Throwing him off the tower sounds better by the minute.

"Ow, okay, easy on the grip," he whines. "I was stuck in the human world, and your Ever-Place solution was the only way out. So I—"

"You came through the portal with me? How long have you been following me?"

"I needed to get back to the Supreme Court. Once I was there, I—"

"Watched what that scale did to me and did nothing to help me?" Hurt blooms in the bruised piece of my heart. How long has he been following me? Since before I left Philly? How long did he just watch from afar, knowing I was waiting for him to show up . . . ? He saw how lonely I was and never came out of the shadows.

"You're not a good friend. You watched me suffer and did *nothing* about it. You said you were jealous—of what? Of me being shut out by my dad? Of not knowing if I even have powers, or where I belong? We could have been looking for answers *together*, and instead you just—"

"I'm selfish—is that what you want to hear? I claim that. I'm a bad friend too. Maybe that's why I'm cursed. Maybe . . ." Idris's voice trails off. "Maybe I did something to deserve it."

"And finally, we get to my lead." Yaseen looks very smug for someone drowning in books. He never looks up but waves his hand from the pages. "Go on."

Idris continues. "During your . . . judgment, the scale spoke to me. When I asked why I was missing, it gave me a clue. Or a memory. I'm not quite sure." He shudders. "I was . . . chained up and drowning. Somewhere dark and cold. And I was *angry*." He breaks free of my grip and turns to face me. "In the dark, all I could hear was this weird phrase. *But with all magic comes a price. In pieces, chained through mist as cold as ice.*"

"What does *that* mean?"

"If I knew, do you think I'd be here?" Idris's gray eyes are haunted. The usual twinkle of mischief is missing. He reminds me of my mom, and the ocean, and the big gaping hole that can never be filled. "It makes me wonder, who was I? Why do I suddenly have this ugliness inside me that doesn't care who I hurt . . . ?" He looks away. "I'm sorry, Noorzad, for always doing the wrong thing," he says quietly. "My moral compass is a big mystery to me, and right now I'm doing a terrible job at figuring myself out. But I can't stand the not-knowing anymore."

"And I can't stand this painfully drawn-out apology." Yaseen groans in frustration and chucks a book at Idris. "Since Idris can't cut to the chase for the life of him, I will. He's here because he needs access to the academy records and can't get in without one of us."

Well, that's a direct answer if I ever heard one.

"How do you know that?"

"After you spectacularly smashed ghost boy's face in, we

talked, and I had a *brilliant* realization. The scale *hid him* from your memories so the jinn kings couldn't see him, but then it gave him a clue? That has to mean something. My hunch is that you"—he points at me—"and him"—he points at Idris—"are tangled up in this"—Yaseen gestures at all the books—"and we've just got to figure out what it all means."

"You mean how his curse fits in with my prophecy?"

"Bingo."

"What prophecy?" Idris leans against one of the stone pillars around the circular tower. Yaseen fills him in.

"I brought all these books in because of Idris, but after seeing King Mudhib's reaction to your prophecy, I think it's a good idea to check and see if he really has heard it before."

"That's—really smart." I blink at Yaseen.

"I have my moments. Now hurry up and look." I catch a book Yaseen throws. "I've got homework in other classes. I can't be doing this all day."

I notice all the books are from around a hundred years ago—the same time period when the jinn world radically changed and Idris got stuck in the ring. I glance back at Idris. "Do you really believe Yaseen's theory?" That somehow Idris's fate and my fate are tied together? "Or are you just using us for another secret plan like last time?"

"I don't think you'd believe me either way, Noorzad." He shrugs, takes a few tentative steps toward me. "But for what it's worth, I wouldn't be here if I didn't believe him. So is it okay if we help each other this one last time?"

"Seems like I don't have a choice in the matter," I tell myself, and settle into the pages of the worn book. "You're gonna help whether I like it or not." When Idris sits next to me, a shield goes up around my heart. I know I made a promise to Idris to help him regain his memories and find his family, but that was before he ran away again, before the scale— before he left a bruise that won't heal if he abandons me, just like Padar did every year. "If it is true, then the sooner we untangle this mystery, the sooner we can untangle our lives from each other's." This prophecy is just a setback. Destiny can try its best, but I've fought fate before, and I'll do it again. Because nothing is going to ruin this simple fact: I will come out of this observation period proving that I am not a threat, and nothing is going to get in the way of that. Not even Idris.

Yaseen looks up from his search to glance curiously at Idris and me but doesn't say anything.

"Then let's get to work, Noorzad."

AFTER HOURS OF PORING OVER TINY PRINT I COULD BARELY read in English (Yaseen had the Arabic covered) and not finding a single written record of my prophecy or Idris's clue or the prophecy from one hundred years ago, we end up calling it a night.

As I drift off in my bed, all I can think is *How odd that the prophecy is nowhere to be found.* There were mentions of the treaty that banished mixed jinn from the City of Jewels and paraphrasing of the events leading up to the prophecy, but that's it.

The next day, I'm still thinking about it. "Maybe we're not looking in the right place," I mumble to myself on my way to the dining hall for lunch. We were up way too late, and if I'm ever gonna wake up before noon, I've got to get to bed earlier. Plus, it's not like they *need* me to go back to the tower for the rest of the weekend . . . or ever . . . unless absolutely necessary. Yaseen knows the academy libraries better than I do; he's best equipped to feed Idris a continuous string of books. I can make myself useful elsewhere . . . away from Idris.

I wouldn't want to spend time with someone who enjoyed watching me suffer either. Azar's voice slinks into my head.

"Stay out of my head," I hiss. "You're going to ruin everything!" I speed-walk, keeping my eyes glued to the floor. I imagine the faster I go, the farther behind I leave Azar's voice. When I finally walk into the dining hall, I gasp. "This is where we *eat every day?*" There are high gilded ceilings with frescoes of the seven jinn kings and their realms painted on the ceiling. With stained-glass windows on one side and clear windows on the other, overlooking massive gardens, I couldn't imagine a prettier place to make new friends.

My stomach lets out a loud, angry growl. *And eat.* I got so caught up in the prophecy yesterday, I skipped all my meals. That's not good.

I smooth the front of my silver shirt, spritz one more

spray of the perfume for good measure, and slide into one of the seven long tables, next to Sufia, who is sitting with Tamira and Laila.

"If it isn't our local celebrity," Tamira says slyly over a pile of books as she scribbles notes over *Dragons, Vermilion Birds, and Other Fire-Breathing Beasts*. "Surprised Yaseen let you out to mingle with the commoners."

"What's that supposed to mean?"

"*Tamira,*" Sufia hisses, "that's so rude."

"But true." Laila slurps from a big steaming bowl. (It looks like a cross between oatmeal and pudding.) "You are the talk of the academy." To prove her point, she snaps her head toward the tables behind her, and a dozen students quickly look away, keeping their whispering to themselves. "See? A bunch of gossips, we are." She sighs before turning her big eyes on me. "Rumor has it that you're on an active prophecy track, and it's a big one."

"*Laila!*" chastises Sufia.

"If everyone else is talking about it, why can't we?" She flips one end of her scarf over her shoulder and leans across the table, pushing plates of bread and pastries out of the way. "The sun king rarely sets up private meetings like that."

"It just happened yesterday. How do you already know?" I ask.

"So it *is* true." Laila's eyes light up in excitement.

"D-doesn't everyone go through the Arch of Oracles?" I stutter. So much for lying low.

"We get checked, but not like that," says Laila, her voice a conspiratorial whisper. "I'm from the sun king's realm, and everyone from our realm knows that the Golden King only does personal checks for other kings' kids. . . ."

The silence is huge, with Sufia and Tamira blinking curiously at me.

"So is that your secret, Mars girl?" asks Laila, her eyes wide and bright—they remind me of the glow that comes off the sun king. It feels like she's staring right into my soul again. "Are you the Mars king's kid? Are you the spawn of the Red King?"

"Why would you think that?" I choke on a sip of water. "King Ahmar is definitely *not* my dad."

"I'd hide it if that was my dad," mumbles Tamira through bites of a bagel. "Unstable, that whole realm. I hear half of them don't even make it past twenty with their brutal training."

"Well, he's *not my dad*." I nervously pick at my bracelet.

"Hmm, she doesn't seem to be lying." Laila chews on her lip in thought. She blinks once more, and the glow fades from her eyes. "Well, I had to ask— What?" She raises her hands defensively when Sufia glares again.

"It's rude to use your power as a lie detector." Sufia smiles apologetically at me. "They're not normally like this—"

"Yes, we are," Tamira cuts in.

"But if *someone* were to keep using her soulstare power, I'd just make sure to wear your protection charm to block it." Sufia glances at my uniform when she notices I'm not wearing mine. The other girls are—their pins are displayed brightly on their lapels.

"Way to ruin all the fun," Laila grumbles.

"Um, well, I kinda broke my protection charm when my best friend needed help, so—"

"You broke your charm?" Tamira gasps.

"Not on purpose. I made a charm for her and didn't realize that'd break mine."

"You *made* a charm?" Sufia looks impressed. "It's a big risk, to give up strong magic like that. Your friend is incredibly lucky."

"I'm the lucky one, really." Best friends like Arzu only come around once in a lifetime. I checked, and none of my texts to her went through; plus, now my phone's fully run out of charge, so I don't have any way to feel connected to her. She's going to be so disappointed when she realizes . . .

"Spring break!" I gasp. What's she going to think when she shows up at my aunt's house and I'm not there?

Laila opens her mouth to ask a barrage of questions—but a small breeze wafts through the dining hall, bouncing along the stained glass, creating a tinkling chime sound. Miss Cerulean, the building spirit, trails behind the breeze, shooing us. "Disperse, all of you! Lunch hour is nearly over. No time like the present to get a head start on your studies for the week. And yes, I'm talking to you, Esen Zulmani—don't you dare think of skipping Dream Theory again!"

"It's not my fault the academy put a class when I need to be asleep in the *morning*." A boy with dark wings and sharp red eyes glares at Miss Cerulean before getting up from his table. His wings flutter behind him as he marches out of the hall alone.

"That's King Maymun's nephew, Esen Zulmani," Sufia mentions when I keep staring. "Most steer clear of him. He's the only student here from the Winged Nightmare's realm."

And just like that, the focus is taken off me and my mini freak-out.

"For good reason." Laila helps Tamira gather her books. "Dream vapor's been leaking out of their gateway for weeks! If you're worried over my soulstare messing around in your head, try getting a heavy dose of dream vapor in your system. You'll never wake up." They continue complaining as they walk off and out of the dining hall.

"She's exaggerating." Sufia reassures me, patting my arm. "You wake up eventually." She smiles, holding out her hand. "Hey, you want to spend the day with us? We were thinking of hanging out in the courtyard. That is—if someone *else* hasn't already made plans?"

An image of Idris and Yaseen hovering over dusty books flashes in my mind. "Nope, my day is free." The prophecy can wait.

"Perfect." Sufia smiles wide, and I let her guide me out of the hall, down a spiral staircase, and out into the sunshine of the courtyard. "It's a tragedy to spend such a pretty day indoors. Plus, Miss Cerulean can get grouchy when she feels like we're making a mess of her castle."

Miss Cerulean reminds me of a certain germophobe brother of mine, who I'm sure is obsessing over every word in every prophecy record. I sigh. Maybe I shouldn't skip out on a tower session today. Yaseen did seem really invested in figuring out this prophecy, and fast.

"Is everything okay?" Sufia glances quizzically at me.

"A-okay."

"You sure?" She passes by a row of rosebushes, her hands gliding gently over them. "You sighed, like, three times in a row."

Busted. I sigh again. "I'm just . . . a little nervous."

"About your classes? Do you have your schedule? I could always take a look," she suggests. "Let you know which professors are the worst." She settles into the grass and basks in the sunlight. "I mean, technically, they're all the same, but some are nicer than others." From the window, the plants looked perfect, but up close, they all look a little wilted and weathered. Sufia frowns. "Dunno why the grass has gone so yellow. It's not usually like this."

Because I don't want to start a conversation about *grass*, I pull my class schedule from my pocket and smooth it out. It appeared last night when I got in late from prophecy-searching. I was so exhausted, I didn't take a good look at it.

In big looping letters, it reads:

Prophecy Track
Prophecy Seminar with *Professor Lena Lilac*
Introduction to Jinn History with *Professor Amias Amaranth*
Essence Study for Beginners with *Professor Ulric Umber*

"That's weird. You've only got three classes and no power training?" Sufia looks up at me. "Maybe it's a prophecy-track thing?"

"What do you mean, power training?" I ask as she takes a pen out of her pocket and writes down directions to each classroom.

"Every jinn has an inherent power, something that's special—you've seen Laila's, obviously. Usually it's important to be able to master it." Sufia hands back the schedule.

"What's yours?"

"What's the fun in telling? Let's make it a game. Next time we see each other, try and guess mine, and I'll guess yours." She winks and gives me a dazzling smile, leaving me a little dazed and nodding in agreement as she goes back to lounging in the sun. "Though, if I could choose, I'd love to have Tamira's power. Wait till you see what she can do with a dragon. She says they speak to her *in her mind*. Isn't that wild? Wouldn't be surprised if she met us with one trailing behind her."

While Sufia relaxes like she doesn't have a care in the world, a question pops up in my head.

Why don't I have power training?

THAT QUESTION IS STILL ON MY BRAIN ALL WEEKEND WITH MY new friends, even when we were stargazing, especially when I see how seriously they took mastering their individual powers, and it's all I'm thinking about when Monday rolls around while I'm headed to my first class.

Ask your father. I'm sure he would know, Azar hisses in my head.

"Like he'd give me a straight answer," I mutter reflexively before stopping short and slapping a hand over my mouth. I can practically see Azar's smile wrapped up in my reflection on the floor, as if to say, *If he won't help you, you can always come to me.* "Stay out." I trample through it and ignore his buzzing presence in my head.

But his idea isn't a bad one either. Why is it so easy for everyone else to access their true power? I examine my hands and try to remember what it was like, that burning feeling from before, waiting for a burst of light, but nothing happens. All I feel is a dull, pressing weight in my chest. What triggered my power in the first place? Maybe that's the first step. . . .

Somehow, I get hopelessly lost.

"Where *is* this classroom?" The Golden King was right about one thing—school is different here. Normal schools don't shrink and grow, adding corridors and rooms whenever they feel like it. The moving plant staircases don't help either;

some of them have flowers in the shape of tinkling bells that laugh every time I take a wrong turn.

I'm following the directions Sufia scribbled on my schedule and somehow double back into a golden chamber that is decorated with sun mosaics all over the walls. I keep a lookout for other students, but it seems totally abandoned up here. When I reach the seventh floor, a little light floats out of my schedule and taps the wall in front of me. Magically, a door appears. *Good luck*, the light twinkles before vanishing into the classroom.

"Where were you when I was lost?"

Three of the classroom walls are made of glass, letting in globs of light. There's a view of a park, a sweets shop, and a bunch of skyscrapers (seven, to be exact). In the center of the room are one desk and another building spirit.

"You are three minutes late," the spirit snaps. She floats down to the ground and claps her hands together. "Today, I have a tight schedule and cannot make any exceptions, even if my pupil is highly irregular."

"Oh, sorry, I'm not used to the halls yet." I hurry to my seat and pull out a notebook and a pen. "Wait, does that mean you know—"

"Who you are? Past that silly illusion? Of course." The spirit stares down at me from her glasses. "While that perfume may trick those around you, it cannot mask who you truly are to the academy. And as one of the many spirits bound to this institution, I am simply here to teach. I've witnessed many students with many incredible secrets pass through these halls—yes, your father included." Her shoes click against the floor, a knowing smile on her face. "But I digress. My main concern is the education and protection of this building and those within it. Anything else can be left at the door. Is that understood?"

I nod. "Yes, Professor . . . Um, which name do I call you?"

"I have many and no names," she says. "I am the academy, in her many forms, from students and wisdom past. But if a name is necessary, then you may call me Professor Lilac."

"Lilac?"

"I'm quite fond of the color." She points to her outfit— a soft purple sweater with a gold belt cinching her waist. Her plum pants taper at her ankles. Rows of lilac bracelets, anklets, and earrings tinkle as she starts writing in the air. Words glitter where her hand loops. "Now, I'm told we're to start with the very basics for you."

"I'm a fast learner," I assure her. "I'm the best in all my classes back home."

"For your sake, I hope that is true," she says, peering over her glasses at me. "Prophecy tracks are difficult for even the most seasoned students. For an outsider . . ." She tuts. "It will be nearly impossible. Deadly, even."

"What could be worse than the Realm Beneath?" I joke.

"Danger lurks beneath glittering beauty. You'd do well to remember that." Professor Lilac goes back to the floating words. "The goal in our sessions during your time here is to

aid you on your prophetic track and uncover the true meaning of what is contained in this orb." She turns just as the
mentioned orb appears in the middle of the floating words.
It's the same one King Mudhib gave to the Arch of Oracles.
Inside, gray smoke swirls. "The prophecy will glow depending
on level of completion. Gold indicates a successful conclu-
sion." The orb glows lightly to demonstrate. "Silver for half
completion." It spins and shines like glitter. "And lastly, red
for interruption or failure. Let's hope it doesn't come to that."

"What about gray?" It seems like a lot of colors to keep
track of.

"The color it is now? That's simple," says Professor Lilac.
"It means you're resisting the calling." She places both palms
on my desk and leans in very close.

"It knows that?" I sit, embarrassed.

"Of course; it is your prophecy, and as such, a reflection
of yourself," explains Professor Lilac. "It's fairly common,
the initial resistance, but that is where a guide such as me
steps in to ensure your focus is solely on completing your
prophecy."

"But what if it's . . ." I whisper the last part. "Bad?" I'm not
sure Professor Lilac knows the exact wording of my prophecy,
but she can't blame me for not jumping for joy to complete it.

"Ignoring it will be worse, I assure you." Professor Lilac
taps the top of my head. This close, I can see the galaxies
shimmering within her skin and clothes. "Denial leads to
failure, and should whatever be in this vial turn red and

become unleashed, well . . ." She clears her throat. "It will devour you."

"*Devour me?*"

"Indeed. This world is not like the one you grew up in. It is not so easy to disobey what is predestined." She crouches down to my level and looks deep into my heart. "Is your fear over the outcome of this prophecy worth refusing the call?"

"I'm afraid . . ." I hesitate, thinking of the seven glaring faces of the jinn kings and the way they all see me as the threat—Padar included. "I don't want to accept this prophecy if it means proving my dad right," I say in a small voice. I thought breaking the ring of fate meant choosing my own destiny. I don't like not having control over what happens to me. It's my life; it should be my choice, not a glowing crystal ball's. "If the end really is coming, then the kings were right all along. That I'll never be accepted. That I'm—"

"*A threat to their careful order?*" Professor Lilac floats a little off the ground, fluttering her wings. "Let me tell you this: this academy is ancient and has stood the test of time. She is older and more powerful than even the kings. If she has accepted you, you will always have a placc here. Prophecy or not."

"How do I know if I've been accepted?"

"Didn't she welcome you when you first arrived?" asks Professor Lilac.

"Well, yeah, but—"

"Then you're accepted. The academy has made its choice already. The kings think they are all-powerful, but limits apply, even to them," Professor Lilac says knowingly. "You were destined to answer this call, one way or another. And they cannot stop that, nor can they deny you your place here after that ends."

"Even though I'm half-human?" And totally against the rules.

"Half what?" She glances at me. "I do not see half of anything in front of me. I see a whole girl with a mixed heritage, that's all." She scoffs. "I'll never understand this *half* nonsense. You are not oil and water, two halves separated by an invisible line. You are a whole of both."

Something hopeful and fiery sparks in my chest, lifting a piece of the weight that's been on my shoulders.

"You mean I can stay after all this? After the observation period, if I want?"

"Of course, but that will only happen if you let go of those fears that hold you back." Professor Lilac points at the swirling gray vial. "Now, if you can do that, then your first homework assignment is to allow yourself to discover what destiny has in store for you and to not let your fears shape the outcome. Think you can do that?"

With a tiny glimmer of hope, I nod. "I can try."

"Splendid, then we can continue with your basic prophecy education to get you up to speed." Professor Lilac shares a warm smile before turning back. "Let's begin. . . ."

I DON'T KNOW HOW IT HAPPENS, BUT BY THE END OF CLASS, the dark gray mist disappears from the vial, leaving a bright and delicate white light in its place. *Acceptance.* It's progress— maybe not as fast as Yaseen would like it to be, but it's something.

I just wish my mom were here to see it. She would want to hear all about it—every single detail. I imagine her now, proudly writing my prophecy on the fridge. Like it's something to show off. *I know you'll figure it out, janem,* I imagine her saying. *And I know, whatever it is, it's gonna be good because that's who you are.*

Good.

I hold this daydream version of my mom close and pray that she's right.

CHAPTER THIRTEEN

AM I THE BAD GUY?

B y the time Thursday rolls around for my check-in with my dad, I feel a whole lot better. I got so used to the feeling of dread because of the jinn kings telling me what I can't do, I didn't realize how much I needed someone to point out what I *can* do, who I can be, without letting those worries get to me.

It made the rest of my first week at the academy zip by. (Only having classes four days a week really helps, and if I ever get back to the human world, that's the first thing I'm going to convince Arzu to petition for at her school too.) And even though Arzu isn't here, I decide it can't hurt to record the highlights of my week so she doesn't miss a single detail.

- Stayed awake in all my classes (even though I was dangerously close to snoring in Jinn History—Professor Amaranth is not the most . . . engaging speaker).

• Aced a quiz about the Great Jinn War (which was really just a millennium of ancient jinn fighting each other until they formed their own realms) and how the City of Jewels came to be (aka seven jinn kings who were tired of fighting against each other and decided it'd be easier to unite). (Also, who gives a quiz on the second day of class?)

• Found out some of my new friends' powers: soul-stare and dragon telepathy. (Still haven't figured out mine yet.)

• Tried looking for that prophecy that caused the treaty one hundred years ago. Cleared out the whole first-year and second-year libraries. It's gotta be somewhere around here. . . .

Oh, and the most important one:

• Have not caused total destruction of the jinn world . . . yet (joking, not really).

I bring the note with me as I exit the academy doors and trek out into the city. I may not be able to send the list to Arzu or my mom, but maybe my dad will appreciate hearing about my first week at the academy. It's a pretty short walk to the Supreme Court of Jinn, but I could never get tired of bursting through hazy clouds in the streets or listening to a chorus of singers just casually practicing in the square around the court. Right before I slip into the court, I crane my neck to check out the tallest peak of the Qaf Mountains, to the simurgh nest.

"Haven't seen you fly around in a bit," I say. "Kinda miss those morning wake-up earthquakes." The clouds around the peak are a little darker than normal. Hmm. Maybe it's gonna rain today. I wonder what rain is like when you're actually up in the clouds.

With that thought, I hold my breath and walk through the barrier into the courts (which is just as bad as the first time) and follow signs to my dad's particular court, which is thankfully only on the fifth floor, and not the seventh, like the moon king's.

"Here goes nothing." After a nervous twist of my bracelet and a check that every hair is neatly in place and my shirt isn't too wrinkled, I march into my dad's court and say, "The world hasn't ended. Aren't you proud?"

"That's one way to put it," Padar mumbles while sitting on his throne. He's reviewing a long scroll that's rolled in a zigzag around his feet. He doesn't look up at me. Instead, he says, "Is that all you have to report for me?"

"Um." I wave and twirl to show him that I've kept my identity secret, as promised. "Notice anything different?"

"Is there something different to notice?"

I spray the perfume again for good measure. He still doesn't look up. "I just thought, maybe you'd notice the illusion. I feel like I kinda look like . . ." *You.* I stop when he picks up another scroll. It feels very cold-shoulder. "Did I do something wrong?"

At that, Padar glances from his page. "Quite a few things, actually." He adjusts the bark ring on his finger. "I would think you'd catch on after watching your brother, but it seems you feel like you are immune to the rules."

"I'm sorry?"

"If you want my attention in my court, there is an etiquette to be followed." Thunder booms behind him. He seems very annoyed with me. "In this room, I am a king before anything else, and I have ordered you to report to me weekly, as I would order any patron of my realm. When reporting information to a king, you speak with respect, relay the information, and nothing more. Is that clear?"

"But . . . you're my *dad*." I take a step back, shocked.

"Here, I am your king. You said you wanted to be part of this world. Next time, come prepared," he says, leveling me with a stare. "Is that all you have to report?"

Don't tell him about your prophecy track. Azar's voice mingles with my own.

I have to inform him, I answer back in my head. *The sun king wouldn't hide it from him.*

Why tell him when he hides so much from you?

"I'm on a prophecy track," I mumble, kicking the floor with my shoe. Any confidence I got from Professor Lilac flew out the window. "I don't know what it means, but if I had to guess, it's what the observation period hinted at."

My dad nods in approval. "Yes, I have been informed."

"Okay, well . . ." I really don't want to share my note now—it all seems so silly. Except for one thing. "Why can't I find the prophecy that banned mixed jinn from the City of Jewels?"

"Why would you be looking for it?" he asks, and then goes deathly silent.

Mistake, little one, Azar warns.

"I just thought . . ." I can't tell him the truth—to confirm if the sun king *had* heard it before. That would be the equivalent of running around with a big red flag, to my dad. I gulp. "It'd help in my Jinn History class. That's all."

My dad examines me closely. I shrivel under his stare. All I want to do is run out of here and never come back. After it feels like I've been holding my breath for hours, he finally says, "There are some prophecies that are too dangerous for young minds—especially young minds under *observation*—to stumble upon." He pauses. "Is that clear?"

"But—"

"Is that *clear*?" Thunder cracks behind my dad's voice, and I shake under the weight of his power.

"Yes."

"Good." Padar returns to his scrolls and waves his hand away. "You are dismissed."

I'm almost out the door when my dad says offhand, "Take this with you. It's the last one that will be allowed."

In between two fingers is an envelope addressed to me. From my mom.

I NEVER THOUGHT PAPER WAS WORTH MUCH.

But after *that* unpleasant conversation, my mom's letter makes me feel like the richest girl on Earth.

I rip open the letter while in the middle of withered landscaping in the plaza around the court, desperate to know how my mom is, if she's getting out of bed and brushing her hair, if she told Arzu I didn't cancel our spring break plans on purpose, if Bibi jan is having a blast in Khala Fazilat's brand-new kitchen, if they all miss me the same way I miss them.

But the letter is just two lines on a blank sheet:

I told you not to go

do you see now

I don't cry the whole way to the dormitories.

I am very proud of that.

I am less proud, however, of screaming when I see my room invaded by a certain white-haired boy, who has his inky fingers all over my desk.

"How did you get in here?" After my horrible afternoon, the bubbles of hurt are close to overheating into rage-seeking missiles, and their current target is Idris. "My door is pure lava for anyone who tries to get in that isn't me."

"I tried the door, nearly burned off my hand," Idris jokes.

"But then I remembered I can do this nifty trick." He takes a step in my direction and vanishes and reappears and vanishes and reappears. "Which comes in handy when I need to be in places that would normally melt my hand off."

"Great, now take your power and vanish out of here." I gesture toward the door. "Now's not a great time, so—" I wave him out.

"I know you're avoiding me." Idris sits on the chest next to my bed. "You haven't been to the tower since last week. It's just been me and your brother trying to help *you*. And now he's telling me you're avoiding him too?"

"I've been *busy* with classes." Have I been steering clear of Yaseen this week because I don't want to deal with his pressure to rush through solving a prophecy I've only just accepted? Maybe. Is that a crime? No way. Plus, I *have* been working on it—just not with them. "And speaking of *helping me*"—I smack my mom's letter down on my desk, shaking some loose paper and jostling a jug of water—"don't pretend like you're here to solve my prophecy out of the goodness of your heart. If the Scale of Deeds didn't give you your own little clue, you wouldn't be *here*." Hot tears burn in the corners of my eyes because I'm so mad—at myself, at Idris, at my mom, at my dad, at everyone making this impossible weight on my shoulders even heavier. Big fat tears cannonball off my face and splash onto my mom's letter. Great, and now I'm crying. In front of Idris. How *embarrassing*.

"I didn't mean to upset you—" Idris springs up from the

chest with a panicked look on his face. A classic *Oh crap, I made a girl cry, now what do I do?* response.

"Not everything is about you!" I'm about to go full rage-mode on Idris, because being angry is a lot less embarrassing than crying, when I notice something odd on my mom's letter—the spots where my tears fell. It looks like the ink smudged, but there isn't ink in those spots to smudge.

Unless.

"Invisible ink," I whisper, grabbing the jug with shaky hands. I dip my hand in the water and sprinkle it across the page. More words bloom instantly.

"Your mom can use magic?" Idris casually leans over my shoulder.

"It's not magic." I wipe my hand on my skirt. "It's science." Everything goes quiet, like someone turned down the volume on the outside world, when I walk away from the desk and lean against my bed. I barely register Idris peering over the other scattered sheets on my desk. All I can feel is the fact that I'm touching the same paper my mom touched, reading the words she carefully tucked away just for me.

I never meant to be cruel when I told you not to go for your dreams.

All I ever wanted was to protect you, but do you see now from exactly what?

I hold on to your protection charm now, hoping there's some way for me to reach you. It helps. It brings light to these unusually dark days. A cold fog rolled in from fires up north that makes it hard to get out of bed, but I'm sure it will pass.

Until then, I'll hold on to your sunshine.

Love,
Madar

A string, tightly wound, snaps somewhere within me, and that claustrophobic pressure is back, pressing so hard on my chest, it's getting hard to breathe. *My mom is sad again.* And I'm not there to fix it. The ocean roars loud in my head as the words *bad daughter, bad daughter, bad daughter* pummel my bruised heart like comets flying through an asteroid belt. I feel it push me over the edge until all I can hear is the dark water pulling me down, down, down . . .

"Earth to Noorzad." Idris snaps his fingers until I finally look up.

"*What?*"

"Where did you see this?" He points to some sketches on my desk—it's a combo of class notes, background on the essence of matter, and a drawing of what I saw in the Arch of Oracles with the words of my prophecy written over it. He points again at the tree. "Why are you drawing this?"

"It's what I saw during my oracle test." I shift uncomfortably from foot to foot because I'm still drowning inside. *Can't breathe, need air.* That burning pressure is still in my chest.

"It was in the arch, but I couldn't get a good look at it, so I don't know if that's what I saw or—I mean, it's a tree with burning feathers. It can't be right."

"A tree with burning feathers." He stares at the shape. "It—it looks familiar." He holds his head and blinks a few times. "It's right there; I can *feel* it. These shadows around it—it's like the tree is drowning . . . like my memory." He looks up at me.

"Drowning?" I look closer at the drawing. I don't even remember adding this much detail, but my mind must have remembered more of the vision than I thought. The tree is withered, with blackened feathers, gnarled roots, and shadows all around. "I guess it could look like that. But trees can't drown."

"*Without its roots, all things shall die . . . ,*" Idris mutters, staring at the drawing. "*In pieces, chained through mist as cold as ice . . .*"

I picture Idris, drowning in cold mist. *Wait.*

I freeze, then reread my mom's letter. "*A cold fog rolled in from fires up north that makes it hard to get out of bed.*" *Think, Farrah, think!* "Do you think whatever my prophecy and your memory are about . . . is somehow affecting the human realm?"

Idris squints. "I mean, maybe? But—"

"I need to see my family. I have to make sure," I blurt out, panicking. The ocean roars so loud in my head. "What if this is what the prophecy means? What if the beginning of the end isn't just for the jinn world?" Every breath burns as the dark shadow of the ocean grows within me. A little spark shoots from my hand. Is there danger back home? "I need an Ever-Place solution or a cloud or—"

"You can't leave the jinn world, remember?"

"Says who?"

"The scale, remember? Just calm down." Idris moves to plant his hands on my shoulders to get me to stop pacing. "It's only fog. I think you're panicking because you got a letter from your mom."

"Don't tell me what to feel!" The pressure of that ocean bursts—dark and heavy—when Idris's palms touch my shoulders. "I can't just forget the people I care about like you can!"

Idris gasps.

"I'm sorry—that came out wrong."

"I think that came out exactly as you meant it, Noorzad," he says quietly before vanishing.

"Wait!" I try to grab his arm, but my hand swipes through thin air.

Red alert. Red alert. Red alert.

The weight of guilt is crushing me as I sink to the floor. It squeezes every worry together from this crummy day until there's no air left to breathe. I lean my hand against my chair and yelp when the burning pressure bursts from my palm and winds slowly along the chair—transforming into a dark, swirling energy, like deep ocean water, that eats away at the chair until it cracks and crumbles . . . into dust.

"What is happening to me?" I crawl away from my desk and bump into my dresser. "W-what is going on?" I flip my hand and notice a dark spot on my left palm. "What is *that*?"

That, little one, is what you've been waiting for. Azar's oily voice slithers down my spine. *It just needed the right trigger to reveal itself.*

"Reveal what?" I try to wipe the dark spot off my hand, but it won't go away.

Your true power, of course.

"There's no way. It didn't look like this before!" Little bursts of darkness spark from my hands again, but I'm afraid to close my fists. What if I turn myself into dust too?

Oh, little one, when will you allow yourself to accept your truth?

"What truth?!"

The truth that was hidden from you with that elephant pin your mother painstakingly created for you, giving up her most precious love. The pin she clings to now, to keep the shadows at bay. Azar's words shake the room as the roaring gets louder in my head. *All that foolishness to suppress the power that's now ready to emerge.*

My power couldn't have picked a worse time to emerge.

"Did you get any sleep last night?" Sufia asks at lunch the next afternoon.

"You look like you got punched by a glass hornet." Laila bites into a fluffy bun filled with custard.

"I got enough." If you count forty-eight minutes of total sleep enough after grappling with anxiety all night, trying to make sure nothing else came out of the dark shadow that is now chilling on my hand. I scowl into my bowl of soup, which is looking more like regurgitated mush by the second. I keep my spoon held tightly in my left hand and continue stirring. "Totally rested—everything is fine. . . ." So long as I don't think about drowning trees or cold fogs or the fact that I feel swallowed whole by all this pressure to be good when in reality—

A dark and burning spark zips into my spoon—crumbling it into dust.

Maybe I'm not fine.

"Never been better!" I yelp, covering the evidence with my right arm hiding the bowl. As if on cue, Yaseen comes into the dining hall with a frown colder than the Ice Age. "Um, on second thought, I think I'm late for a class with Professor Lilac."

"Fridays are independent study days." Laila raises an eyebrow.

"It's an emergency session." I stand up, ready to get out of here.

"So it has nothing to do with Yaseen about to have a full-on meltdown in three, two—" Laila looks sidelong at Sufia the moment Yaseen bursts, red-faced, to the table.

"I need to talk to you," Yaseen grits out. "Privately."

"Everything okay?" Sufia asks, looking between us.

"Peachy." His smile is so frosty, Sufia freezes in her seat. "Just have an issue with a *missing* inkpot that isn't where I last left it—on a pile of books in a very *specific place*—and I remembered Farrah was the last one to see it before it *went missing*. And I need to know if she did something to the inkpot and left a cryptic drawing in its place."

Yaseen's face screams *Where the heck is Idris?* when he looks at me.

"I have no idea where your inkpot is," I say back, trying to get out of the dining hall, but Yaseen stands in the way. The handful of students lounging in the hall nosily glance over.

"Are you sure?" he asks. "Because it would be a big problem if the inkpot is lost, for the both of us."

"Something tells me this isn't about an inkpot," murmurs Sufia, deeply fascinated.

"Obviously. I have ears." Laila chomps on a stick of licorice. "Care to share with the group what's going on?"

"It's nothing." I quickly wave my hands before remembering the spot on my palm and hide them behind my back. Not fast enough to miss Yaseen's attention.

"Is that *ink* on your hand—"

A rumble rips its way through the dining hall, causing Yaseen and me to topple over.

"What was that?" shrieks Laila, holding on to the table as silverware and cups rattle, clattering to the floor. Vibrations buzz through the hall, zapping my skin like a rubber band.

"Mountain quake!" students in the room yell.

"Students, stay away from the windows!" Dozens of building spirits order us, flying above and darting around swinging chandeliers. "I said, do NOT rush to the windows!"

"Whoa, look at the mountain." A student gapes with their face pressed against the window we weren't supposed to be near.

Sufia twists to get a good look. "What is it—" Through the windows, I see the simurgh soar out of her nest and circle the top of the mountain. She looks distressed. "Is something wrong with her?" When she gets near the nest, instead of flying into the entrance, she hits the side of the mountain, swoops around, and does it again before blasting fire from her mouth and flying straight for the academy.

"AWAY FROM THE WINDOWS!"

Fire bursts out of the simurgh's wings, and she screeches in pain, flying up and away from the academy at the last second. It looks like dark mist is wrapped around her ankles and spread all along her tail. Mist that looks a lot like shadows. . . .

A few blackened feathers float in her wake. I think of my drawing. The tree with the withering feathers.

"Does the prophecy . . . ," I whisper to the simurgh, "have to do with you?"

Gasps ripple through the room.

"She went berserk. . . ."

"That never happens. . . ."

"Did you see the way she smashed into the mountain?"

"I've never seen the simurgh act like that before." Sufia shares a worried look with us. "Maybe a few times, she's hit a building or a wall, but never like *that*."

How does the saying go again? Azar mutters through the chaos. *"But should the end come rear its head, there will be more than kingdoms dead."*

"How do you know those words?" I snap, racing out of the hall. My body aches from the roar of the ocean that won't leave me alone. "Are *you* the one attacking the bird?" Yaseen catches on. I can practically hear the question in his face: *What is the old fart saying now?*

Now, that's quite rude. I've been nothing but helpful to you. I can hear the smile in Azar's voice. *Why would I hurt such a majestic creature?*

"Because it's what you do. Create chaos." Chaos in my head. And chaos in the world. It's exactly what Azar wants. The beginning of the end of the jinn world. "I know you! You're trying to get back at the jinn kings. You breaking out of the ring—you're the reason for the prophecy!"

While I would love to take credit for inconveniencing those so-called kings, Azar sneers, *this current situation has nothing to do with me and everything to do with you.*

"I'm not doing anything!"

Exactly, he says. *Prophecies are tricky things. Your little academy is failing you. All it takes is one small mistake, one wrong step, one delay too long. And it all comes tumbling down.*

"Stop listening to him," Yaseen hisses as we run, turning randomly left, right, up a set of stairs—until we've found ourselves within the Mercury wing of the academy.

You should have listened to your brother. Azar needles me. *You should have rushed.*

This isn't my fault. The pressure is worse than ever, my chest is on fire, and I can't breathe again. *This isn't my fault. This isn't my fault.* I rush past potted plants lining the hall and enter a huge sunroom filled to the brim with bright light and plants of all shapes and colors twisting and snarling around rows of glass beds. "I didn't sign up to save the jinn world." All that means is, I'm going to let them down, the same way I let my mom and Arzu down; it's too much pressure on my shoulders.

The roar of the ocean explodes from me as I yell, "I just want to be left alone!" I bump into vines of ivy and pots of blossoming sunflowers, that dark and heavy pressure bursting out of every part of me.

"Farrah, slow down!" Yaseen calls out.

Perhaps that is the problem, little one. Azar pauses. *Perhaps you're not destined to save them at all.*

It starts with the ivy—my power bursts from my hand and runs from one leaf to the next—a chain reaction that moves into a glass flower bed. One by one, it ripples through the plants until all is dust.

Perhaps your fate is chained with mine. His voice winds its way around my thoughts, tangling into the crushing pressure in my heart.

"What is this power?" I stare at my hand in horror as the dark shadow grows a little bit bigger. I look up at Yaseen, whose jaw has dropped in shock. The reaction keeps going, spreading to every other plant, flower, and shrub until it's all gone. "Why am I destroying everything I touch?"

"I—I don't know." Yaseen bends down, squinting. He seems afraid to even touch the remains of the plants. "But you've got to find a way to control it, Farrah. This is dangerous."

"What if I can't?"

"Then maybe we have to tell Baba." Yaseen's lips purse in a thin line. "He did say—"

"NO," I roar as I stand up. Yaseen jerks back, like he's afraid I'll hurt him. "None of the kings can know, especially not our dad." If he finds out, he'll think . . .

That his suspicions were true. That you're no hero at all. Azar whispers my biggest fear. *That perhaps you're like me.*

The villain.

IDRIS

BEING TANGLED

———◈———

I dris was tired of disappearing.

He was tired of the holes in his life turning him into a monster who hurt the people he was supposed to care about. He was tired of not being able to answer simple questions like *Where am I from?*, *Who is my family?*, *What is important to me?*, and *What kind of future would I have had?*

But most of all, he was tired of it being thrown in his face.

"You think you have it bad, Noorzad?" Idris grumbled as he flickered out of the academy and onto the roof, in the tower where he sheltered most nights. "It must be nice to be able to turn off the puzzles in your life. To hide the parts that you don't want to look at." Anger coursed through Idris as that familiar rage suddenly rushed to meet him. He had no idea where it came from—the anger that he could barely control—and that in itself made the feeling worse. It pierced his head, shooting a stabbing pain into his temple. He was used to it now—the headaches that made him see double and want to vomit—but this time, something odd happened. This time, it triggered his power. His eyes clouded over, and the river of recollection bloomed in his mind. Without warning, he was sucked into it.

"Argh—not again!" He always fell back into the same vision. He was drowning, and no matter how hard he struggled against his chains, he kept sinking into his icy grave. This was it for him—just as it was predicted—the end. Idris squeezed his eyes shut, willing the vision to go away, to gain back his control. Instead, when he opened his eyes, his body blinked in and out of sight—first at the top of the academy tower, then at the entrance of a shadowy gate. Its icy mist was a vise grip on his ankles. Pain burst behind his temples as he continued to teleport wildly out of control. "What is going on?" His eyes blazed completely white as he was thrown back into that vision the scale gave him. He clung to the words he hoped would save him one day. *In pieces, chained through mist as cold as ice. In roots, dreams of sons all come undone. In wait for—*

Pain. In his head again. Those words were new. "In wait for what?" Idris moaned, holding his head as he blinked and disappeared and reappeared—this time he stumbled off the ledge of the clock tower in Philadelphia. "I can't make any sense of it. My head is splitting in two."

He fell down, down, down toward the concrete floor where people strolled lazily in the grassy plaza. Right before he crashed into the ground, he clutched his head again and disappeared and reappeared on Broad Street, the main street that led toward Farrah's old neighborhood.

"Make it stop," he groaned. "I don't want to see any more. *Please.*"

But Idris was tangled in the river of recollection, and his power had no intention of letting him go. Before, when he used his power, it felt like he was the one looking in on what was, what is, and what will be. Now it was like he was *living* it.

Like it was happening directly to him.

"Idris?" a girl with curly hair and a scarf covering her mouth called out. "Is that you?" She coughed as dark mist swirled around her. Her protection pin shimmered on her shirt. "Have you heard from Farrah? Something weird is going on here."

"I—" *Something weird is going on with me,* Idris wanted to shout to the phantom vision of Arzu. *I don't know what's real and what's not.* Instead, he turned in pain again to face the clock tower. It pulsed once, twice, before he blinked, disappeared, and reappeared back in his icy grave, the cold water dragging him down. The chains wrapped around his body snagged against something in the water. Raindrop leaves bumped against his face. Before he could reach for them, the numb from the cold took over and ripped the words from his mind.

"*In roots, dreams of sons all come undone,*" the voices roared as Idris was thrown again into another vision, "*in wait for . . .*"

This time he was standing in front of the Arch of Oracles, holding a small red orb in his hands. *Whose is this?* A hairline crack splintered along its side as the red mist began to swirl out. . . .

"I can't take it anymore! Stop!" yelled Idris, dropping the orb.

And then, as quickly as the teleporting began, it stopped, and Idris found himself violently shaking on a deserted street in the City of Jewels. The mountains seemed to be shaking with him, spewing giant chunks of emerald debris from the sky, which were crashing into the street.

But even though the teleporting stopped, and the pain finally receded in his head, Idris was still lost, and the worst part of it all was that he had no idea if this was what was, what is, or what will be—and that terrified him.

Because there was nothing scarier to Idris than being tangled in time.

CHAPTER FOURTEEN

A THOUGHT YOU WALK AGAIN AND AGAIN

We don't run out of the destroyed room of plants fast enough.

"What did you do?" Sufia gasps when she finds us. Her eyes go wide at the sight of the conservatory.

"I—I can explain," stutters Yaseen. "Er, it's not what it looks like. I mean, it *is* what it looks like, but not."

"Yaseen, you do know you're a horrible liar," Sufia says flatly. Her hands tremble, gripping a napkin between her fingers. "And if you're not going to be honest, then I've got no other choice but to alert the academy."

"Wait, please don't." I rush toward her and flinch when she flinches first. I keep my hands behind my back. "It's . . . complicated." Problem is, I can't tell Sufia the truth; otherwise it'll ruin everything—for me and Yaseen.

"Complicated where you've got Yaseen lying for you?" Her eyes narrow. "Is this what *inkpot* was code for?"

"Um, no, that was something else."

"Something else!" Sufia purses her perfectly glossed lips. Voices float from beyond, along with footsteps coming in our direction. Her eyes dart toward the outer hall, and we all think the same thing: it's only a matter of time before we're all discovered in a very bad situation.

I have to think quick. "If they find us here, it'll be bad news for me, but worse for Yaseen." I try to move past her, but she's a brick wall.

"Why would it be worse for Yaseen?" She glances his way.

"Because . . ." He pulls at his ear, debating if he should tell her.

Don't, I mouth.

Sufia crosses her arms, and I know we've lost this battle.

"Okay, we'll tell you," Yaseen says in a panicked rush. "But it can't be here. There's not enough time."

Sufia is silent for a beat. "You promise?"

"I'll do you one better. I'll owe you one," Yaseen says instead. At that, a bright light bursts from his uniform, and a tiny bead forms, floating onto Sufia's bracelet. A debt. "Now will you let us go, please?"

Sufia doesn't say a word, just steps to the side.

I don't give her a second to change her mind. I sprint out of the conservatory and don't look back, leaving both Yaseen and Sufia behind.

Now I really need a session with Professor Lilac.

"Hello! I really need your help—it's an emergency!" I throw my academy jacket on the desk and roll up my sleeves. On my way here, I managed to keep my power contained, but I can't stop fidgeting, afraid that destructive darkness will burst out of me again. "I don't know what's going on with me!"

Villain, villain, villain roars in my head.

Professor Lilac appears in a *poof* with her arms crossed. Today she's wearing a floor-length purple dress in the shape of petals. "Maybe you should start from the beginning, and we can figure it out from there."

"My hands! They're out of control!"

"Shouting will not improve the situation," snaps Professor Lilac. "Now let's take a deep breath. Yes, good. Exhale. Now another—a real deep breath. Good. Yes. Let it out slowly."

The heavy pressure in my chest starts to lighten, calming me down, and I feel a bit better after my fifth deep breath.

"Now show me your hands." She reaches out to touch them, but I jerk back.

"I don't want you to turn to dust too." I grip them into fists.

"Turn to dust?" Professor Lilac frowns.

"Yeah, I . . ." *Just demolished the entire conservatory, and I'm afraid the shadow is gonna swallow me whole.*

"Ah, I see now." Professor Lilac clicks her tongue and gently extends a hand. "Sometimes when we live with secrets for so long, we forget how to stop hiding." Her dress sways just as another tremor hits the school. "Strange." She pauses to glance out the window, a worried frown tugging her mouth down, before turning her attention back on me. "It can't be easy carrying those secrets—both known and unknown to me. Especially if you're afraid of what releasing some of them would mean for you and the things you want." Her purple eyes sparkle with concern. "But I am here to help you shoulder some of that weight, if you need it. And it seems like you need it, unusual one."

My lower lip wobbles, and embarrassingly, big fat tears splash onto my cheeks.

"The academy will not reject you, if that's what you fear," she says, "no matter what hides in your heart."

"I just want to be good," I whisper. "But I'm afraid . . . I'm not." Slowly, I release my hand and bring my palm face up for Professor Lilac to see. The shadow on the palm of my hand itches, growing bigger until it's almost swallowed my palm. "I destroy everything I touch—what if that's what the prophecy means? Am I the end of the realm?"

"Slow that racing mind. One problem at a time." Professor Lilac spreads her hands, just as my words are plucked from the air and written in looping, glowing words. She lets them hang there to read and circles *I destroy everything I touch*. "This is a problem, yes. We can't have that, now can we? Let me shoulder that weight for you."

"How?"

"Until we understand what is lurking within you, we need to keep it under control." She gently wraps her hands around mine, spinning a web of starlight around my left hand. It looks like a glove made from a constellation of stars.

"My power?" I whisper. "It's bad, isn't it?"

"I do not know the true extent of this power that lies within you, but what I do know is this. . . ." The professor passes her hands over my arm one more time, and the glove melts into my skin. I can't see it, but I can still feel the ancient magic lingering. "What happened in the conservatory was a warning that cannot be ignored again."

"A warning for what?"

"For that inner voice inside your head." She points a finger at my forehead and taps it just once. "We become what we think. A single thought is harmless, but a thought you walk again and again creates a path. You must decide: What is the path you choose to wander? Are you the end of the realm? Or are you something else?"

I look up at the glowing words and grip my hands into fists.

"I am . . . something else, something good. I can belong. I can prove it." I close my eyes shut and think it again and again.

I am good, I belong, I can prove it is lassoed around the old words and creates a chain around them.

"Isn't it nice when you don't have to shoulder all that weight by yourself?" Professor Lilac asks.

"It is." I wipe away the dried tears, feeling a little bit lighter. With this power locked away, I feel like I've got one less thing to worry about.

That is a mistake, Azar warns.

I ignore him. Letting *him* into my head is the mistake.

"Since we're already here, why wait until next week to discuss your prophecy status?" suggests Professor Lilac. "Maybe I can help you bear that weight too."

"That . . . would be helpful." I tell her about the tree I saw in the Arch of Oracles, and how it looked like it was drowning, and now the simurgh is in distress. "There was a darkness on her feathers, just like I saw in the arch!"

"That is troubling." The professor worries her lip. "And I'm surprised I didn't see it before."

"See what?"

"The bird's deteriorating state," she explains. "You see, at the beginning of all beginnings, before humans populated the Earth, there were the jinn. Fashioned with smokeless fire, they were the custodians of the land and nature, entrusted to protect our home, including all creatures that live within it."

"Like dragons and faeries and simurghs?"

"Especially the simurgh." The professor nods sadly. "Perhaps the most burdened of the legendary birds." She picks at a spot on her forearm while staring out the stained-glass window at the nest. "The phoenix plays a great role. She purifies our land and the waters below, hence bestowing fertility. She represents the union between Earth and sky, serving as mediator and messenger between those of us above and those of us below. And within that nest, she protects the Tree of Life, to keep our world's careful balance."

My head snaps up at the mention of *Tree of Life*. Is that what I saw in the Arch of Oracles . . . ?

Professor Lilac carries on. "The simurgh is ancient—older than our seven jinn kings. It is rumored she and the tree have seen the destruction of the world three times over."

"So the tree and the bird are linked?" Which would make sense of the withered feathers on the tree. "That's what I've been drawing—the Tree of Life?"

"I believe so." Professor Lilac nods. "And if this is true, then I believe that is where your prophecy is leading you."

"To the tree?"

"Perhaps, although it is not an easy task to enter the simurgh's nest to gain access to the tree." Professor Lilac stares at me warily. "But with the state of the bird, I fear there isn't a moment to waste. I expect a full report during our next session on what you find there."

How am I going to get to the simurgh's nest?

I don't want to go it alone, but when dusk starts to set in, and after knocking on every boy's dorm room door on Yaseen's floor gives me the weirdest stares and rudest responses, I decide to make an executive decision.

I've got to go now.

I hesitated for over a week, and look what happened to the simurgh. If I had answered the call earlier, if I had shared the details of my drawing earlier, maybe whatever is hurting her could have been fixed earlier.

I step out into the cool early-evening air and carefully walk along the clear glass sidewalk. Down below, I see the ocean through a wave of clouds. And past the ocean, somewhere far away, is Long Island, where my mom is clinging to my protection charm, waiting for her sunshine to come back, completely unaware of the danger coming from the jinn world.

That's why I can't fail this observation period—if the simurgh and the Tree of Life create balance for the human and jinn worlds, then I've got to get through this prophecy and make sure whatever is hurting the bird stops. Which means I've got to get up to the simurgh's nest. But how?

"I wouldn't advise going up there alone." Idris appears right over my shoulder.

"Where did you come from?" I yelp. "You can't sneak up on me like that."

"Sorry, I'm just a little—disoriented." Idris tugs nervously at his wristbands, scratching at the skin underneath. "My head, it's . . ." His hair is wilder than normal. "What day is it?"

"It's Friday. . . ." Now that I'm looking at him, he's so much paler than before—he looks like a ghost come to life.

"How many Fridays has it been since the last time you saw me?"

"I just saw you last night." I look at Idris in concern. "Are you okay?"

"Yeah, just got"—he glances around before rubbing his head—"hit by falling debris after that mountain quake."

"You felt that too?"

"That's one way to put it," he mumbles, still clutching his head. He seems really tired and hurt.

"I'm sorry," I blurt out. "I freaked out on you because I was freaking out, and if I hadn't been so mean, you wouldn't have gotten hurt and—"

"Water under the bridge." He smiles weakly. "So, any reason why you've been staring at the mountains for the past five minutes?"

"We've got to go there." I point at the simurgh's nest. The tallest point in all the Qaf Mountains.

"Wish I didn't ask . . ." Idris's face turns green. "But since I'm a sucker for punishment, I feel compelled to also ask, *why*?"

"The prophecy is leading us up there to figure out what's bothering the phoenix. So any suggestions on how to get there would be great."

"I suppose I might have an idea . . . but—where's your brother?" Idris glances back at the academy as we walk down the street. "After all that prophecy-studying, wouldn't he want to be here too?"

"He wasn't at the academy." I wince in guilt. "We'll fill him in later. It's just me and you this time."

"The original duo," he jokes.

"Yeah . . . the original duo . . ." It's quiet after that. The shield I put up makes it hard to joke back. Is it possible to let go of the shield when Idris and I have both hurt each other?

Maybe it starts with a question.

"Have you . . . had any luck with your memories?" I ask as we cross the glittering streets, keeping an eye out for any more rogue simurgh attacks. "I mean, I know I haven't asked in a while, but—"

Idris stiffens. That seems to be the wrong move. "My memories are what they are, Noorzad." We turn a corner. Huge chunks of emerald, peridot, and chrysolite litter the street. "Oh, that's going to be a problem."

"What?"

"I literally just remodeled the shop," a frustrated jinn groans while sweeping away the smaller pieces of debris. The store—named MOUNT QAF TOURS AND EXPEDITIONS—lies in ruins. "Knew it was a mistake to renew the agreement in this location."

"You and me both," another jinn a few stores down agrees. "She's been acting strange for quite some time."

"The phoenix?" I ask, jumping around a huge block of green chrysolite. "Acting strange? For how long?"

"Oh, no, we're closed." The frustrated jinn wags his finger. "Come back another day for a tour." His weary gray eyes appraise Idris and me. "Last time I let an academy kid take one of my clouds, I nearly lost my license. Boy thought he could pluck three feathers off the simurgh! He's lucky he only lost an eye. Never again. Shoo now. I'm busy."

"But, sir—" Idris gets interrupted.

"No buts. We're closed, and the mountain is unstable," the jinn replies. "Now scram before I make you."

"Well, there goes that idea." Idris rubs his face.

"You don't have your cloud pen we could refill?" I ask hopefully.

"They break when left empty for too long." He takes out his pen, clicks it a few times. "It's just a sparkly piece of junk at this point. Can't even hold ink . . ." He trails off. "Hey, do these stones . . . look weird to you?" He crouches down and picks up a few smaller pieces of fallen green peridot.

"Looks like a green rock." I take a few pieces from his hand and hold one up against the sunset. It's so clear, I can see the sun behind it. I can even see a dark cloud moving across the sky, blocking the sun. Wait a sec. "Something's . . . squirming inside it."

"It's in all of them." Idris's arms are full of gems now. "Little shadows wiggling around."

"That's so weird," I say. "Do you think it's the same shadows hurting the simurgh? Or the tree in my vision?"

"Your guess is as good as mine." He studies the stones before pocketing a few. He's thinking about something, his eyes fixed on the mountain. "Any other ideas on how to get up there?"

I stare at the mountain. Even if I had my super strength

back, it's too high to climb. With the falling rocks, there could be loose holds all over the place. One wrong grip, and we'll look just like these shops—destroyed. Plus, these days, climbing leaves a sour taste in my mouth.

"In three, hold air," a boy's voice shouts from above us. "Three, two, one, hold!" A whistle blows.

A flurry of short, cloudlike tubes floats over our heads. They remind me of boats. On the side of each one, Al-Qalam's insignia shines.

"All right, team, take a sip of water. We're going to power-ten it all the way back to the airhouse for the night," the boy shouts again.

"Aw, come on, you've got to be kidding me!"

"Have some mercy on us—you nearly steered us into the mountain!"

"POWER TEN, NOW!" The boy blows his whistle, and the floating cloud boats row away.

"Whoa," I breathe, staring at them as they float toward the edge of the city. They disappear through a passing cloud.

"You've got that gleam in your eye," Idris comments. "Which means . . ."

"I think I've found our ride," I whisper, grabbing his hand and chasing after the cloud boats. "And I know just how we'll get them!"

CHAPTER FIFTEEN

THE TREE OF LIFE

"**A**nd now we're back to stealing," Idris grumbles.

"*Borrowing*," I correct Idris. "We'll return it when we're done." We sneak through the row of fluffy airhouses. It reminds me a lot of Boathouse Row on the Schuylkill River, except instead of boathouses made of wood and stone, these airhouses are made of big panels of stained glass with clouds wrapping around the roofs. "I think this is the right one."

Inside the airhouse are six bays. Each bay has rows of gleaming boats stacked on glass racks. A small group of academy students are tightening ropes, putting away cloud oars. A short boy blows his whistle and claps his hands. His silver long-sleeve shirt and green pants are pristine while everyone else's clothes are covered in sweat. "Group huddle, team. Great work today . . ."

"Now's our chance." I urge Idris to go deeper into the bay

in the back. "While they're distracted. Help me untie these." We get to work untying one of the small boats that has two seats.

"I hope you know how to fly this thing, because I don't," whispers Idris.

"Can't be harder than riding a bike."

"Riding a bike was *very hard!*"

"But you still did it." I groan, shouldering one end of the boat while Idris holds the other. "This is a lot heavier than it looks."

"Why isn't it floating?" Idris's face gets sweaty as we slowly walk out of the bay. His hand touches the academy insignia—it glows red against his palm. We both have an aha moment.

"It's like a fingerprint lock. Genius!" I slap the insignia on my side. It bursts with green light, triggering the boat to rumble and groan. Instantly, it becomes as light as a feather. Little wisps of white fluff pour out of the insignia and coat the shell of the boat. "Whoa, on second thought, I don't think I *want* to give this back." I flip the boat over, admiring the shiny inside. The sleek seat that rolls back and forth. There's a little spot to buckle our feet in. It's the most amazing thing I've ever seen.

"Hurry up before they notice us!" Idris tosses one long oar at me. I catch it. "How . . . does this attach?"

"If it's anything like rowing, I think it goes here." The oar snaps in place on the right side. "Try the left for you." Idris's oar smoothly snaps in. "All right, Mount Qaf, here we come," I whisper-shout. We jump into the boat and are still strapping in our feet when the boy with the whistle appears.

"Hey, what do you think you're doing?" He blinks in surprise. "There's a no-fly curfew after dark!"

"So sorry, I owe you one." I frantically try to get the boat to go, but I realize Idris needs to move his oar too. A small bead appears from my chest and floats toward the boy. *Oh no, a debt.* "On three, just follow me," I whisper over my shoulder. I mimic the way I've seen rowers row on walks through Fairmount Park with my family and Arzu's family. There's a tiny squeeze in my heart thinking about them. "Three . . ."

"Noorzad, you didn't tell me we'd be moving backward," Idris whispers angrily. He follows my lead when I lean forward. "Two . . ."

"Oi, Hassan, get Coach Celadon," the boy shouts.

"You got it, Jal!"

"ONE!" I shout, pushing back as hard as I can. The boat moves—fast. It bursts through the airhouse, and we are zipping away. "KEEP GOING!" We fly away from the city and out to the open sky. The airhouse and Jal's angry face get smaller and smaller, but so does the mountain. "We're going the wrong way!"

"It's not like I can see where I'm going," Idris shouts back.

"You've gotta steer us."

"IT'S DARK. HOW?"

If the airboat goes straight when we row together, it should turn if one of us stops, right? I stay still and watch Idris continue to row. Slowly, we start turning. As we make a big loop heading back to the mountain, I feel the weight of the ocean of my worries fall away. The wind blows against my neck. This is a different feeling from climbing—where I was always chasing the high, always striving to impress, to be the best, to go farther than before. To please my dad.

With this, I don't have to do anything but sit above that heaviness instead of drowning in it. Just sit, breathe in, and row. "This is . . . amazing!" It's the lightest I've felt in months.

"I'm sure it is when I'm doing all the work." Idris huffs and puffs, taking quick peeks behind him every second. "Okay, I think we're set now." Together we row our way up, up, up. Past the skyscrapers of the city, and higher still. We crash through layers of clouds. The little wisps bubble and burst on my skin. We're so close to the nest.

"Keep an eye out for anything that doesn't belong," I warn Idris.

"You mean other than us?" Idris huffs again.

"Yeah, like *you-know-who*'s shadow creeps . . . ," I mutter.

"Why would he want to bother the bird?"

"I'm not sure." The breeze flutters my uniform, shaking loose a single button. "My professor said the phoenix guards the Tree of Life, and together they keep the balance in the seen and unseen realms." I think about the darkness in the mountain gems and on the simurgh's tail. "What if he's trying to upset the balance on purpose?"

"But why?"

"Maybe it'll break his chains. I don't know," I say, frustrated. "It's not like he's going to tell me his master plan."

"Break his chains . . . ," Idris mumbles. "Is that what the visions mean?"

"What visions?" When Idris doesn't answer, I turn around to quickly look at him. "I'll keep asking until you answer."

"Recollections," he says hastily. "At least, that's what I think they are."

"Do you get these . . . recollections often?"

"No." He sighs. "Yes. It depends. But they're nothing like how they used to be. Sometimes they feel like visions. Other times, memories, I don't know, but what I see scares me, Noorzad. It's"—he stops rowing, allowing the boat to drift—"not good."

"Do you see me in those visions?" I ask quietly. "Is this . . . our fault for returning to the jinn world?" Yaseen had said it himself months ago, that Azar and the shadow jinn were never a problem until we showed up. And now . . . there are even more shadows lurking around.

"I wish I knew." Our boat bumps against the entrance of the nest. Idris jumps out of the boat and holds out a hand to me. "But maybe this will lead us to the answer."

"Hope so." *Think good thoughts, Farrah.* Just like Professor Lilac said. *I am good. I belong, and I can prove it.* I take Idris's hand and face the cavernous nest.

The *dark*, cavernous nest. With a *spider* crawling right by my foot.

"Don't tell me you're still afraid of dark places?" Idris squeezes my hand.

"I'm not *afraid*," I say, scurrying past the rogue spider. "I just prefer to avoid them." To prove my point, I stride into the nest, keeping myself alert for any disturbances. I hesitate when I see three deep claw marks in the stone. "The simurgh isn't . . . dangerous, right?"

"Depends on your definition of *dangerous*." Idris's pale eyes glow through the dim light. "But let's hurry so we don't find out."

"Great." I gulp. *That* doesn't make me feel better. Our steps echo through the cave. Pieces of dust rain from overhead, tickling my nose and eyes. "Achoo!" The sound echoes in the cave, followed by rustling of leaves. Deep within, a spotlight shines down on the biggest tree I've ever seen in my life. It looks a lot like the tree I saw in the arch. "The Tree of Life . . ."

"Looks like we're not alone," whispers Idris.

Standing in front of the tree is a girl with blinking red eyes. Holding a long feather.

"It's you!" I shout, running to face her. Shoulda known, where there's chaos, Azar's minions aren't far behind.

"Whatever you're doing to the phoenix, you've gotta stop it now!"

"Me?" The shadow girl looks up, surprised, and blinks.

"Stop infecting the bird with your shadows!"

"Why would we do something like that?" asks the girl.

"Because . . . that's what the old fart wants." I point a finger at her, keeping my distance. I brace myself for the attack, for more red eyes to blink from the shadows. When things go wrong, Azar isn't far behind. He's got to be playing a mind game with me. These disturbances have to be because of him; otherwise, why send one of his minions?

The girl steps farther into the spotlight and illuminates the shimmering jewel-toned feather. The branches of the Tree of Life sway behind her.

"If you want to know what the *old fart* wants . . ." She beckons toward us. "Then why don't you come closer? Take a look. Don't worry, I won't bite."

"Seems unwise, but . . ." Idris takes the bait. "Any funny business, and we bolt."

"Sounds like a plan." I walk closer to the girl, who extends her arm out to give me the feather. "Why are you giving this to me?"

"Curious to know what you see," she says.

Idris and I huddle together under the spotlight. The feather is beautiful, soft to the touch, crackling with the tiniest bit of electricity. It almost hums with magic. Except . . .

"Noorzad, it's the same darkness," whispers Idris.

The very end of the feather has gone murky with wisps of darkness coiling around it. But why? I look up at the tree, and now that I'm closer, I notice something that makes my stomach drop. "The leaves . . ." I reach out to the lowest branch and touch them. They blacken and disintegrate through my fingers. The branch snaps off, brittle and old and worn. Little trails of sap run down from the broken spot. They look like tears. *The tree is crying.* The same shadow runs through the tree, seeping through the branches into its core. Bright pulses of energy flash from its core and are sent down to its roots. "It looks like the tree is . . ."

"Dying," the girl answers.

"But why?"

"I don't know." The girl shrugs. "But we were sent to find out." There are two other shadow jinn lurking in the corner of the cave. Silent and waiting.

"Noorzad, this is worse than bad." Idris pales as he touches the tree's trunk. "If the Tree of Life dies . . ."

"*Without its roots, all things shall die,*" I whisper. "It's about the tree."

I turn on the shadow girl, my eyes narrowed. I don't buy this innocent *I'm here to find out what's going on* act. This is *exactly* something Azar would do. "How is your boss poisoning the tree?"

"I am here to simply obey orders. I was told to enter the nest when the phoenix was gone and take a feather." The girl shrugs. She picks up another feather from the ground. "It is not in my nature to ask questions, or to have thoughts, or feelings." Her voice is clipped, and her eyes turn down. "A simple *puppet* meant to obey."

"Then why did you stay?" If that's all she was meant to do, then why is she still here? Something isn't adding up.

"Just wanted to see if you remembered" is all she says.

Idris and I blink in surprise.

"Remember what?" I ask.

"I thought . . ." The shadow girl shakes her head. "Silly me. I don't have thoughts. Or feelings. Or a name. Just a shadow and nothing more." She holds tight to the feather. There's a small burst of light glowing from her palm. Before I have a chance to ask her any more questions, she and the other shadow jinn fly up into the opening through the ceiling.

"Be careful, Farrah Noorzad," she warns. "Nothing good ever comes from dealings with jinn kings."

"What was that supposed to mean?" asks Idris.

"No idea." Holding my hands together, I stare at the light at the top of the cave, filled with more questions than answers. Why would they just leave? If this is Azar's doing, wouldn't he want to eliminate me and Idris so we can't expose what's going on with the tree? The cave rumbles, causing tiny debris to rain down on us. In the distance, something roars. "Let's get out of this cave before a certain phoenix decides to have us for lunch."

"Um." Idris freezes in place as something large blocks the entry to the cave. "I think it's a little too late for that."

The simurgh's golden eyes blaze in anger as she opens her mouth and roars.

Golden fire erupts from her mouth, heading straight for us.

CHAPTER SIXTEEN

THE LIVING SANCTUARY

"We're gonna be fried bird food," Idris yelps, jumping backward. He desperately climbs up the Tree of Life. The branches are so brittle, they snap immediately. "Oh no!" He tumbles and falls onto the hard cave floor.

This makes the phoenix madder.

"Easy there, birdie." I nervously keep my hands out and back away. The simurgh is *huge*. At least two times taller than me. From far away, she seemed smaller. But up close, she could swallow me whole. I'm not sure if giant birds are like bears, but the last thing I want to do is give her something to chase. "We were just about to leave. Please don't eat us." My back hits the end of the cave. This can't be good.

Her front paws scrape against the floor, creating deeper claw marks in the stone. Her face—more doglike than birdlike—snarls as she sniffs the air and comes closer. Her wide-open mouth is the last thing I see before I squeeze my eyes shut. The heat from the blast charging in her jaw burns hotter than my worst sunburn, and I think, *Here comes the end. Prophecy failed. Game over.*

The blast never comes.

"Huh?" I open one eye to see the phoenix staring curiously at Idris. She lowers her head, sniffing the air until her large nose is pressed against Idris's belly.

"Noorzad, help me," he hisses. His whole body is shaking as one sharp tooth grazes his shoulder.

"How?" I whisper-shout back. "It's not like I can shoo the bird away!"

At that, the phoenix stares sharply at me, growling low. It's like she's saying, *Watch it.*

"Sorry, sorry," I mumble.

Slowly, the simurgh does something strange—she lowers herself to the ground at the base of the tree.

"N-nice bird." Idris tentatively strokes her head. His fingers are covered in ash.

"Wait a second." I take the smallest step toward the bird and smell charred smoke. She breathes heavy and roars again, a little softer now. On her body, there is a deep orange glow. "She's glowing. . . ." No, not glowing. Little embers crackle beneath her skin. "She's *burning.*"

Her body sparks without warning, and a blast of fiery energy erupts from her mouth again, this time feeding into the tree.

"Watch where you're blasting!" Idris jumps away in the

nick of time. He stumbles toward me, and we exchange horrified glances at the way the Tree of Life lights up. It pulses bright. Suddenly, the bark improves. The leaves turn lush and green, like jeweled raindrops. The strange, shadowy mist surrounding it shrinks away.

"She's fixing it," Idris marvels. He reaches up and plucks a raindrop leaf. It hums in his hands. "There are no shadows in this—look!"

The phoenix wails as she rests her head on the ground. The moment she stops, the wispy dark shadows return with a vengeance, flowing out of the tree and over her body. Her golden eye never leaves Idris.

"I've got a bad feeling about this, Idris," I say. "This doesn't look like the shadows the old fart uses."

Idris is transfixed by the bird. "She looks so tired." He kneels closer to the simurgh. "What's hurting you?" he whispers to the bird.

In response, a tear glistens in her eye.

"She's been trying to fix the tree." Stroking the bird's head, Idris examines her feathers. "It looks like she's been taking in whatever is hurting it. All her feathers are infected with this stuff." More tears pool in her golden eye.

"She seems awfully familiar with you." The phoenix is ready to bite my head off but is fine with Idris.

"Wish I could remember," he says sadly. She blinks, and a tear falls on Idris's knee.

"Maybe you could . . ." In all the fantasy stories I've read, if a phoenix gives you her tears, it's supposed to fix something broken inside you. "Use her tears?"

"Wait. You're right." Idris looks at the bird. "Do you think you could give me my memories back?" he asks. "Can you fix me?" He cups his hands together near her eye.

The phoenix rumbles and closes her eyes, letting one big tear drop.

"I don't want to be lost in time anymore," Idris says as he splashes the tear against his face. He keeps his face buried in his hands. "I just want to wake up from this bad dream." His shoulders shake as he kneels before the bird. "Please."

"Idris . . ."

The mist has turned the bird completely black now, except for the orange embers that are burning brighter, getting hotter. Almost like she's getting ready to combust—

"Idris, I think we need to get away from her." I get up and start backing away slowly.

"Not yet, it's not working." Idris grits his teeth and tries to gather more tears to splash on his face, but they've all dried up. "Nothing's changed. I need to know who I am. I need to stop the disappearing—" Now the whole bird is changing—burning from orange to red to icy blue. I've read enough stories to know what comes next.

"Idris, we've gotta get out of here!" I grab his arm and jerk him away from the bird.

"Just leave me alone," he cries.

"You're going to get hurt—" I grab his torso and pull.

"So LEAVE ME!" He pushes free from me. Shadows from the glowing bird cast eerie shapes all over the cave. "If the simurgh's tears can't break the curse, then what's the point of trying anymore?"

"You don't mean that—"

"I am all *alone*, Noorzad," he cries. "I'm a stranger in my own head. You have *no idea* how that feels. The scale was right. I'm not in anyone's mind, not even my own! This curse is impossible to break. I could disappear from time, and no one would even remember me."

"I would." I hold his shaking hands and gently tug him away from the burning phoenix. "I would always remember you, no matter what. And your memories are out there, but you'll never get them back if you give up now."

Reluctantly, Idris blinks his tired eyes at me and quietly concedes, "Okay, Noorzad."

We make a run for it. Just when we get to the entrance of the cave, the simurgh explodes in a wave of dazzling fire and searing heat, throwing us back onto the cloud boat as pools of smoky mist spill out of the mouth of the nest.

We stare at the chaos in shock.

"We should probably get out of here before the smoke clears," Idris says. "Otherwise it's gonna look like *we* killed the simurgh."

I grab hold of the cloud oar and start to row away.

I AM A CHARRED MESS BY THE TIME I BURST INTO MY PROPH-
ecy seminar room. But this can't wait for Monday.

"It's game over." I throw my jacket to the ground and
slump over my desk. I've failed. The phoenix exploded, and
the Tree of Life probably went up with it. And without either
of them . . . *"There will be more than kingdoms dead. They will
be—the beginning of the end,"* I wail.

"It is not game over, unusual one." Professor Lilac appears in a frumpy purple bathrobe, with her hair in a lavender towel. "Please. You'll wake everyone in the academy with
those antics."

"But I failed to save the simurgh!" I also tell her what happened with the tree.

Professor Lilac snaps her fingers and shows me my prophecy orb—my perfect, not-red, uncracked orb. "If the Tree of
Life had died, you would have failed your prophecy, but as
you can see, all is fine."

"For now," I mumble.

"The phoenix will be reborn. That is her role." Professor
Lilac pushes her glasses up her nose as she paces around the
room with her lips pursed. "Let's give her time. Sometimes
the best way to purify ailment is to burn it away. Perhaps that
is what she did. To keep the tree going. She will reemerge
from her cave, and all will be well. I'm sure of it."

"And if she doesn't?"

"We will cross that bridge when we get there" is all she says. "Now, off to bed. Everything will look clearer in the morning."

I WAIT SEVEN DAYS.

In those days, I trust in Professor Lilac, and continue going to class.

On the third day, I listen to Professor Amaranth, who continues his lessons on the planetary realms that make up the City of Jewels and cites, "A phoenix rebirth cycle takes approximately one hundred sixty-nine hours and thirty-two minutes."

On the fourth day, I wait, even when the worries nestle deep in my head when Idris doesn't come out of the impromptu fort I made for him under my lofted bed.

"You don't want to come out to meet with Yaseen to talk game plan?"

"Just leave me alone, Noorzad," he mumbles from inside the fort.

On the fifth day, I sit with Yaseen in Divine Delights, the magical bakery that sells tarts that tell you the truth and cupcakes that boost brainpower. Yaseen bites into a cupcake, hoping it'll help us make sense of what happened in the simurgh's nest. "I still can't believe you went up there without *me*," he grumbles.

"In my defense, I did look for you," I say. "Where *were* you, by the way?"

"I went to the living sanctuary to clear my head and avoid Sufia," Yaseen replies.

"A living what?"

"It's easier if I just show you. Maybe after your weekly meeting with Baba?" He peers over at me with his eyebrows raised. "You might need it."

"I'll need a miracle to get through my check-in with our dad. At least with my power being sealed, I won't have to worry about him discovering it," I mumble into a milkshake—especially since I haven't worked out exactly what to tell him. At first, I thought Azar had something to do with the disturbances, but the shadow jinn didn't even bat an eye at Idris and me. "Just wish I knew what was hurting the tree . . ." If it's not Azar, then *who*?

"You said the bird was taking in what was poisoning the tree?" Yaseen taps his fingers against the table while staring out the glass walls of the café.

"Yeah, she was burning the sickness away. . . ." But even though the simurgh is all-powerful, everything has its limits. And she did look so tired. . . .

When Yaseen and I get back to the academy, I painstakingly sit in Professor Umber's class while trying to catch a glimpse of the simurgh's nest out the window. *What's taking so long?* I barely pay attention to his lesson on the ways jinn essence manifests in the seen and unseen realms.

"It's a common misconception to think our realms are separate—jinn and human—seeing as we are scattered far and wide and divided by the Great Veil." Professor Umber lectures in the moon wing of the academy. He adjusts his monocle while pacing the silvery classroom. "But just because humans cannot sense our essence, it does not mean they do not benefit from it." He snaps his fingers and cycles through a range of shimmerfields, each one sneaking a glimpse into a modern human city. "When the unseen realm shifts out of balance"—he glances at the simurgh's nest—"so does the seen realm. What do you notice here?"

"They all look pretty normal to me." I squint at the shimmerfields, careful not to touch them and accidentally get stuck in one.

"This looks normal?" Professor Umber flicks through each. "Raging fires across eastern Canada, four major hurricanes brewing in the Atlantic, unheard-of heat waves in Europe in *April*—all of this happening at once." The professor shakes his head. "Our realms are out of balance with one another."

"Could you show me . . . Long Island—for my own personal notes?" I nervously pick at my bracelet, trying to ignore the building pressure in my chest again—that itching suspicion I've been putting to the back of my mind.

He casually cycles through until he finds the Long Island

shimmerfield. "You know what they're calling this haze?" asks the professor as he shows it to me. "Smog." He snorts. "When it is very clearly dream vapor."

"Dream vapor?" I whisper in alarm. "But how did it get all the way there?" That should only be coming out of the Winged Nightmare's realm. My nose is nearly touching the edge of the shimmerfield as I squint, staring deep into the mirage to make sense of the thick fog of a gray haze moving through the streets. But from here, I can see it infiltrate homes, parks, trees—turning brittle and dying . . .

"Have you not been paying attention to a word I've been saying?" He drags his hand down his face in frustration. "It all boils down to the very basics of essence theory, which we will obviously go over again, since you fail to retain the absolute basics. . . ."

I can barely pay attention to Professor Umber because I can't believe I didn't put it together sooner. Why the shadow jinn were peaceful—the shadows weren't Azar's; they were King Maymun's. But if what Professor Umber is saying is true, then the big question is, *why* is the nightmare king's realm imbalanced?

When I leave his class for the day and the simurgh still hasn't emerged from her nest, I've made up my mind. I can't wait seven days. If the root cause of all this is a realm imbalance with the Winged Nightmare's realm, then I've got to go to the ones with enough awesome power to fix it.

The kings themselves.

THE NEXT DAY, ON THURSDAY, I DO WHAT I'VE BEEN DREADING and ask my dad for help.

Back in my dad's court, I've got the routine down pat. He always sits on his throne, and I always enter softly, with my head bent low, gaze down, and say, "Good afternoon, Padar jan."

"Anything to report?" he asks.

"Yes, actually," I say, eyes on the ground. "In prophecy seminar, we've pinpointed what the prophecy hinted at—it's the problem with the Tree of Life." I pause because, for the first time, my dad's eyes are zeroed in on mine.

"Go on."

"I think dream vapor is poisoning it . . . and, as a result, making the simurgh really tired trying to fix it."

"Hmm. Yes, it has gotten a little out of hand for Maymun," my dad agrees, relaxing into his seat. "But nothing that cannot be handled. I'll talk to him about it. You are dismissed."

"So . . . you're not worried about it?" I ask hesitantly. "Or how it's affecting everyone in the city, not knowing what happened to the phoenix?" Or not letting them know that the tree is literally *dying* without the bird?

"What makes you think I'm not?" His dark eyes glance at me, and I feel super nervous. No matter how many times I see my dad in his true form, I can't get used to it. Everything about him says *don't mess with me*, and I wonder if I made up the caring dad who would take me climbing on my birthdays, if I dreamed all the laughter and hugs.

"You seem . . ." I shrug. "Like you don't care."

"Farrah, you see one moment of my day. Believe me when I say I am aware of the situation. It will be handled. All I want to know is if anything unusual happens with *you*."

I gulp. "Unusual like—" Harboring an illegal mixed jinn in my bedroom. Or sealing an extremely destructive true power that has left a scary mark on my palm (and won't go away). Or talking to an evil ancient fire jinn king because sometimes he feels more interested in me than my own dad does and it feels nice to have a consistent male figure in my life (even if he is *evil*). Though he's been quiet too lately.

Padar leans forward. "Like?"

"Nothing," I say, swishing my skirt as I turn on my heel. "Nothing at all."

"I can't believe I wished to spend more time with our dad last year," I complain to Yaseen when he meets me outside the Supreme Court of Jinn. "What was I thinking?"

"Sounds like it went great, is what I'm hearing." He hands me purple rock candy on a stick. Then, licking his own green stick, he gazes up at the empty nest of the simurgh. "That mist is still seeping out." He frowns as we walk through the glittering main square.

"Well, our dad's not worried. Everything's *handled*." I grumble, too stressed to even think about eating candy. "So long as I'm not getting into trouble, he can't be bothered." Even though the longer we don't fix the situation, the worse the realm imbalance will get, which means things could get real bad at home.

"You get used to it." Yaseen sighs. "But"—he looks behind his shoulder just in case we're being listened to—"he doesn't know everything."

"Obviously not."

"Which is why we need somewhere private to talk." He glances around before leading the way down the street, and after zigzagging through a few blocks, he enters a building made of vines, twisting fifteen stories into the sky. Little gem flowers bloom all around. Though a bunch are very droopy and wilted. Crystallized butterflies flutter around them. "This is where I go to do my best thinking and scheming."

"You think?"

"Ha ha." Soft grass squishes under our feet as Yaseen wanders deeper into the building. One second we're in the bustling City of Jewels, and the next we warp into a dazzling jeweled jungle.

Or what I assume once *was* dazzling.

Instead of vibrant greenery and lush canopies of jeweled trees, there's an overall gray-and-brown drying to everything.

"What happened?" Yaseen looks horrified.

"Is it not supposed to look like this?" I lean closer toward another swarm of crystal butterflies, but the second I get too close, they screech and leave a trail of shimmering mist while they fly away. Tiny flashes of light burst from the beat of their wings.

"No, this is a living sanctuary for rare creatures, insects, and plants. It's supposed to be living, not dried out and . . ."
Dying.

"Like a zoo?"

"A what?"

"Um, a place where people pay to see wild animals?" I explain. "They're usually in cages, though, and the exhibits are mainly fake, so technically they're not wild anymore, and sometimes you can feed and pet them."

"Is that what humans do for fun? Cage creatures?" Yaseen sounds distressed as he continues to walk through the sanctuary. "Living sanctuaries are meant to be a refuge for the creatures within the seen and unseen realms. You'll see a bunch of them scattered through the city. Jinn share space with them, especially when they no longer feel safe in the human world."

My fingers run through the thick and brittle vines as they stretch up into a canopy of jeweled trees. "I've never seen plants like these before." Energy hums through their leaves, with the tiniest bit of light gently glowing around the edges— and something else. A dark mist. The leaves turn brittle in my hand, like the Tree of Life.

This has got to be because of the dream-vapor imbalance.

How can our dad be so calm when the living sanctuary looks like this?

"Of course you haven't," Yaseen says, walking deeper into the sanctuary. "That's the whole point. To seek refuge from the things that hurt you. At least, that's what it's supposed to be." He makes a sharp left turn and then a right before stopping short in front of a distorted portal. "Please be fine, please be fine." He steps through the portal. The space transforms, and now we're in the middle of a field of dark red flowers along a riverbank. *Spider lilies.* The same flower that's on Yaseen's protection charm. "This really isn't good. The sanctuary is suffering."

"Yeah, this is so much worse than I imagined." I watch Yaseen sit down on a dry spot next to a patch of flowers. His face goes sullen.

"These were my mom's favorite flowers," he says quietly. "She was into planting and gardening. Could talk to them, knew what they wanted." A breeze ruffles his hair. "She used to joke that my eye color was a gift from them." He sighs and stares at the dried-out spider lilies. "She would know how to fix this."

"I bet she would," I say. I know how hard it is for Yaseen to talk about his mom. I can't imagine what it's like to be without your mom. She seemed much kinder than our dad. It seems cruel to let her favorite place waste away like this. So I admit something scary. "I don't think the simurgh is going to be reborn."

"Yeah, I think the same," says Yaseen.

"And if the simurgh isn't going to be reborn, then it's only a matter of time before the tree dies too." I stare out into the living sanctuary—or at least, what's left living of it—as proof of the tree's weakened state. "If our dad isn't willing to do something about it now, then we've got to go to the source of the imbalance that's hurting the tree."

"To the nightmare realm?" Yaseen's eyes go wide.

"If that's what it takes." My words are braver than I feel, but I can't stop thinking about everyone I care about back home—my mom, my grandparents, my best friend—and the image of the mist infiltrating Long Island. "Then that's where we'll go."

CHAPTER SEVENTEEN

I OWE YOU ONE

T here's a big ruckus by the time we get back to the academy.

"We know your king's realm is the problem," one tall boy threatens. A jeweled sun pin glitters on his uniform lapel. He's pressing a finger against a boy with wings. I recognize him—it's the Winged Nightmare's nephew. Esen narrows his red eyes but doesn't say a word back. "Your realm's flooded the entire lower city with . . ." The boy shudders. "Your dream magic!"

"Tell your king to keep his nightmares to himself!" a second boy growls, while a third boy nods in agreement.

"Let's not get involved in that." Yaseen tries to slip around them in the great hall, but something feels wrong about watching three bullies gang up against one.

"Esen isn't doing anything."

"I know, but you know not all the realms get along,"

explains Yaseen quietly. "And see those guys—they're all from the sun king's realm. Everyone knows the Golden King and the Winged Nightmare are enemies at heart."

"But why?"

"Because he's a total nightmare," Yaseen reiterates.

"Doesn't mean Esen is . . ." Yaseen thought humans were even worse than nightmares before he met me. If seeing the good in me was enough to get him to change his mind, why isn't that same logic applied here too? Before I get a chance to think, I shout, "Hey! Fighting won't get us anywhere! We need to work together, not tear each other down."

Esen grips his hands in fists right when the three boys get in his face.

"What did you say?" the boy with the sun pin says.

At that exact moment, Esen unfurls his stone wings and flies up and out of the hall. He zooms through the grand open doors, leading out to a balcony overlooking the court-yard.

"Stay out of conversations that don't concern you, Mars girl." The sun-pin boy looks me up and down. "Don't think we aren't watching your king's realm too. Everyone knows the Red King and the Winged Nightmare are close. That's why the other, better realms stay away from them. I'd watch who you keep company with, Yaseen, unless you want to drag your father's realm in with them." With that, the boys stalk off.

"See?" Yaseen scrubs his face with his hands. "Focus on things we can change. Focus on getting rid of all that mist before it gets worse. Come on."

I CAN'T BELIEVE I'M SAYING THIS, BUT WE NEED IDRIS'S POWER.

"If the answer to fixing the mist imbalance problem is in the nightmare realm, then we need to keep two steps ahead of it," Yaseen reasons. "Using Idris's recollection is the only way to do that." We almost make it to my dorm to get him.

Almost.

"Hold on!" a girl calls out.

Yaseen is about to scream. "Please don't tell me that's—"

"Sufia!" I spin around. "What's the occasion? I mean, it's so great to see you, but we're—"

"Avoiding me like the plague?" Her eyes narrow. "Is that what your power is, Mars girl?"

"Avoiding or the plague?" I nervously laugh while trying to slip into my room.

"You're going to tell me what's going on *now*." She marches toward Yaseen and me, a frown on her face. Her normally kind eyes are glowering. Yaseen shrinks back a little. She can be scary when she's mad. "I waited long enough. But ever since the conservatory, Yaseen's been acting strange, the same way he did when his dad disappeared. Missing class, borrowing books on things that have nothing to do with the judicial track—"

"Can't a guy have other interests?"

"Avoiding me and not showing up for our usual hangouts." She shakes her wrist where her bracelet sits. "Remember when you had *other interests* our first year when your mom was sick—"

"That is *none of your business*," Yaseen snaps, yanking out a chunk of his eyebrow. His spider-lily pin twinkles against the molten-lava glow of my door.

"It is my business when I was the one who was there for you!" Sufia has angry tears in her eyes.

"And now I'm great," argues Yaseen. "Better than great!"

"No, you're not!" Sufia shouts back. "You're keeping secrets again!"

"Because it's none of your—"

I don't want Yaseen and Sufia's friendship to have problems because Yaseen is protecting me. I march between them and throw my hands out. "You're both giving me a headache. Yaseen can't tell you the truth because it's not his secret to share." I throw a *thanks, but I got this* smile toward him.

"You don't have to—"

"I really do, Yaseen," I say. "I don't want to get between friends." I take a brave breath, turn toward Sufia, and continue. "I can tell you the truth, but once I do, there's no backing out. Once you know, there's no untangling yourself from our mess."

Sufia chews on a manicured finger, shooting a hesitant look between the two of us. "You're not . . . *dating*, are you?" A deep blush spreads across her cheeks.

"That's the grossest idea I've ever heard." My face goes beet red in mortification.

"Would rather eat slugs." Yaseen gags.

"Then tell me, Mars girl." Sufia clasps her hands together, waiting.

"You'd better come in." I sigh, letting Yaseen and Sufia slip into my room. "Because it's a long story."

To Sufia's credit, she doesn't immediately sprint out of the room and alert the entire student body about what she's just heard, and she only screams twice.

Once when she notices a bleary-eyed Idris emerging from a huddle of blankets under my lofted bed, and the second time when the Eau de Illusion wears off and she gasps, *You're the girl I saw in the library last year! I knew you looked familiar!*

"So let me get this straight. For starters, you're not from Mars—you're actually a Jupiter girl. Well, half. Other half human." Sufia sits cross-legged on my desk, looking horribly confused. "Your dad is also Yaseen's dad, and the only reason you found out was because *you-know-who* enchanted your dad to give you a cursed ring of fate to make a wish on, which then trapped all the jinn kings in it, who you then had to save."

"We call him *old fart*," Yaseen chimes in, "but yeah."

"And after you saved them, they put you on trial, which put you on house arrest at the academy until you finish out your prophecy, which means fixing the problem with the simurgh and the Tree of Life. Which you think is because of the Winged Nightmare's dream vapor. And we have to do something before it dies and we all die as a result."

"Yep," I say.

"My head is spinning," says Sufia.

"You're not going to . . . expose us, are you?" asks Yaseen.

"I mean, if Tamira and Laila were with me, the whole city would know by now, but no," she says seriously. "If the jinn kings know and are keeping it a secret, then . . . not keeping your secret would get me in trouble with them too. Since I'm not supposed to know at all."

"And you're okay that we're . . . part human?" I gesture at me and Idris, who has yet to say a single word but has shuffled with a blanket over his head to sit by the window. His pale eyes stare out into the twinkling dark.

"It is a little weird, I won't lie, but . . ." Sufia wraps a strand of hair around her finger. "It's already tense here with the realm divisions. I don't want to throw y'all into the mix."

"Not when we've got a bigger problem on our hands," Yaseen agrees. "Thank you, Sufia. It means a lot."

"But you still owe me one." She nervously waves a hand.

"I owe you a million." Yaseen and Sufia share a small smile (and a second of too-long lingering eye contact). I cough because, awkward.

"There's a storm outside," Idris mumbles to himself. Clouds are heavy across the city, lightning flashes in a few of them. "Lots of mist all over the place. It's flooding some parts of downtown."

"The realm imbalance is getting worse," says Yaseen.

"Do you think she's just too little to fly right now?" Sufia asks. "If she's reborn, maybe it takes a little more time to gather her strength."

"I'm not sure if she had enough energy to survive again," I say quietly. "You didn't see her. She was . . ." So tired. Like she couldn't go on carrying the weight of the sky and the Earth on her shoulders any longer. Something caused her to break.

Or cause a cycle interruption, Azar suggests.

I blink, trying to keep my face still to not give anything away. *You've been gone for a while.*

I don't like being called "old fart."

Seriously? That's why you've been quiet?

Azar is frustratingly silent after that, but his comment gets the gears turning in my head.

"Since the dream vapor has gotten to the tree . . ." I try to piece it together. "If you breathe in too much of it, it'll put you in a deep sleep, right? So if the simurgh stayed too long next to the tree when she combusted, what if she fell asleep before she could be fully reborn?" I remember the way the simurgh's eyes fluttered shut right as she burst into flame. She was covered in the mist by the time Idris and I ran out.

"That's why she hasn't emerged from the nest." Yaseen gasps.

"How do you reverse the effects of dream vapor?" I ask.

"You'd need an antidote." Yaseen jumps up and scans the books on my desk shelf. He opens the one from Essence Theory. "Since the tree is infected with dream vapor, that mist is coming out nonstop, and if the bird is asleep, she's still inhaling it. That's a lethal dose. Even if she's managed to be reborn, her new body will be too tiny to fight it off."

"Yaseen's right, but even if we could get our hands on an antidote, it doesn't solve the problem," adds Sufia.

"Because the problem is in the realm of nightmares itself." I finish Sufia's thought. The mist is just a symptom of something that's gone wrong in the nightmare realm. All our faces are grim. "We've got no choice. How do we get in?"

"It won't be *easy*." Sufia tucks her hair behind her ears just as the curfew bell rings. "But I know someone who can take us."

"Who?"

"Are you sure you want to go? Truly?" Sufia worries her nails. "On second thought, maybe an antidote could be enough. I'm not an expert, after all." She smiles nervously at Yaseen. "Where could we get one?"

Yaseen scans the book and laughs. "In the nightmare realm, apparently."

"So we've got to go either way." I stand next to Idris, who has done nothing but stare out at the glittering city. I nudge him. "You're not scared of a little darkness, right?"

"*Through mist as cold as ice,*" he mumbles, so quietly, I can barely hear him. "*In roots . . . dreams of sons . . . all come undone. . . .*"

"What was that?"

"Huh?" Idris blinks slowly, his eyes moving slowly toward me.

"Sounds like you were saying something?"

"Was I?" He furrows his brow. "I was just . . . looking at the storm."

I frown. I don't want to press him in front of Yaseen and Sufia, and I don't want them to pry, so I turn my attention to Sufia and say, "Who can take us to the nightmare realm?"

"If you're dead set on going . . . don't worry about it," she says, gathering her stuff into her bag. "Just meet me at the tallest turret in the moon king's wing at three a.m. tonight."

"Why can't we go now?" Time is of the essence. The longer the bird stays asleep, the weaker the tree gets, the worse the imbalances will become.

"Because that's when the barrier between the realms is the weakest. If you want to sneak into a king's realm undetected, that's your best shot," explains Sufia. "Oh, and to stay on the safe side, wear all black."

CHAPTER EIGHTEEN

THE REALM OF NIGHTMARES

⎯⎯⎯ ◈ ⎯⎯⎯

When Sufia and Yaseen leave to rest before Operation Infiltrate the Nightmare Realm, I hunker down to recharge too. Idris, though, is still staring out the window, fixated on the nightmare realm gateway.

"What was up with you before?" I ask with a yawn. "You were mumbling something about sons' dreams? I didn't quite catch it."

"It's . . . something that keeps playing in my head," he answers vacantly. "From the scale. It's hazy, but something about this storm is bringing it up."

"Well, that's good, right?" It means he's remembered something. "Maybe if you sleep on it, something else will pop up."

"I've slept enough." He keeps his nose pressed against the glass. This is the most he's said in days, and I nervously try to broach a subject I've been afraid to ask him about.

"Hey, do you remember a while back when I said I didn't want you to use your power on me?"

"Sure do."

"Well . . ." I hesitate. "Do you think, this one time, you could? To see if there's a way to find the antidote, or even better, fix the problem with the nightmare realm entirely! If we had a leg up, we could—"

"You know my power doesn't work like that, Noorzad."

"I know, but—"

"Please don't make me." Idris's eyes are sunken. "If I do, I'm going to disappear, and I just want my head quiet. No more questions or searching. Just quiet."

"Disappear?" What does that mean?

All Idris does is nod.

"Well . . . that sounds a lot like giving up." I crawl over on my bed to get a better look at Idris. "I know the phoenix tear not working was disappointing, but you can't give up on breaking your curse."

"It's not giving up, Noorzad. It's making peace." He bows his head and taps his two index fingers together. "I think I just want to move forward. Maybe that's what is causing the recollection glitches. I should stop looking back."

"But—"

"You know, I think you're right. It's probably better to get some rest." He shuffles back under the lofted bed. "We've got a tree to save in less than five hours." Within minutes, Idris knocks out, snoring softly.

I can't seem to fall asleep. Idris isn't making any sense. What is he talking about, recollection glitches? And I have no idea what to expect in the nightmare realm. My nerves are pretty bad. I tap my butterfly bracelet. I wish Arzu were here to give me a pep talk. She would know the right thing to say to me, to Idris.

What if I told you there was a way? Azar asks. *To reach her.*

"How?" I whisper.

I can offer you a peek for a price.

"No thank you." I don't need anything with a catch.

Pity . . . And here I thought you cared for your friend.

Nope, not listening to him. Not tonight. I take my pillow and plunk it over my head.

If that's what you want to do, so be it, Azar says before vanishing from my thoughts. *I only hope you don't regret it.*

You're just trying to mess with my head. Azar might not be the cause of what's happening in the nightmare realm, but I'm sure he doesn't want me fixing it either. He wants the jinn world in chaos. He's being a distraction. Arzu is fine. Madar is mostly fine. Everyone is *fine.* Once I complete the prophecy, fix what's hurting the tree and the bird, then I'll have all the time in the world to fill Arzu in on what's happened. It'll make up for missing spring break.

With that thought, I fall into a restless sleep.

At two-fifty a.m., Idris and I walk out to the top of the agreed-upon turret.

Yaseen and Sufia are already waiting for us—decked out in dark pants and sweatshirts that camouflage with the sky.

"Why do you look like you?" Yaseen whispers, stalking over to me. "If anyone sees you like this—"

"Oh shoot." In my rush to get up and dressed in the dark, I forgot all about my perfume. "Why didn't you remind me?" I ask Idris, who sleepily mumbles, "Was hard to see in the dark."

"I have to go back and get it."

"No time." Sufia comes over and pulls the hood over my head, tugging the strings tight. "You're wearing long sleeves, and this hood covers the parts that would give you away. Just don't smile and—" She sniffs my shoulder. "I can still smell a little bit of the perfume, so maybe it'll be enough to mask the human scent for now."

"What about Idris?"

"Smells like vanilla." Sufia sniffs him too. "Should be fine."

"Still, to be on the safe side, maybe we should double back for—" Yaseen clams up when he notices a shadowy figure hopping onto the tower's roof. A large shadowy figure with wings. "You brought *Esen*?"

"He's from King Maymun's realm," says Sufia, like he was the obvious choice. "Who else did you think I was going to bring?"

"Not Esen!"

"I owed Sufia seven favors." Esen rubs his tired eyes and yawns. His wings unfurl, spreading wide. "And this knocks them all out."

Sufia shakes her bracelet to prove it. Seven beads glow before disappearing.

"Um." I tie the strings tighter on my hood and turn away so Esen can't see my face. "You do know what we're asking you to do, right?"

"Break into my uncle's personal apothecary to get an antidote for the bird?" Esen scratches the back of his head. "And other stuff? Sufia wasn't very clear."

"Great. That's sooo great. Can't believe we're working with the Winged Nightmare's nephew. . . ." I lean next to Idris to further shield myself and not collapse from anxiety. I haven't forgotten when King Barqan had slipped Yaseen those enchanted pills inscribed with King Maymun's magic to take over our bodies. "So . . . great."

"Contrary to popular belief, jinn from my realm are not all nightmares." He rolls his red eyes. "Is my uncle one? Sure, but so are most uncles. Doesn't mean everyone else is, and if getting this antidote will put some balance into the city and get jinn off my back for the dream vapor, I'm all in." Esen uncomfortably picks at his arm. "So long as no one knows I went back home."

"I mean, can't you just say you were visiting home?" I get

why it would be bad if we were caught in his realm, but why would it be bad for Esen to return for a night?

"Once we start our studies at the academy, we live here full-time," Esen explains. "We can only go back when we're done. Whenever that is."

"What?" I glance between Sufia and Yaseen (who has also conveniently stood in front of me to block Esen's view of my face). "You mean you haven't gone home—"

"In three years? Yeah." Yaseen shrugs, staring up at the starry sky. "Yeah," he says again quietly.

"It's a rule put on all academy students," Sufia adds. "It's to keep us focused on our tracks so we don't have any distractions to interrupt us."

I gasp. "You mean you couldn't go home when your mom—"

"I don't want to talk about it." Yaseen keeps his eyes toward the sky. "Just want to focus on what we came here to do."

It's uncomfortably silent for a few seconds.

It gets way more uncomfortable when Esen clears his throat and asks, "New girl, why are you hiding from me? Afraid I'll steal you away?"

"Uhhh . . ." I blurt out the first thing that comes to mind. "Yaseen gave me an illusion potion for the mission, and I'm self-conscious about it."

Esen furrows his brow. "It can't be that bad."

"Well, if I look weird, that's why." I hear Yaseen's audible *way to make things awkward* sigh and try to get the conversation back on track. "So you really weren't there when—"

"Enough, Farrah," says Yaseen.

Sufia keeps throwing worried glances Yaseen's way.

"I don't know why it's a surprise. Are you telling me you can go home whenever you want, new girl?" Esen asks.

"No, I can't." For different reasons, but Professor Lilac's words come back to me. *If she has accepted you, you will always have a place here.* That rule can't apply to me, though, if the academy considers me a true student. . . . *Focus, Farrah. Don't think about it!* "So, um, the gate? What's the plan?"

"If you've met my uncle, he can be a bit dramatic." Esen kneels and opens a front pouch around his waist. "But when he monologues, it makes it easier to swipe things, like this." He pulls out a gleaming black helmet.

"What is it?" asks Idris, suddenly interested.

"It's my uncle's helm of darkness," says Esen. "Anyone who wears it can slip undetected through the gates. To the guards, you'd be nothing more than another storm cloud passing through."

"Why does your uncle even have that?" I ask.

"Why does King Barqan have a lightning spear?" Esen shrugs. " 'Cause it's cool."

"So it's settled, then." Sufia claps her hands together. "We'll go in two groups. Esen will fly in on his own precisely at three a.m., which is only two minutes away, ha ha. . . . We only get one chance to pass through undetected. If we arrive a minute too late, it's all over. So we'll all ride on Yaseen with Farrah wearing the helm."

"Excuse me?" Yaseen sputters. "Why do I have to carry everyone?"

"Because you're the only one who can shape-shift, duh." Sufia bops Yaseen's nose, which makes him more furious.

Idris stifles a small smile. It's the first time I've seen him smile since the failed phoenix tear. The shield I once had starts to lower. I nudge him. "Don't let him see you laugh," I whisper. "Shape-shifting is hard on him."

"Of course not," Idris retorts, "then we'll never hear the end of his insufferable complaining."

I smile. A sarcastic Idris is better than a silently sad and confusing Idris.

"It's go time!" Esen flaps his wings to get our attention. "If anyone wants a chance at sneaking through the portal tonight, we've got to go *now*." Without warning, he leaps off the roof, plummeting down into the inky night before spiraling back up.

"Can't believe I have to carry all of you again," Yaseen grumbles. He closes his eyes, letting out a deep breath. One by one his bones snap, breaking into odd shapes before they lengthen and re-form into two giant wings on his back. He kneels. "Well, climb on already!"

"I'll never get used to that," mutters Idris, his face a bit green.

"Same," I agree.

"How about this? I'll owe you one for carrying us," Sufia promises, hopping up on Yaseen's back first. A bright bead of light bursts from her chest and floats into Yaseen's pocket.

"That makes it a little better," Yaseen admits.

I get on next, slipping my arms around Sufia's waist. Idris is last.

"Oof, I don't remember it being this heavy last time!" Yaseen groans as he takes off and soars into the sky with Esen.

"Maybe you're just out of shape," taunts Idris.

"I can kick you off right now for that!"

Sufia turns her head over her shoulder. "Are they always like this?"

"Sometimes," I admit.

As we fly closer to the portal, Esen hovers on my right side. "You know what to do." He nods before throwing me the helm. The second I catch it, its energy crackles in my hands.

"Whoa, this feels . . . dangerous." I place the helmet on my head. Instantly, all sound—the rush of wind, the scrape of wings flapping, Idris's breathing, Yaseen's complaining—vanishes. In its place is a silent world. Then, like magic, we vanish too.

Esen signals for us to follow.

We swoop through the glittering city. Weaving between the spires of the Supreme Court of Jinn. Spiraling past skyscraper after skyscraper. Clipping the marshmallow top of Divine Delights. And finally, we pass through the dark, foreboding gates of the Realm of Nightmares.

The second we reach the gates, Idris's hold gets super-tight around my waist.

"What's wrong?" I ask, but I can't hear a thing. Can only feel Idris bump his head on my back a few times and squirm. "I can't hear you!" The gems on the two spires lining the gate begin to spark, charging with a distinct hum.

When we pass through, everything goes bright white as energy zaps right through us.

"THIS REALLY HURTS!" I shout, as it feels like every cell in my body is being ripped apart and squeezed into the tiniest tunnel ever. "SOMETHING'S WRONG. WE'RE ALL GONNA DIE!" And then, after an eternity of being squeezed so thin, the light goes away and we're flying gently into some-place new.

"That was awful," I say while ripping the helm of darkness off my head.

The world comes back in full volume.

"Portaling through the gateways always sucks," Sufia gasps. "But never quite like that. I don't know how Esen stands it."

"Ughhhh," Idris moans, still tapping his head against my back.

"What's going on?" I whisper, but he shakes his head.

"My head . . . is killing me." He's got a death grip on me. "It's"—he continues groaning—"tangled again."

"It'll pass. It's probably from the portal," I reassure him.

"It's not my favorite feeling," Sufia adds. "It's way too

essence-draining." She shivers, her eyes wide as she takes in the new realm. "Hopefully, we won't have to be here for long. I don't like the look of this place."

"Hopefully," groans Yaseen. "Because you guys weigh a ton after that. Just do me a favor and don't fall off."

The Realm of Nightmares lives up to its name. A hazy mist claws at our ankles, swallowing up where the ground should be. Dozens of floating buildings, filled with long, spindly archways and towers, scatter endlessly in the realm. A single bright spot in the sky—the planet Saturn—casts a halo around the dark mist beneath our feet. "Wait, where's the ground?" I ask.

"There isn't any," Esen calls out, swooping in happy loop-the-loops up into the dark sky. "Flying's the only way to get around."

"Well, that's not very accessible," mutters Sufia. Her hand holds on to something in her sweatshirt. "What happens if you drop stuff?"

"It probably gets swallowed up by whatever that is." I point down when the mist breaks, revealing an endless inky ocean.

"What is that?" Yaseen squints, trying to get a better look. He flies us lower until his feet nearly touch the surface. The water is so dark, I can see a perfect reflection of us—only, in the reflection, our eyes are closed, like we're fast asleep.

All of us minus Idris.

He's the only one that's missing.

"I wouldn't get too close," warns Esen. He swoops close

by, his wings fluttering against the wind. "It's the Other-world."

"Otherworld?" asks Yaseen.

"The part of you that lives in your dreams. That's my realm's domain," says Esen. "Your *other* world. When you're awake in this world, your other you is asleep."

"I thought King Maymun was only responsible for night-mares," I mumble, shocked. Dreams aren't real, right? There's no way there's another me in another world living another life. . . .

"No wonder he keeps his realm so private; if everyone knew, they'd freak out. Surprised the academy keeps it out of the curriculum," says Yaseen, swooping even lower to get a good look at himself. In the water, his other self slumbers peacefully. "You're saying that's me?"

"Yep," replies Esen.

"But if that's me, and I'm me, then . . ." Yaseen's fingers nearly graze the dark surface. "Which me is the *real* me?"

"Don't touch!" Esen grabs Yaseen's hand and yanks him up and away, causing all of us to hold on for our lives as we go up, up, up and away from our sleeping reflections. "If the other you takes hold and drags you into the dream vapor, you'll never be able to get out."

"But what if . . ." Idris grips my waist tighter. He struggles to speak. His head must really be hurting. "Your other you is missing from the water?"

"I noticed that too," I whisper back.

A worried line pops up in between his eyebrows. "Why am I always missing?" He quickly swipes at his eyes. "Why am I always forgotten?"

"We're going to figure it out," I say quickly.

"This curse is forever. There's no point."

"Don't think like that." I press my head against Idris's. Our hair tangles together in the wind. His tears hit my cheek. "Curses always have solutions."

"Not always . . ."

"Let's stay away from the main cluster. We have to go the long way to the apothecary," Esen advises, cutting across the floating buildings toward a line of thin archways that weave in and out of the perimeter of the main city. "And whatever you do, don't—"

"Oof!" Yaseen bumps into the side of an arch, struggling to keep up.

"Touch anything!"

"If I didn't have a million pounds on my back," complains Yaseen. He tries flapping his wings away from the arch. A shrill siren goes off, followed by a bright white light erupting from the arch. "Ahh, my eyes!" He veers to the side. A silver mist sprays from the design in the arch, coating Yaseen's hair.

"Watch how you're flying!" Sufia is thrown up and over Yaseen's head.

"Sufia!" we all yell as Yaseen scrambles to grab her hands. Her manicured fingers slip through his.

"Help meeeee!" wails Sufia.

Intruder alert, there is a waking soul that does not belong, the arches whisper one by one. *Intruder alert, there is a waking soul that does not belong.*

So much for being stealth.

More arches light up, spraying their silver mist all over us. Dark, shadowy figures burst up from the main city, zipping high into the sky.

"You've got to get her!" I shout, shaking Yaseen's shoulders. That only causes us to collide into another arch. Its screech blasts through my eardrum.

"The point is to NOT hit the arches!" Idris death-grips my waist as I hold on to Yaseen's shirt. It starts to rip from the pressure.

"I can barely see!" Yaseen shouts back. The silver mist settles over his eyes, causing them to droop. "I need . . . a quick . . ." He yawns. "Recharge."

Esen zips down, down, down. He curls his wings tight against his body and spirals faster. "Almost . . ." His hands are outstretched as Sufia screams, falling closer toward the Otherworld.

"He's not gonna make it," I gasp.

"*We're* not gonna make it if your brother doesn't find a place to land," worries Idris when Yaseen drops fifteen feet. His wings barely beat. "He's too tired!"

"Yaseen?" I tap the back of his neck to get him to open his eyes. "Earth to Yaseen, this is the worst possible moment for you to pass out!"

Does not belong, the arches continue to wail. *Does not belong.*

The dark figures soar closer to us. For a second, I think they're shadow jinn, but their eyes don't glow red, and their faces are angry. *Very* angry. Their wings pump harder. They shout at one another before encasing themselves in the darkest mist I've ever seen.

No, no, no! This wasn't the way it was supposed to go. We barely even looked for the antidote or discovered any hint at why the nightmare realm is out of balance. The mission can't be over before it begins!

We're losing air fast. Yaseen can barely keep us afloat, and there's nothing close enough to grab on to to give him a break.

There's only one option.

"Idris, I need you to look inside my head," I say, attempting to remain calm.

"Noorzad—"

"You've gotta use your power. *Please.*" I'm near tears when the ocean of dream vapor gets closer to swallowing Sufia whole. "It's the only way we can get out of here alive. Tell us what to do!"

"I really can't—" His shirt whips in the wind. "My head— you don't understand—"

"PLEASE!" For Sufia. We can't lose her like this.

"I really—don't—want—to—" Idris's eyes flash from clear

gray to milky white as his power takes hold. I can feel him poking around the avalanche of open boxes in my head. He grimaces and presses his head against my back. "Argh, it hurts." He squeezes his eyes shut and whispers, "Esen needs to vortex faster."

"VORTEX FASTER!" I shout.

"What do you think I'm doing?" he yells.

"GET ME OUT OF THIS REALM NOW!" cries Sufia.

Esen is closing the gap, his fingers inches away from hers.

"Please tell me he's going to make it, Idris."

Idris doesn't say anything. I don't think he can hear me right now. His head is in the future. After the longest second, he mumbles, "She won't fall into the Otherworld."

Relief bursts in my heart. Esen's going to catch her. But Idris's eyes stay squeezed shut. His grip digs into my waist a little too painfully.

"Idris?"

"Tangled—" Idris groans and flickers in and out of sight. "I'm—" One second I can feel his arms around me, and the next I can't. Yaseen continues to spiral farther down. A loud snore bubbles from his mouth.

"What's happening to you?" I try to hold on to Idris, but he keeps flickering in and out.

"My head—" He tries to hold on, but his fingers go slack. "It wants—me—"

"What wants you?"

Sufia shrieks. "Get away from me!" A dark, misty figure catches her milliseconds before she collides into the ocean of the Otherworld.

"Let me go!" Esen struggles as two other winged jinn trap both of his arms with glowing chains. The moment the shackles touch his wrists, his entire body freezes.

Three more dark blurs head straight for us.

"Yaseen, wake up, they're going to catch us!" I tug on his topknot, but it does nothing. The silver mist crawls its way up my arm and into my nose. The heavy scent of honey and chamomile zaps against my brain, making me very warm and cozy. "Wake up, they're gonna . . ."

My eyes get heavy, followed by my arms and fingers. I'm about to slip off Yaseen's back, but Idris pushes me forward. My arms hold on to Yaseen, and slowly my eyes start to close.

"Sorry, Noorzad." Idris grits his teeth before fully letting go. "I can't fight it anymore—I just want peace."

Moments before the world goes dark, and the three dark blurs catch Yaseen and me, Idris falls into the ocean of darkness.

"Peace and a quiet head." Idris collides into the dream vapor.

The Otherworld swallows him whole.

BEING QUIET

---

*I*cy cold impact.

  Golden chains.

    Drowning down, down, down.

      A raindrop leaf.

        Screaming.

And then pure, blissful silence. That was all Idris ever wanted.

CHAPTER NINETEEN

A RUDE AWAKENING

✦

"Get up, you're drooling all over the floor."

The world comes back in fuzzy pieces. An inky darkness cuts through with glowing shards of amber light. A cold, slick floor and designs made out of lead embroider the hall of the chamber we're in. The smell of burning dreams gets me up. "What happened?" I mumble, rubbing my face in my hands.

"Yaseen's horrible flying skills are what happened." Esen yawns, trying to stretch his wings wide before remembering the chains of starlight binding them together. "Oh right. We're prisoners."

"Prisoners?" Yaseen groggily stands, shivering in the misty castle. "For what?"

"For breaking and entering into King Maymun's realm," a guard announces from the shadows of the chamber. Five more figures march out, glaring ominously in their onyx uniforms. "When you know it is expressly *forbidden* for academy students to traverse through the great planetary realms."

"That doesn't mean you can imprison us," mumbles Yaseen. He throws on a shirt after fishing it out of his endless pouch. I guess he really doesn't travel anywhere without it.

"It does when one of your group is of a forbidden class," the guard hisses at me. He pulls down my hood to prove his point. "Round ears and the faintest whiff of rotting cabbage. We could tell the second it passed into our realm."

"I'm not an *it*," I snap back.

"What?" In the bright light, Esen gets a good look at me. "You're mistaken. It's a disguise. . . ."

"You are what I say you are," the guard barks as his companions step in closer. They are all as dark as night with galaxies stitched into their midnight-blue uniform jackets. Their wings extend ominously as they corral Esen, Sufia, Yaseen, and me into a tighter circle.

"You can't hurt us," Sufia says calmly. "And you know it. So why don't you let us leave, and we'll never come back here again."

"Now, wouldn't that be easy." The guard looms closer, his sharp teeth glinting against the glowing star-filled lanterns that are spread around the chamber. "But you have us all wrong. Who said anything about hurting you?" Sufia shrinks back as dream vapor rolls from the guard and the rest of the figures. "Any terrors we induce in that sleeping mind of yours stem from the dark thoughts that reside in your head."

He leans even closer, touching Sufia's cheek. She freezes instantly, with her eyes wide, mouth frozen into a scream. "And your thoughts are quite dark for one who appears so innocent."

"Get away from her, kabus!" Esen shouts, pushing the guard's hand away. "That is against the rules. You can't inflict a nightmare on an academy student, and you know it!"

Sufia gasps. She burrows into Yaseen's shoulder, shaking.

"What did he do to you?" asks Yaseen, but Sufia only trembles.

"They're kabus. Jinn from my uncle's realm who can sink into your worst nightmares and paralyze you so even if you wake up, you can't escape the terror," explains Esen in a measured voice. His eyes narrow as the kabus all smile wide. "They're employed to protect against threats, not intimidate the king's nephew and his friends."

It's official. King Maymun's realm is a million times worse than the Realm Beneath. Can confirm I *never* want to come back here again.

"Of course. How could I forget?" The kabus guard bows in mock apology. His eyes sparkle in mischievous delight. "After all, we are just the messengers, fetching our king's nephew and his friends to have an audience with the great winged king himself."

"We're what?" I gulp.

"Well, what did you expect?" the guard taunts. "You could break into a king's realm unannounced, arms empty, and not say hello?" He *tsks*, clicking his shiny shoes together. "Now that you're all awake and well, I can escort you to the Winged Nightmare himself."

The remaining kabus poke us forward.

"Hey!" Yaseen evades one's touch. "We got the message. We're going."

I loop an arm around Sufia's. She hasn't stopped trembling. "Are you okay?"

Her brown eyes are clenched shut. "I . . . I need to get back to the academy." Her forehead is sweaty. "It's . . . too much."

"What's too much?"

"The essence drain from the portal. I'm running too low," she whispers as we are corralled along a wispy hall. Stars flicker in lanterns, lighting the way. I try to remember the path, but the more I focus on the twists and turns, the more I forget. "I have a condition. I can't manage it without my essence pen. . . ." She grips my arm tight.

"Without what?"

"It helps me balance my essence levels." Sufia can barely get the words out. "I need . . ."

"Enough chatter," the kabus guard warns. "When stepping into a king's hall, do not speak unless spoken to." He ushers us into a huge glass room. The walls fall away, replaced with floating shards of glass that orbit the throne room. A towering waterfall crashes down from one side of the room, splitting it in half with its dark dream vapor. It pools around a shimmering throne in its center. The vapor flows and falls down, past the glass to the abyss below.

In the center of the throne is King Maymun.

"Well, this is a . . . surprise." He looks up from his work. Parchment, books, and jewels float in front of him. He looks extremely stressed. "Strange to see this eclectic group in front of me. Especially the half-human."

Dark dream vapor swirls around my ankles, grabbing at them. I yelp, jumping away. Sufia latches on to Yaseen, swaying dizzily.

"Do you know what the punishment is for trespassing into a realm that is not one's own?" asks King Maymun.

"Stop it, Uncle," Esen shouts. His wings strain against the chains. If Esen is shocked by the revelation that I really am half-human, he doesn't show it.

"And to steal one of *my* helms?" King Maymun snaps his clawed fingers. The kabus guard runs over to him, offering the helm of darkness. I gasp, suddenly realizing I don't have it on me anymore.

"I took the helm," Esen says.

"Even more unsettling." King Maymun frowns. "My sister will not be pleased to see her son *stealing*."

Yaseen grips his free hand into a fist. He's about to shout when Esen waves in warning.

"Let me handle this," he whispers to us. Esen walks toward his uncle, totally calm and composed. He does not back down when King Maymun gives him another death glare.

"My sister will be especially displeased when she finds out why you brought others into our realm."

"They were curious." Esen breezes through his lie. "After learning about the realm's expansion and bottling of diluted dream vapor to—"

"Do not waste my time with a lie," snarls King Maymun.

We all shrink back when he stands, growing taller with each second, his wings unfurling, casting shadows along the floating glass walls.

"I dared him," Sufia whispers. She can barely lift her head from Yaseen's shoulder, but she does, just enough to show the bracelet on her wrist. "He owed me a favor. And I wanted to see if the Realm of Nightmares is as bad as they say."

"Ah, the debts." King Maymun smiles. "How I remember them." His eyes go misty. "And the havoc I caused with my own favors." When he stares back at me, his expression goes cold. "But that is not the truth, is it, half-human?"

"No, it's not," I admit.

"Farrah, don't tell him—" Yaseen mutters, but I cut him off.

"Your realm is infecting the City of Jewels, and you know it," I say bravely. Out of the corner of my eye, something blue glitters within the waterfall.

"Bold claims, half-human. It seems no one can temper the human in you, not even that brother of yours." King Maymun walks across the stream of dream vapor, hovering over the Otherworld like it doesn't scare him.

Maybe it doesn't. If he controls it.

"Your realm is out of balance, and it's hurting the Tree of Life and the simurgh." I gulp, taking a few steps back. "We want to know why."

"You barge into my realm and want to know *why*?" King Maymun advances closer until I've walked all the way to the edge of the throne room. "You think I haven't noticed the imbalance within my realm? You think I haven't been working to stop the spillage into the city? You think I haven't noticed the *bird*?" The orbiting glass whooshes past my head, fluttering my bangs over my eyes. "You think I haven't observed that the disturbances all began when *you* entered the picture?"

"Me?"

"You think I didn't notice a certain someone who stole an airboat and conveniently paid a visit to a shadow puppet?"

"Y-you saw that?"

When King Maymun is close enough where he could push me out of the room and into the dark waters below his floating realm, he crouches so his gold eyes are level with mine. "I think there is a reason for my realm's imbalance. I think there's someone whispering in that cursed head of yours. And I will not play into that jinn's games."

"I— That's not true!" He thinks *I'm* helping Azar? Is that why he sent a shadow puppet to the scene of the crime? To blame the chaos on *me*? "I've got nothing to do with him!"

I'm just following my prophecy track. I'm doing what the scale told me to do.

"So you expect me to believe that you just randomly chose to disguise yourself as a patron of Mars? That you had no intention to be spotted by the general public moments before the simurgh caught fire? That the rumors about *the jinn kings of Mars and Saturn ruining the city* are pure coincidence? Because linking the realms of war and nightmares doesn't send a dangerous message?"

"I—I didn't think of it that way. . . ."

"None of this would be happening if you didn't set foot into our world. *You* interrupted that bird's cycle by going into that nest. There is a reason why we do not interfere with nature," says King Maymun. "Consider this your last warning, foolish half-human, to stay out of matters that do not concern you. While academy law protects you now, it won't forever."

"The simurgh was already sick when I went to the nest. Besides, you can't hurt me. My dad—"

"Your father what? Will *protect* you?" King Maymun growls. "Are you sure about that? When that little prophecy of yours is over, I wouldn't count on it." His voice grows dangerously soft. "You should be very, very afraid for that day. *Now stay out of my realm.* If I catch you sticking your nose where it doesn't belong again," King Maymun warns, a huge, threatening grin across his face, "nothing will save you from what I can do. And I will gladly sever my ties with the other kings should they not be able to control their children from poking their noses in places they don't belong." He leans away, letting me run back to my friends.

"Let's get out of here before he changes his mind." Yaseen grabs my hand and yanks on it.

"Who is your father? And what did he mean by jinn kings' *children*?" Esen is shocked. "There's only one jinn king kid here."

Weird that *that's* the part that shocks him—and not the half-human part.

"Yeah. Um." My mind is having a hard time thinking under the roaring noise of an ocean of pressure inside me that is only getting bigger, heavier. *This isn't my fault. What King Maymun said can't be true. I didn't cause this. I'm good. Aren't I?* "Let's get out of here." I look up at the raging waterfall. The dark waves crash down, down, down. It reminds me of the waves of sadness that keep wanting to pull me under, that follow and seep into everyone I know, into my mom, into Idris. . . .

"We can't leave yet." I gasp. "Idris is still missing!" How could I forget him?

"Idris . . ." Yaseen scratches his chin. "Why do I feel like I've heard that name before?"

"I'm getting the weirdest déjà vu," agrees Sufia. "Was he a new recruit for the national kite-fighting team?"

"No, no, no. He was my friend, and he was with us when we . . . when he . . ." *Why can't I remember? What is going on?* Everything feels so fuzzy in my head. We flew into the nightmare realm, and then we . . .

Again, something sapphire blue glints in the waterfall.

King Maymun snaps his fingers, releasing the chains from Esen's wings. "Kabus, escort my nephew and his guests back through the portal. And let's make sure this doesn't happen again." He spreads his wings and soars out of the throne room in a cloud of dark mist, spiraling up to another tower.

"You heard the boss." The guard pokes Esen in the back.

Esen growls, making the guard take a step away from him. "One day, I'll have to come back home," he warns. "Remember that." Esen kneels, spreading his wings for me to climb on. Yaseen's bones crunch and break, forming wings of his own. He holds Sufia in his arms, who has promptly passed out.

"Sufia can't be here much longer. She needs an essence injection," Yaseen reminds us as we are escorted out of King Maymun's castle. "She has backup pens at the academy." Yaseen takes a running head start, flapping his wings until he's soaring up, up, up.

"Remember . . . ," I mumble, holding tightly on to Esen as we leap and twirl into the glittering night sky. From this high, I can spot the hundreds of floating buildings and craters. King Maymun's castle glimmers like a jeweled centerpiece. But there's something else. A sapphire-blue glow that follows a golden chain that plunges deep into the Otherworld. "Do you see that?" I point down.

"See what?" asks Esen.

We're level with Yaseen and Sufia now.

The portal back to the City of Jewels grows bigger, and the blue glow gets smaller, following the path of the chain.

"What is that?" The farther away we get, the worse the burning pressure in my chest gets. *Go down*, it urges. The pressure thrashes against Professor Lilac's enchantment keeping my power sealed. I resist it, but it is so heavy, and I'm getting so tired of finding the energy to fight it. *Go down*.

"Promise me you won't be mad," I shout at Yaseen as he flies into the portal.

"Why would I be mad?" he replies.

"Because I'm about to do something stupid."

"Then I'm definitely going to be ma—"

Right when Yaseen and Sufia disappear in a blaze of light, I give in to the burning pressure. I let go of Esen and fall into the dream vapor.

CHAPTER TWENTY

THE OTHERWORLD

I fall into a nightmare.

Only this time I'm sinking through the darkness of the Otherworld. The dream vapor invades my hair, moves through my clothes and up my nose.

"It's f-f-freezing." The cold steals the air I'd need to say anything more.

The mist zips straight into my mouth and down my throat. It feels like a million ice cubes are fighting to get into my lungs. *Can't breathe. Need air.* The burning pressure continues thrashing until it manifests an eerie glow from my hands, traveling up my veins, igniting them, chasing the chill of the dream vapor away.

"Whoa." My voice is garbled in the water. Whatever my power is doing, at least I'm not icy cold anymore. In the glow, little tendrils of mist from the dream vapor screech the second they pass through and touch my skin—disintegrating into dust.

It's so quiet, I think as I continue drifting down. *I feel like I could sink forever.*

In the silence, King Maymun's words come back to me. *The disturbances all began when you entered the picture.* Another king's voice chimes in. *You are a threat to our careful order.* And another's. *Off with her head.*

Drowning in the Otherworld, I wonder, maybe they're right. At least without my head, I wouldn't have thoughts or worries, wouldn't have the impossible weight of everyone's expectations—to be good, to be my mom's sunshine, to be the best—on my shoulders anymore.

After sinking for what feels like an eternity, I hit rock bottom. Literally. There's solid ground down here. I look up and see the *other* Otherworld (or maybe it's just called *the real world*) rippling above.

The portal home flashes angrily. The kabus fly in circles around it, probably searching for me.

A dark figure soars above me. Her agile body flaps through the water, with her sapphire-blue feathers shimmering behind her. *The simurgh.* "So you *did* fall asleep."

Because if the real phoenix fell into a dream-vapor sleep, interrupting her cycle, then her *other* self would have to wake up here.

"Hey, wait up!" I chase after her as she roars, soaring ahead. She dives up and down, following the trail of a golden chain. With each rippling step, the Otherworld morphs until I'm right back to the last place I want to be.

The gate to the Realm Beneath the Unseen.

"No! Bring me back, this is wrong!" I take one step, then another, down the ruby staircase. "I never want to see these gates again!" As far as my eye can see, there are so many sprawling levels to Azar's realm. The phoenix keeps flying farther away, searching for something.

"If that's true, then I wonder why your dreams always bring you back here?" a girl says from the bottom of the stairs.

"Hura!" Her name comes to me instantly. Somehow, seeing her triggers so many past dreams . . . of all the times I've been here. With her.

"Finally." Her grin exposes her sharp teeth. Her smile is so wide, it nearly cracks her shadowy face. Her red eyes shine brightly. "Took you long enough to finally remember. That's a really good sign." She tightens her ponytail and flicks the end, so it sways behind her back.

"You're . . . different than before." For a shadow puppet, she could almost pass as my sister. It's the way she stands, so like me but not. There are now slight differences. She's a little taller, eyes slightly harder. Teeth sharper.

"Having this helps, makes me less puppet, more . . . real." Hura raises her palm, showing the center filled with light. It's the opposite of my dark shadow. "Dunno what it is, but the bigger this light gets, the better I feel."

"Strange. The bigger mine got, the worse I felt. . . ." Until Professor Lilac sealed it.

"Well, we are connected, remember? Ever since that day in the observatory." She cocks her head to the side, still grinning. "If it weren't for Azar interrupting, it'd be me standing where you are. Still, a tiny piece of your soul latched on to me."

I shiver at the idea. For once, I'm glad Azar stepped in.

"Tricky, tricky, these jinn kings. They create and play with us, no matter the cost. They'll chew you up and spit you back out. Make you free them and then expect you to slither away into the shadows without a single *thank you, Hura*. I suppose that's what happened to you when you freed your father from the ring too, huh?" Hura twirls, marching toward Azar's throne. She follows the line the chain makes as it wraps round and round the throne.

"Wait a sec—*you* freed that old fart from the ring?"

Hura just giggles, ignoring me. "A dangerous thing, those kings—especially that old fart." She giggles again. "But maybe that's why you're drawn to him."

"I'm not *drawn to him*." I'm about to argue that I'd love to get rid of Azar's voice in my head, to stop being used for his games, but the words get stuck in my throat. Deep down, if I had to admit it, he can be helpful.

A fire bubble floats in the center of the throne. Within the bubble is an upside-down Idris. His hair fans out over his sleeping face. "Idris!" I run up to the throne, tripping over the chains, trying to reach him. "There you are! I thought I lost you. Get him out of there *now*."

"No can do," says Hura.

"Why not?!" Through the bubble's orange glow, I notice something not quite right about Idris. "What did you do to him?" His hair—normally white—is midnight black. His skin looks more tanned, like mine. And weirdly, his silhouette is fuzzy at the edges—like he's a phantom or a ghost. "Why does he look—" Different. My fingers press against the bubble. Electricity zips and whirls through my hands, shocking me with zaps of static.

The jolt lifts the veil, and the scene changes.

Azar's throne in his fiery kingdom warps into something else . . . someplace else. I'm floating in the inky darkness of the Otherworld. It was all an illusion. The dream vapor hisses, burning away from the eerie light in my veins. My power pulses, wanting to break free, but it can't. It's trapped within me. The pressure makes me feel like I'm burning up with a fever.

When the illusion is finally gone, I gasp.

In front of me is the Tree of Life—only it's upside down. Its roots furl and grow up toward the surface of the Otherworld. It stretches in every direction, piercing through the top of the Otherworld and into the waking world. Wound through the lower branches is a golden chain. Idris has somehow gotten tangled in the chain. It's wrapped around him as he sleeps. At least—I think it's Idris.

"How is the tree here?"

"Every being must rest—be it a person or a jinn or a phoenix or in this case . . ." Hura keeps smiling. "A tree."

The Tree of Life pulses a deep, dark red. Ever so slowly, its branches *move* toward Idris.

"I'm not sure this tree is resting. . . ."

"No, I don't suppose it has, at least not here." Hura's hair floats gently around her face as she swims closer. "Though I don't suppose I could rest with all *that* stuck in my branches."

Suddenly the simurgh appears, ramming her way into the branches, only to be hit with a force field, throwing her back.

"Why is she doing that?" I hold on to a branch to not be swept away by the rippling water.

"Seems like they're trying to get to him." Hura hovers near the phantom Idris. Her shadow hands pass through his dark hair.

"W-what happened to my friend?" I try to get closer. Idris looks peaceful like this, like he's got no worries in the world. The branches have grown over his body, slowly encasing him in a sort of cocoon.

"Your friend?" Hura's eyebrows knit together. "This is not the friend you seek. No, this one has been here for decades, a century maybe."

"A century?" I gasp.

"This is something else"—Hura swims up, searching around the tree—"something precious, something lost—"

"Something cursed," I whisper. Is this phantom image . . . Idris's stolen memories? Is this the source of his curse?

But why would it be hidden here in the Otherworld?

I swim next to this see-through Idris and hold on to a branch to really look at him. The words from my prophecy come to mind.

"*An endless age, a fate defied*," I whisper into the water as dream vapor shrieks around us. "*Without its roots, all things shall die.*" I gasp just as the tree pulses red again, illuminating his face. Memories could be roots, right? They are the core of who we are—without them, a person is only a shell, a ghost. "Is my prophecy . . . about you? Am I . . . meant to break your curse?"

Idris has technically been an endless thirteen for over a hundred years. And without his roots—his memories, his identity, his sense of self—he's been losing himself, his joy, his spark.

Maybe Yaseen was right. Maybe our fates are intertwined.

"Aha, there he is." Hura swims down, tugging at the Idris I know—with his snow-white hair and skin. His eyes are wide open, frozen in shock, his body stuck in an uncomfortable position. "Seems like he's not having a great time either."

"It's his curse. It's not letting him close to his memories," I think out loud.

If you want to break your friend's curse, I know a way. Azar's voice slithers in my head. *Just move closer.* His voice buzzes all the way to the tips of my fingers, through the shadow trapped in the center of my palm. He whispers, *Closer, closer, closer,* until my hand rests against the chain across Idris's chest. My power pulses in my hand as the phoenix roars again.

"Is that the solution—break the chain?" I call out to the bird. Is that what she's been trying to do? "Break the chain, break the curse. . . ." And possibly unlock what's wrong with the tree? "Is that why they cursed you and split you from your memories?"

Did Idris know something he wasn't supposed to?

Did he know what was causing the imbalance?

"Only one way to find out," Hura shouts, "and I'd hurry up. I wouldn't want to be frozen alive like your friend here for much longer."

If there was ever a time I was grateful to have a power that could turn gold to dust, it's now. *Please, please break the link.* My heart skips a beat when I reach out, veins blazing with eerie light, and grab hold of the chain. *This is the one time I want you to work!* Bright light wraps around my fingers and the link. For a second I think I've done it—until the invisible glove Professor Lilac placed on my hand squeezes so tight, it feels like it's about to rip my hand off. Then the pain starts—so much pain. The tree pulses, throwing me into a kaleidoscope of moments—a prophecy, a wish unraveling. "ARGH, BREAK!" It feels like my head is splitting in two. "LET IDRIS'S MEMORIES GO!"

The pain is too much.

It's no use. I can't break it, not with my power sealed. I let go of the chain, and immediately, the squeezing feeling in my hand goes away. "I am not leaving Idris's memories behind." Maybe I can yank his memories out. I try to pull on his arm, but my hand goes right through him. Now, that is super annoying. Little bubbles pop, pop, pop out of his mouth. "Come. On. Get. Out. Of. There."

I just need one win.

Please.

In response, the Otherworld starts to bubble and screech.

Intruder alert, there is a waking soul that does not belong, it wails. *Intruder alert, there is a waking soul that does not belong.*

"Not again!" I groan.

"Uh-oh. Don't you know the rules of places like this? You *never* touch the treasure," Hura warns. "It seems you're out of time." She pushes white-haired Idris into me. We both go tumbling backward, flipping through the water. "I'd run if I were you, if you want to get out of here alive."

"How?" I scream through the alarm. Everything is flipped upside down. I don't even know which way is up! In the distance, the dream-vapor clouds bubble and swirl, colliding into each other until they turn into shadowy sharks—deadly nightmare sharks. They swim right for us.

Oh great. This just keeps getting better.

Their fins move slowly through the vapor, their mouths chomping the bubbles in their way.

"This way." Hura spreads her arms and kicks her feet,

heading farther away from the tree. I don't have time to think—I grab Idris's hand and start kicking as fast as I can.

"Don't look back, don't look back." The last thing I need is to picture Idris and me becoming shark food, so I keep my eyes trained on Hura as she leads us farther, past the thickest parts of the tree's roots that have grown along the surface of the Otherworld. When we get closer to the surface, I can see the portal out of King Maymun's realm.

"Let us through!" My hands push against the surface, but it doesn't budge. It's like a wall of water keeping us trapped. The nightmare sharks have caught up—one tries to chomp on my foot; another tries for Idris's hand. For Idris's sake, I really hope he's *not* awake, and just sleeping with his eyes open. "Hura, how do we get out of here?"

"We?" asks Hura. Her glowing palm grabs the shark biting near Idris's feet. It screeches and swims away.

"I can't leave you here either." I punch the nightmare shark attached to Idris's hand. It growls before joining its friends that are circling around us. "Or the simurgh. If we could get her to wake up without an antidote, then she can be reborn, and her cycle interruption will be over. It'll give the jinn world more time." I glance in the direction of the tree about twenty feet away where the simurgh is still hovering. "Come on! The world needs you! You've gotta wake up!" I shout at the simurgh. Her golden eyes stare intensely at me before she flaps her wings and turns away, continuing her assault on the chain around the tree. "Why is she staying where she's trapped?"

"Maybe she's not trapped" is all Hura says.

"Of course she's trapped, like we're gonna be if we don't find a way out of here." The nightmare sharks continue to circle around us.

"There is no *we*," says Hura. "This *is* my world. Haven't you figured it out by now?"

"What do you mean?"

"I'm not real. Not really." Hura glances around, smiles a sad smile. "Here, I'm just a figment in your dreams." To prove it, she plunges her marked hand up and through the surface of the Otherworld. The ripple from her hand creates a small opening.

"So why are you helping me, then?"

"Because even in your dreams, you give me a choice," answers Hura. She reaches out her other hand to me and Idris. "And here, I can choose. So I choose to save you, Farrah Noorzad. Because in some small way, saving you feels a lot like saving me. Well, the me that's out *there*."

"Hura," I whisper, taking her hand.

Against the endless waves of the dream vapor, I hear it again. The crash of the ocean, of a growing emptiness, too big for one person to hold. I feel that weight wrap around Hura, the same way it wrapped around my mom, around Idris, around me.

"Just try not to forget me on the other side," she whispers back.

"I pinkie-swear, I won't." I squeeze her hand one last time and try my hardest to remember her, remember the way her face starts to morph, looking more girl and less puppet. "I could never forget a friend."

With Idris in tow, I jump back into the waking world.

CHAPTER TWENTY-ONE

YOU COULD CHANGE THE ENTIRE WORLD

"**W**HERE WERE YOU?**" Yaseen yells the second Idris and I burst through the portal and back into the City of Jewels. Loud alarms are still ringing in my head.

"W-what happened to m-m-me?" Idris is shivering as he rolls on the ground. His clothes are sopping wet from the dream vapor. "Th-that was a n-n-nightmare. I c-couldn't move."

"GET AWAY FROM THERE!" Yaseen is sprinting toward us.

"Oh, not this again," Idris groans. Wispy black vapor is pouring out of King Maymun's realm. He scuttles out of the way.

"Don't breathe unless you have a death wish." Yaseen grabs my hand and races away from the mist. I can't tell if the alarms are ringing through the portal or the city itself, but it's giving me the biggest headache. We pass by the living sanctuary, where the vines have rotted and sloped down.

The mist has invaded everywhere. This part of the city has become a ghost town.

"Where are Sufia and Esen?" I cough with my sleeve covering my mouth.

"Back at the academy. I stayed behind to make sure you came back. . . ."

We eventually find a higher point of elevation and break through the mist.

"FRESH AIR." Idris breathes huge gulps of it.

My heart is racing in my chest. All I want to do is lie down and—

"You can't just do stuff like that!" Yaseen shakes my shoulders. His words are angry, but his eyes are big and puffy "I thought you were *gone*. I thought—"

"I told you not to be mad," I weakly joke, and try to wiggle out of Yaseen's death grip.

"I'm not mad, I'm *furious*," he replies.

"Well, everything is fine, so you don't have to worry."

"Nothing is fine," Yaseen cuts in sharply. "Have you seen the city?"

"Oh." The dream vapor is pouring out of the nightmare realm, spilling over half the city and pushing against four other jinn-king realm entrances. The moon winks up at us, and I notice something odd. "Is it just me, or is the moon smaller than usual?"

"We are *sinking*," Yaseen says in a panicked voice. "And

everything is *dying*. The plants, the . . ." He hesitates. "Sanctuary, just like with my mom. I don't know what to do!"

Alarms continue to blare, causing us all to wince.

"Let's get back to the academy and regroup in the morning. Everything is clearer on a fresh head." I glance at Idris. "We can't stay here. Someone is gonna see us."

"Thank you for stating the obvious, Noorzad," says Idris.

Below us, the portal to King Maymun's realm flashes a bright red before a huge shield walls it off from the rest of the city.

"That can't be good," I mutter, pulling my hood over my head as we run back to the academy.

THE NEXT MORNING, THE ACADEMY CALLS AN EMERGENCY assembly.

I slip onto the bench next to Sufia, Tamira, and Laila in the dining hall. My knee jiggles nervously as I count down the minutes until we can regroup. My thoughts are all hazy, and trying to hold on to what happened last night feels like a dream slipping out of my fingers.

But I know one thing for sure—King Maymun is hiding a very big secret.

And I think whatever that secret is, Idris knew it.

King Maymun is the one who cursed Idris.

"Um, so there's a rumor going around." Laila butts into my thoughts, nudging my side not too gently. "That *someone* was seen leaving campus grounds past curfew last night." She raises an eyebrow at Sufia.

"Really?" Sufia seems unfazed. She flips her glossy hair over her shoulder and takes a bite of crunchy bread. When she puts the bread down on her lap, her fingers shake. "I wonder who."

"There's also a rumor that the last time the simurgh was seen, *someone* had tampered with her nest." Tamira glares at me.

"Are you trying to insinuate something?" I ask.

The air gets tight between Laila and Tamira.

"Just seems strange that chaos is ripping through our city the moment *someone* entered it," hisses Laila.

"When you say *someone*, do you mean m—"

"Oh darn, it seems I forgot my books for class today," says Sufia. A sweet scent wafts from her, reminding me of sunshine and warm honey. The tension melts away. "I really hate to bother you, but I'm feeling a little dizzy at the moment. Laila, Tamira, could you please fetch them for me? I'll owe you one."

"Why would I—" At first Tamira opens her mouth to argue, but her expression goes syrupy sweet. "Sure, we could go for a walk." Two beads burst from Sufia and attach onto Laila's and Tamira's bracelets. "Be back soon."

"You're the best." Sufia waves as the two girls walk, relaxed, toward the staircase.

"What did you just do?" I whisper next to Sufia, who continues to smile sweetly.

"Whatever do you mean?" She bats her eyelashes at me, blowing more sunshine and warm, fuzzy feelings my way. Her smile stretches over her face, and she keeps it there until Laila and Tamira are out of earshot.

"That." I nod at Tamira and Laila. "One second they were grilling us, and the next—"

"I'm surprised you hadn't noticed earlier." Sufia drops her smile. The warm fuzzies immediately go away. "The charm."

"The *what*?"

"My power. The happy feeling jinn get when I'm around." Sufia finishes off her bread. "The wow-she's-really-nice-I-want-to-be-her-friend feeling." At that, she gets nervous and picks at her fingers. "I'm sure you felt it the first time we met?"

"I— Actually, yeah." The first time Sufia noticed me was the first time I thought I could belong in the Qaf Mountains. The way she smiled at me, with her sparkling eyes and glossy hair. I gasp. "That's your power?"

"My mother's an enchantress jinn. We're from the Venus king's realm. It's what she does, enchant and charm. She's very influential in the politics of our realm. One day, I'll do what she does," she explains softly. "I'm still trying to get a handle on it, so if I accidentally charm you, it's never intentional. I try to follow the rules, but sometimes, well . . ." She peeks at me nervously through her perfect hair. "It's easier to charm the questions away."

Now Yaseen's reaction around her makes so much sense. I have so many questions. "How—"

"Enough morning chatter!" Professor Jade yells, silencing the entire academy. Standing next to her is an army of professors—including Professor Lilac, Professor Amaranth, Professor Umber, and Coach Celadon. "Until further notice, the academy and its students are under lockdown."

Yaseen sits across the room and shoots us a tense glance. Esen looks equally bothered.

"That's not good," Sufia whispers.

"It's because of them!" Jal, the student from the airhouse, stands up and shouts. He points at Esen and me. "Their realms are putting us in danger!" The other students chatter nervously, throwing dagger glares at us. "Where is the phoenix?! Why is her nest overrun with your nightmare mist?!"

"Yeah, where there's Mars and Saturn, there's trouble!" his friend Hassan chimes in.

"Oh no, no, no." I grip my fists supertight. "This isn't looking good for us."

"No, it's not," Sufia agrees quietly. "And I can't charm the *whole* school to look the other way."

"Settle down," Professor Jade interjects. "It is the duty of the academy, first and foremost, to protect all within it. That means every student, Jal. Not just the ones we like. Our careful society can only thrive when we are working *together*, not against each other. It's the guiding principle of the city, after all, but it's clear the jinn kings have allowed the rifts in their realms to go on for too long.

"As a result, I regret to inform you that a few students have broken a critical rule of the academy and, yes, entered the Realm of Nightmares— Settle down!"

Angry students chatter and move far away from Sufia and me—and Esen. Yaseen is helplessly surrounded by a handful of students whispering in his ear. He frowns.

"To prevent more students from trying to take matters into their own hands, we are on lockdown until the jinn kings resolve this issue. Doing anything else would further fragment the balance between the realms and would have dire *consequences* for anyone who wants to take shortsighted measures."

Sufia and I exchange nervous glances.

"Is that understood?" shouts Professor Jade.

"Yeah . . . ," the students grumble.

"Know that we are always watching," says Professor Jade. "And for the students who breached King Maymun's realm, know how lucky you are to have come back alive." She looks directly at me. I shrink back. "Do not attempt another breach again. With that, you are dismissed."

WE ARE CAREFUL NOT TO BURST INTO THE UNDERCROFT AT the same time.

"Oh, I'm not feeling well all of a sudden. I think I'm going to take a nap." Sufia throws a hand over her face while march-ing through the crowd to her room.

"I suppose I should head to prophecy seminar . . . ," I say, striding to a different staircase, one that is obscure and out of the way. As I turn the corner and race down the plant stairs, I am uncomfortably aware of the many eyes that were glaring at me. *And that's with my disguise.* If I ever thought I could belong here without it, that future has shattered into a million pieces.

I'm not even sure I *want* to belong here anymore. I knew the jinn hated humans, but if they can't even get along with each other . . .

"Took you long enough." Idris appears from a dark spot under the shadow of a statue. "I've been waiting forever. It's creepy in this part of the academy." He looks around. "Where are the others?"

"On their way. It's not great in there," I admit. "Before the rest of the group gets here, we need to talk."

"About?" Idris bristles.

"What we saw in the Otherworld." I glance at him. "You did see . . . something, right?"

"It's a blur, I can't explain it." Idris shudders. "But it was the worst experience of my life. Everything was quiet, which was nice, until the cold hit me and I couldn't move, couldn't breathe, couldn't think."

"I'm sorry," I say quickly. "I should have listened to you when you said you didn't want to use your power. I didn't know—"

"It's fine, Noorzad," he says quietly.

"It's not. I was only thinking of myself and the prophecy and the tree when I should have been thinking about *you*."

He stiffens. "Why me specifically?"

"Because of what I found in the Otherworld. I found—"

"The answer to all our problems, I hope?" Yaseen bursts through the wrought iron gate from the stairwell with his academy jacket flung over his shoulder. Sufia is a few steps behind. "As in, you've figured out how to get our home to stop rotting from the inside out?"

"Um. Not quite." I wait for Yaseen and Sufia to get situated. Yaseen pulls on a barrel and uses it as a chair. Sufia sits on a broken statue. "But hopefully a step to get there." I tell them what I discovered. Not only did I find the phoenix awake in the Otherworld, but I also found the tree. Which means they're both asleep in our world. But the roots of the tree are so expansive, they cross between both realms.

"So the problem is with the roots," mumbles Yaseen. "The imbalance is causing the dream vapor to spill over and leak through into our world, hurting the tree."

"If that's the case, can't we just cut the roots? Separate the link between the two?" asks Sufia.

"I don't think it works that way." I remember Professor Umber's lecture. "Just because we think all the realms are separate doesn't mean that they are."

"But for dream vapor to get through that way . . . it means there's a thinning of the liminal spaces where this realm and the Otherworld overlap . . . ," Idris mutters to himself.

We all look at Idris in surprise.

"It was in your Essence Theory textbook," he says. "I had a lot of time to read—"

"This theory talk is great and all, but unless someone has a practical solution, soon the City of Jewels is gonna look a whole lot different," interrupts Yaseen.

"I think I might know who has the answer," I start slowly. "I think that person is you."

"Me?" Idris looks surprised.

"I think you knew something important that King Maymun didn't want you to know," I say in a rush, "and so as punishment, he ripped it from you with a curse, stole your memories, and hid them in the Otherworld." I explain my prophecy, the connection to the roots, Idris's memories tangled in them.

"*In pieces, chained through mist as cold as ice. In roots, dreams of sons all come undone*," Idris whispers quickly. "You're right. That's the connection. The memory from the scale. The drowning, the chains, the cold—it's what you saw, Noorzad."

"Your curse is the answer to Farrah's prophecy." Yaseen jumps up. "You must have seen something you shouldn't have. . . ."

"Like discovering my uncle is sucking the life out of the tree that keeps our realms alive?" Esen appears at last, with a troubled expression on his face. We all startle in surprise. "Sorry, I was listening in the stairwell. You guys talk really loud, by the way." His wings are tight behind his back. "But my uncle would only do a curse like that if someone got in the way of something he wanted."

"Whoa." Sufia turns to face Idris. "Who are you, mystery man?"

"If I knew that, I don't think I'd be here," retorts Idris.

"So all we need to do is break Idris's curse and pray the answer to fixing the tree is in his memories." Yaseen ties up his hair and claps his hands. "Shaky at best, but it's better than nothing."

"Yeah, but how do we break a curse?" asks Sufia.

"We need something dangerous." I flip my hands and look at my palms. "Something just as dark . . ." My right palm is charred and scratched from when I first tried to break the chain, but my left hand, with the shadow that's extended to the top of my wrist, is fine.

"You mean like *disintegrate an entire conservatory* dangerous?" Sufia says the words I'm thinking.

"That's exactly what I mean." I tighten my hands into fists. "I'll do my part. You guys find another way back into the nightmare realm."

It's time to pay Professor Lilac a visit.

"Professor Lilac! Professor!" I huff and puff as I run across the academy, past the winding halls and up to the seventh floor. "I need your help." I burst into my prophecy seminar room, where Professor Lilac stands solemnly by the window. The stained glass paints rainbows across her.

"I was wondering when you'd find your way here, unusual one." She sighs, keeping her eyes trained on the courtyard outside—now wilting and being flooded with threads of dark mist. "It seems you're running out of time." With that, she opens her palm, and my prophecy orb appears in her hands. It's glowing silver . . . right on track. Then she spins it around, and I notice strands of red appearing from within. Red means failure.

"No, that's not possible!" I race to meet her, nearly toppling over. My hair is in my face, my jacket long forgotten, and my skirt is on backward, but I don't care because I know what I'm supposed to do. "I decoded the prophecy. I know what it wants me to do."

"Have you, now?"

"Yes! All I need is for you to lift the enchantment you put on me. It's my power, whatever it is . . ." I can't explain it, but it's like there's an ocean of pressure in my veins, bursting to be released. "It's the *answer*."

"Is it?" Professor Lilac purses her lips and moves away from the window.

"Yes, I know it." If with a single touch I could turn an entire conservatory to dust, then I could break the chain keeping Idris's memories prisoner. It's worth a shot. "You've just gotta—"

"Set your chaos free?" she asks.

"Chaos?" I frown. "No, it's my power. Remember? It's all about your thoughts. *I'm good. I belong. I can prove it.* This is how I prove it."

I got distracted by the crushing weight of everyone's expectations, but that was before. I can see it so clearly now. I'll save the day. Idris will get his memories back. King Maymun's secret will be exposed, and we can fix the imbalance. And then the realm can focus on rebuilding, getting healthy again. By the time my observation period ends, the City of Jewels will be better than what it was, and my dad will finally see me, apologize for thinking I could ever be a danger to the realms. They'd let me be me, the real Farrah, and not the Mars girl I'm pretending to be. I could start power training to understand my power better. None of it has to be a secret anymore. And it all starts with Professor Lilac.

I hold out my wrists, waiting for the moment Professor Lilac smiles, says, *Brava, you've finally figured it out,* and sets me free.

But she doesn't.

"Oh, unusual one, I wish it didn't have to be this way." Professor Lilac crosses her arms and gives me an apologetic smile. A chill finds its way into the room. I take a step back.

"W-what's going on?"

"I didn't think you'd actually get this far, but somehow, you did." She *tsks* and shakes her head. "You see, I've also discovered something about you. Something I fear the academy cannot control."

"What do you mean?"

"Professor Umber analyzed the 'dust' that was left behind from the conservatory." Professor Lilac brushes her purple lapels on her blazer. "Usually, when things change form, be it from a magical reaction or what have you, there's a little piece of its essence left behind. Meaning even if this whole room was burned to ashes, we could always bring it back to what it once was."

"So you're saying the plants in the conservatory are fixed?"

"I said *usually*, but this 'dust' you created. Those plants were not burned; they were not magically altered—they were completely undone. Unraveled. Permanently and forever gone."

I don't like the way Professor Lilac flies closer to me. Or the way she's backing me out of the room. "But that means I can break the chain!" My power might be the only thing that can lift Idris's curse and save the tree. "I could change the realm!"

"You could change the entire world," Padar's voice whispers behind me. "Which is why we cannot allow you to free that boy."

"Huh?" I spin around on my heel and see my dad standing in the entrance of the classroom. "H-how did you—" I never told my dad about Idris. Not once.

"I told you I was watching." He nods at Professor Lilac, adjusting the rings on his fingers. The bark one glows red. "This has gone on long enough. It's time to pull the plug."

"You can't just stop a prophecy!" I shout, so confused.

Sparkling dust falls down all around me. One second, I see my dad's somber face—blurry, but there. "What about the phoenix, the tree? They're going to wither away and—"

"Nature will always find a way to correct itself," my dad says. "There are worse fates for all of us if you try to get in our way."

"But—" *King Maymun said something similar.*

"I am truly sorry, unusual one, but this is one prophecy we cannot allow you to complete," Professor Lilac says.

And the next second, I see nothing but the dark.

CHAPTER TWENTY–TWO

DO YOU REGRET IT?

I fall into a nightmare.

But this time, it's different from the others.

"I'm home?"

I blink through sweet sunshine as it filters through my curtains and cascades across my floor, highlighting the organized chaos that is my room. My ocean lights blink because I fell asleep with them on, and there's a mess of open books around me. My academy jacket hangs off the back of my chair.

It's my good old normal room. For a second, I sigh happily and snuggle into my comforter. "I'm *home*."

Wait a second. I bolt upright. "Academy uniform?" I blink, and it's not there anymore. *Must just be seeing things.*

There's something on the tip of my tongue. A thought I can't quite grasp. I stare at the spot where the jacket was for a second longer and shake my head. "Just stayed up too late last night." I push my comforter aside and swing my legs over to gently touch the floor. "Oh, I don't feel so great." I stumble a little on my feet. So weird. Maybe I did too much climbing recently.

That's gotta be it.

I was climbing because I was anxious about the summons . . . and moving.

Again, something tickles in the back of my mind.

Wait. "Didn't we move already?" I walk across my room, touch every little thing, from the string of decorated photos of Madar, my grandparents, and Arzu on the wall, to the piles of colored pencils and stacks of climbing gear. There's even my lucky blue chalk bag. *Huh. Must have been a bad dream or something.* I toss the bag in my palm a few times while gingerly going downstairs.

The house is weirdly quiet.

"Madar?" No one in the kitchen. "Bibi jan?" Same with the dining room. "Baba Haji?" The family room is dark, except for the TV screen. *Weird, usually my grandpa is strict about turning off appliances.*

"A strange storm front has moved into the Northeast, affecting Massachusetts, Vermont, New York, Pennsylvania, and counting," a newscaster reads off a script. "An eerie gray smoke from out-of-control wildfires has made its way south and shows no signs of stopping. Let's take a look."

What is going on?

I kneel in front of the TV, my jaw open. The picture changes from a concerned newscaster in a studio to an aerial view of a large forest fire. Huge plumes of smoke cover the whole area. But I squint at the TV. "That's not fire, though. . . ." That looks a lot like—

"If you are near a danger zone, we recommend immediate evacuation from contaminated air. Toxic air has hospitalized hundreds, with many entering what looks like a deep, un-explainable coma state. It almost looks like they're sleeping."

"Dream vapor!" It all comes rushing back to me now.

But what's it doing here?

I told you, little one, Azar says, *that you'd regret it.*

"Regret what?!" I bolt up, panicked. "What's going on?"

Not taking my offer when you had the chance.

"Madar! Baba Haji! Bibi jan!" I pull the front door open and rush out of our house. The door slams into the wall in our little hall, but I don't care because all I can think is *Where is my family?!*

A wave of cool mist hits me in the face. I cough and splutter as I run to the sidewalk, holding my forearm over my mouth. "Where are you guys?!" I run down the street in the direction of Arzu's house.

Arzu!

Of course, they probably all went to her house. All I've gotta do is get there. And everything is gonna be okay. I know it. But the sidewalk stretches, and Arzu's house gets farther and farther away as the mist gets heavier. I can't explain it, but something drops in my belly, and all I can think in this moment is *Arzu, Arzu, Arzu. I've gotta see Arzu.*

"Might be a little late for that." Hura pops up in front of me, nearly obscured in the mist. "Weren't you supposed to meet her for spring break? Wasn't she gonna travel to Long Island to visit you with her brother?"

"Yeah, but I've got time. We haven't gone yet." Right?

Hura shrugs.

Something tinkles on my wrist. A tiny bracelet with a butterfly.

"Forever bracelets," I whisper. *She gave this to me when . . . we moved.*

The second I touch it, the scene changes, and I'm in my khala Fazilat's house. Only, everything's a mess. There's so much smoke. I cover my mouth again. "Madar! Baba Haji! Bibi jan! Arzu! Is anyone here?"

I turn the corner, and that's when I see them.

Sprawled in the living room. All asleep.

"No, no, no!" I rush over to hold them, shake them, anything to—

"Wake up, please wake up!" When I reach for my mom, who is nuzzled in between my grandparents, my fingers slip through her. "This is a dream. It's got to be a bad dream." I try to hug my mom, but I can't. There's a tear that's fallen down her cheek. I try to wipe it but can't. "Why can't I touch them?!" I look across the room, and I see Arzu. "Arzu, come on, you've gotta get up." I crawl to where she's fallen on the floor, but my fingers go through her too. "Don't you know you're invincible? This can't hurt you." I look for her protection charm, but it's not on her. "Where is it? *Where is it?*"

"You mean this?" Hura nudges the glittering pin with her foot. It's a few feet away. The jeweled simurgh glows brilliantly.

"Yes!" I pull my green shirt over my mouth and nose and pick up the pin. Simurgh and butterfly lie in my hand. I can't help but wonder, *Why isn't she wearing it?*

Maybe because someone broke her promise, Azar needles me. *Maybe because her worst fear came true. That her best friend did forget about her.*

"That's not true!" I could never forget about Arzu. After my mom, she's the most important person in my life. "No, I—" I think really hard. If this is a dream, I've got to remember. "I told my mom what happened." That's right—she wrote me a letter back! "She would have told Arzu."

"But *you* never checked on her," Hura says accusingly.

"Ugh. Just stop talking." My head feels like it's gonna burst. "No . . . this can't be real. This is a nightmare. I know it." I crouch down and cradle my head. "A nightmare. A horrible, horrible dream."

"Sometimes dreams can be just that. A dream." Hura kneels gently in front of me. "But don't you know what also lives in dreams?"

I shake my head.

"Visions. Prophecies." She pauses. "The truth."

"No, I don't believe you." I grip the charms so hard, they pinch my palm. This is a dream and it isn't real and everyone I love is safe at home and awake and there is no smoke, no fires, no dream vapor invading the waking world. "It's all just one bad dream!"

This is what the jinn kings want, says Azar. *This is nature correcting itself.*

"What?"

You've seen your father's precious City of Jewels. A magnificent feat of nature, with seven interconnected realms. I daresay, it's a wonderful place to spend eternity. You didn't think that came without a cost, did you?

"What cost?"

"This." Hura spreads her hands wide. "The human world, of course. The Tree of Life can't sustain all that life without *death*. Whenever the jinn kings take too much, nature has to find the balance."

All those environmental disturbances. Pandemics. Floods. Famine. Uncontrollable fires. Azar sneers. *Humans are the price for the kings' immortality. Do you understand now, little one?*

"No, that can't be true." I look back at Arzu. Asleep and peaceful on the rug. "That's not true!" Tears well in my eyes. "That's not what they taught us." If Yaseen and Sufia knew, they'd never stand for it.

No, they wouldn't. Your father would never reveal such a horrific secret to you. It's so much easier to control with lies.

Is this what they meant by upsetting their careful order?

Was this the balance they were talking about?

"I'm so sorry." I fall to my knees and press my face against Arzu's hand. "For being a bad friend." *For being a bad daughter.* I don't want to leave them. I want to stay here forever.

"What if I told you it didn't have to be this way?" Hura lifts my head from the floor and gently reaches for my hand. "What if you could stop this from happening?"

"I'd do it in a heartbeat." I stare Hura down. "Tell me."

"All you need to do is complete your prophecy." She flips my palm so it's up. She eyes the dark spot on my hand. "And accept your truth." She levels me with a stare. "Can you do that?"

"What truth?"

"That it's time to choose all of yourself—even the parts that scare you." Hura takes a long, deep breath, like she's saying goodbye to something precious. Then she places her hands on top of mine. "*Especially* the parts that scare you." Bright light bursts from her palm and transfers into me. It fills the shadow, traveling up my veins, through my wrists, and into every part of my body.

Something shatters along my arms. The thin veil made of clear, sparkling galaxies explodes into a million pieces.

My power returns with a vengeance—the dark, roaring ocean comes flooding back into my ears, building in my chest, threatening to pull me down, down, down.

"This really is the beginning of the end," says Hura, slipping her hands from mine. Without that light in her palm, she becomes more shadow than girl, more imagined than real.

"Of what?"

Wake up and find out, little one.

CHAPTER TWENTY-THREE

WHO ARE YOU?

◆

I wake up in the Room of Revelations. The only light comes from the rows of orbs full of completed prophecies, but it's enough to see I'm not alone.

"I highly advise you to not be here for this, Shamhurish," says the sun king. "It will not be pleasant for you to watch. Already interfering as we've done has caused signs of major disruption to her orb. It won't be long now."

I crack one eye open and see my shimmering orb floating in the Golden King's palm. It's halfway red now with more hairline cracks all around it.

My dad is silent as he stares at it.

"We know what the prophecy means, Shamhurish." The sun king is insistent. "She is a *risk* to everything we have built here." He hears the rustle of my uniform moving and quickly glances my way.

I shut my eyes and pretend to still be asleep. *Please, please don't notice me.* My heart is racing as the silence drags on.

"She is still my daughter," my dad says so quietly.

"And she is still a problem," the sun king snaps. "She will ruin the world we sacrificed so much to create. The balance is already out of sorts with her arrival. The only way we can get back to normal is to allow her prophecy to fail. Maymun will reopen his realm, and the dream vapor will normalize once enough correction has been made in the human realm. Ahmar has even agreed to increase his plague contribution, and all will be well again here. The cycle will be restored, and all will be as it was."

"But the failure of the prophecy? It would mean . . ."

"It would devour her instantly." There are footsteps as someone walks across the marble floor. "And then we could contain her very essence. Can't have it float around the academy. God knows what chaos would come from it."

"*Her.*"

"Her, yes." King Mudhib clears his throat. "Shamhurish, do not waver. Not now."

Unexpectedly, a soft hand passes over my forehead. My dad brushes my bangs from my face. *Don't do this,* I want to yell at him. *Tell him you won't do it!*

There's a commotion out in the hall.

"What is that?" It startles my dad, and immediately, he pulls away.

"The door is locked," Sufia whisper-shouts from somewhere I can't see. A handle jiggles, shaking a door—probably the entrance—as someone else bangs against it.

"We'll just have to knock it down." There's bone crunching and a collective groan. Yaseen. Oh no, I want to tell them to go back, that it's not safe here. "This is"—crunch—"our only"—crunch—"hope!"

"WHAT ARE YOU DOING TO THIS DOOR?" a building spirit shrieks. "THIS ROOM IS OFF-LIMITS TO STUDENTS."

"Of course, the children are another issue to deal with." The sun king sighs. "I hear Maymun's nephew is also involved. She's really created such a mess for us." He sighs again in frustration when there's more yelling in the hall. "They'll be quiet soon with the academy's sleep dust," he says. "When they're subdued, I'll be sure to have Abyad cast a memory wipe. That should tie up any loose ends."

"Is this the only way?" asks my father.

No! There are a million other ways. I can feel a tear forming in the corner of my eye.

"You know the answer, Shamhurish," the sun king responds with finality. "You just don't like it. Tell me this: Does your affection for her outweigh everything we've built?"

My dad's silence is worse than any words the sun king says.

Don't you see, little one? The only love a jinn king harbors is for himself.

I never thought it was possible for parents to break your

heart—annoy, totally, disappoint, sure—but to obliterate it into something that can never become whole again? Flashes of every birthday I've ever had. Padar's smiling face when he taught me how to climb. His warm embrace when he recited stories of impossible things like faeries and dragons and jinn.

Was any of it real?

Was it all just an act?

Let me help you.

What do you want? I squeeze my eyes shut to stop the tears from leaking out.

The same as you, little one. Freedom.

For one second, I wait. I hope that the dad I used to know wakes up, that he's under some terrible spell and he'll pick me up and hug me and say, *I am so, so, so sorry, janem.*

Didn't you learn from the first time? He'll never choose you. Why do you keep giving him a chance he doesn't deserve?

"Fine," my dad whispers. "Before the imbalance goes past the point of no return."

"I knew you'd see reason, Shamhurish," says the sun king in relief.

Help me, I plead. *Help me get out of here.*

And so it shall be, little one. So it shall be.

Something touches my shoulder, and I stiffen. *No, don't let it be one of the kings—*

"On three, run for the arch, Noorzad," Idris whispers. "We'll do the rest."

Who is we? I want to ask. How did Idris get past the sleeping dust? What happened to the others?

Three, two, one, Azar counts down. *Run now, little one. The element of surprise will only grant you one moment.*

I scramble and make a run for it the second Idris reveals himself across the room and shouts, "HEY! YOU'RE A REALLY HORRIBLE DAD!" and starts chucking prophecy orbs at the two jinn kings.

"What the—" My dad turns to look at Idris for a second.

King Mudhib gasps. "It's you—" A shadow with bright red eyes cuts him off by detaching from the floor behind the kings and rises up to envelop them both. *Hura.*

"Get this shadow off me!" roars my dad.

It's all I need. I run like my life depends on it (I mean, it does) toward the Arch of Oracles. It glows an ominous red as my orb floats in the center—more cracks spiderweb along its glass surface—turning the light within it a deep, dark blood red.

"Now what?!" I shriek in terror.

"JUMP IN!" Idris vanishes, but I can hear the *swish, swish, swish* of his pants as he sprints right into the arch. The dark glass ripples, and I see the Otherworld in its reflection with the same girl standing right in the center. Bright vines of light trail up her veins, and when she looks up at me, she smiles, extends a hand, and says, "Ready to change the world?"

"You betcha." I grab her light-struck hand and fall through the arch and into the Otherworld again.

White-hot fire burns through my palm, running up my arms and spreading through my whole body. Bubbles burst and explode as that familiar pressure sits on my heart again. Dark light is emitted from my left palm, sparking out of control.

"Whoa, watch it, Noorzad." Idris swims quickly to the right, narrowly evading a spark.

"I can't help it." The only upside is, it's chasing away the dream vapor trying to put us to sleep. "H-how did you know this would take us to the Otherworld?"

"The arch is another liminal space. The barriers between the realms are thinner here." He floats, squinting out into the darkness. "In the right conditions, you could fall through realms. Whatever part of me is stuck down here, it's been calling to me. I just had to follow the chain." Above and below us are roots, so many roots—gnarled and brittle and pulsing red. In the distance, I can barely see the shadow of the tree and the gold chain holding Idris's memories hostage.

"You learned all that from my textbooks?"

"Actually, it was Hura who told us."

"*What?*"

"When you left and we were trying to find another way in, Hura just appeared," explains Idris. "Scared the pants off Sufia and Esen, but if she hadn't shown up in time, you would have been toast."

"But for that to happen . . ." Azar would have had to command her to warn them before I agreed to accept his help.

I was always going to help you, little one.

Thanks, old fart. Never in a million years did I think I'd be thanking Azar. But never did I think my dad would allow my soul to be devoured. So. First time for everything, I guess.

"Come on, we've got to reach the tree." We swim as fast as we can.

The Otherworld is just like how I left it. The closer we get, the bigger the tree gets. A dark red glow radiates from it, seeping into the dream vapor and staining it red. It looks like it's actually bleeding. Close by, the simurgh is floating in the water. Her bright eyes barely open.

And there, cocooned by vines, is the other Idris, sleeping peacefully.

"Whoa, that's . . . creepy." Idris furrows his brow. "You're saying those are my memories separated from me?"

I nod. "It's time to end this." So I can go home, back to my family and Arzu. My lungs burn as I swim past Idris and make a beeline for that chain. That's the only thing running through my mind. To go home where I belong—with my mom, my grandparents, and my best friend. Where my family will choose me unconditionally. Where I don't have to be good to be seen.

Because if being good here means sacrificing myself for the jinn kings, then let them be afraid of me. I want them to be scared of what I can do.

I want them to know they can't hurt me anymore.

I want my dad to know I no longer choose to save him.

Not anymore.

I choose myself.

Fiery light bursts from every part of me as I grab hold of the chain across Idris's memories and squeeze it tight. I can barely see as my body burns hot—so hot, it hurts. I scream for every betrayal and let the dark light seep in and drown the chain, transforming it and breaking each link by unraveling its very essence until there is nothing left but dust.

When the light dims, the chain is gone, but Idris's memories are still there—still fast asleep.

Did I break the curse?

"What gives?" The shadow on my palm grows bigger, now racing up my forearm, but I don't care to focus on what that means. "Why hasn't anything changed?" I thought there'd be a flash, an explosion, *some* kind of sign to say, *Prophecy completed, yay, now you won't die!*

"There's something. . . ." Idris swims toward himself. "Déjà vu," he whispers. His hand touches the bark of the tree. "I can't explain it, but . . . there's something I know I'm meant to do. . . ." He really stares at his memories, lost in thought. "Meant to wake up . . ."

"What do you mean?"

Instead of answering, Idris does something strange. "Wake . . ." He draws closer to his memory self. "Up." He stays there, quiet for a long time, only muttering those two words, like it's a puzzle. "Trials are for the waking. . . ." When he reaches out to touch his memory self's face, his hands begin to glow. Impossibly, two globs of bright tears start to form in his palms. He gasps. "The phoenix tears . . . They've come back."

"Idris, I think this is it. . . ." I watch, wide-eyed. "You're gonna get your life back."

"Please, please, please . . ." His face lights up with hope as he gently splashes the tears on his memory self's face.

Idris's memories take a deep breath.

Take a breath?

Everything begins to rumble. Then glow.

"Noorzad! It's working. It's—" Idris laughs. "I'm starting to *remember*."

I'm too busy watching the tree light up and pulse faster. It shakes the Otherworld, its roots groaning as it tries to move away. *Away from what?*

The phoenix flaps her great wings and bellows low. She circles restlessly around us.

"Idris . . . something weird is going on." I spin toward him, but it's hard to see him with the current the simurgh is creating. I start to swim closer to him and try to ignore the pit forming in my stomach. *Everything is gonna be okay.* So why isn't Idris smiling? "What's wrong?!"

"I finally remember, Noorzad." It's so hard to hear him. Is it just me, or is he starting to look a little fuzzy at the edges?

"I remember who I am."

"Who are you?!" I shout, panicked. He's starting to fade now, for real. I'm sure of it. "What's going on?"

For a moment, it feels like time pushes pause.

The simurgh is frozen midflight, right before the roots of the Tree of Life extend farther into the Otherworld and break through the rippling surface into the waking world.

For a moment, it's just Idris and me.

A pause in the galaxies that seems to glitter through his body as he slowly becomes less real and more imagined. More ghost than boy.

A moment where he frowns, his eyes all tears, with ink splotching his fingers.

A moment where he says, "Noorzad, this was a mistake."

"Huh?"

"You shouldn't have woken me. That wasn't my memory you unlocked—" The Otherworld screeches, and Idris clutches his head in pain. "That was—ugh—"

And then the moment is over, and in the blink of an eye, Idris vanishes.

"Idris, wait!" *That was what?* I swim toward him, but all that's left is the boy with the dark hair who looks just like my friend. He is solid now, his silhouette no longer fuzzy at the edges. Right when I reach him, the boy's arm begins to move. I freeze.

"Idris?" I ask tentatively. "Is that you?"

The boy opens his eyes. One black. One red.

He narrows them and says, "That's my name." He pauses, appraising me with a cold stare, and asks, "But who are you?"

BEING TOO LATE

Idris had answers.

And everything he ever thought he knew about himself was horribly wrong.

He was not three-quarters jinn and one-fourth human.

In fact, he was not a *jinn* at all.

He knew now that he was something more—he was a dream. A runaway chance at a blank slate to be whoever he wanted to be in the waking world. A fleeting pause away from the pain that rocked his waking self's mind. A mind that had plans for himself, for Noorzad—plans that scared Idris.

But when Idris finally realized it was a blessing, not a curse, to be wiped clean . . .

It was too late.

CHAPTER TWENTY-FOUR

WELCOME TO FREEDOM

"Don't you remember me?" I ask, feeling scared. "Come on, Idris, it's me. Your friend."

A horrible wail comes from the Otherworld. Deep in its depths, there's movement.

"I don't have any friends, especially not from the academy," he sneers. His mismatched eyes study my uniform with disgust before the red eye goes completely white. *Recollection.*

"No, don't—" I cover my head with my hands and brace myself for the pecking into my mind, for the presence that shouldn't be there, messing up all the broken boxes in my head. But there's nothing.

"Oh, I see now." Idris grins broadly, blinking his eyes back to normal. "I see *everything,* and it's perfect."

A shiver runs down my spine, and I slowly back away. Something feels very off about this Idris.

"What do you see?"

"The beginning, of course." He appraises the dark abyss. Somewhere in the bottom, something huge slithers.

"Of what?"

"I think you know the answer to that, *Noorzad*." Idris's black eye never leaves that shadow. *"An endless age, a fate defied. Without its roots, all things shall die."* He grins so wide, it could split his face in two.

Red alert.

"But should the end come rear its head, there will be more than kingdoms dead." Idris extends a hand to the shadowy figure as it slithers closer and closer. *"They will be—the beginning of the end."* It's bigger than any creature I've seen before. I can see its onyx scales glinting as it swishes past my feet, moving closer, then away. "It's a clever prophecy—I'll give the arch that much."

"H-how is it clever?" I suddenly realize I'm trapped with nowhere to go, with a boy I don't know anything about, and that makes me very afraid.

"Because it's very much in step with mine," he says nonchalantly.

"*You* have a prophecy?"

Sirens sound from above, probably out somewhere in the realm.

A waking soul that does not belong, they scream. *A waking soul that does not belong.*

Four kabus dive into the Otherworld, followed by a fifth figure with enormous wings that just keep getting bigger and bigger, with teeth getting sharper and sharper. He looks like a winged nightmare. *King Maymun.*

"What did I tell you about trespassing?" The jinn king's voice vibrates the dream vapor, causing it to grow larger, like a net heading toward its target.

"I'd tell you all about it, but it seems we have company." Idris sighs just as the giant serpent bumps up against his leg. "King Maymun has always been my second-least-favorite king." Its luminous yellow eyes are two flashlights in the dark. It hisses angrily when Idris hops on. He extends a hand out to me. "Well, are you gonna hop on, or are you gonna stare all day?"

"W-why are you helping me?"

"Because you helped me?" He raises an eyebrow. "If it weren't for you and that escaped other me, I suppose I would have been cursed here forever."

"Other you?" Light flares from my left hand again, but I keep my fist shut. "Was Idris—my Idris—*real?*"

"I mean, I had to signal for help somehow in this eternal hellscape." The giant serpent makes one more loop around me, bringing Idris uncomfortably close. "But don't get too bent out of shape about it. He was never meant to last forever. And now that his purpose is gone, so is he."

Idris is gone.

"So, not to be insensitive, but are you coming or what?"

It's either this new Idris or King Maymun who'll drag

me back to the academy to the other jinn kings who were ready for me to be devoured by my prophecy.

You better not make me regret this, I think to Azar.

"Let's go." I take Idris's hand and slide on behind him.

"Hold on, it's gonna be a bumpy ride out of here." The serpent is *fast.* I can barely hold on to Idris, who seems to know each kabus's attack before it happens. "Here comes the fun part. See that weak spot in the barrier? I need you to unravel it. Now."

"I can't—" Everything happens too fast. I throw my hands out, the pressure inside me roaring to life right when we hit the barrier.

And then everything goes black.

"Ugh."

I have the worst headache of my life.

"I feel like I got hit by a truck."

"It was an Otherworld barrier, actually," Idris calls out.

That's right. My whole body feels so heavy—and everything is so hard to move.

"I didn't have much warning," I groan, and blink my eyes open. "Not like I can just turn stuff to dust on command." I can barely get my power in control under normal circumstances. There's no way I can unleash it under a ticking clock.

"That's okay. After this, you'll have time to control your unraveling."

"After this?" I get up woozily. I bump into the massive onyx serpent circling the room. "Where are we?"

Idris flicks his dark bangs out of his eyes and glances back at me. "Academy education is slipping these days, huh? This is the consciousness of the nightmare realm." He shrugs. "I like to call it *the brain.*"

It doesn't look like a brain—unless brains resemble an open galaxy embedded into the floor. Then maybe it could. Bright purples, blues, and streaks of white glitter between the tiles. But even more interesting are the walls, if you can call them that. They sparkle with a pulsing network of vine-like synapses, stretching and branching out, just like a tree.

"Why is this giving me mad-scientist-evil-lair vibes?" I walk over to a window and notice we're on the top floor of King Maymun's castle. The Realm of Nightmares stretches out endlessly—an infinite horizon of floating cities—all glowing an ominous dark red. It would be pretty if, you know, its king wasn't out to get me. I can barely hear the sirens from up here.

The serpent hisses at me when I reach out to touch one of the glowing vines.

"Wouldn't do that if I were you." Idris moves calmly, precisely. He taps different parts of the growing vines, searching for something until he says, "There you are."

In the center of the room, the floor hisses, and the tiles

fall away to reveal a bubbling white fog. A large silvery stone floats up. It pulses gently, kinda like it's breathing.

"Idris . . . this might be a silly question." I hesitate. "But why are we here?"

"I'm . . . returning a favor." He is bewitched by the stone. Gently, he cups it in the palm of his hand.

A waking soul that does not belong, the alarm blares here now. The control room shakes violently. The snake's giant head snaps alert.

"Now." He mutters to the snake. He's not fazed at all. One eye is completely white, caught up in recollection as he keeps his focus on the stone. The serpent rushes out of the chamber, slinks down a hallway, and disappears.

"Um. What favor?" A heavy weight drops in the pit of my stomach.

"Of what the jinn kings did to me," he says simply. "I'm giving them a taste of their own medicine. I'm sure you know what that's like."

"You mean, something like a curse?"

Instead of answering, Idris pulls a jeweled pen out of his pocket. "A drop of ink to signify the recording of time." He pops the top off and tilts it so slightly. One drop falls on the stone. It hisses, changing color from white to dark gray. The color pulses out through the whole room, lighting up seven specific vines, each a different color. They match the seven gem colors in the ring of fate—quartz white, ruby red, emerald green, amethyst purple, carnelian yellow, pearl gray, and sapphire blue. "A white hair." Idris picks a lone white strand that was stuck to my shirt. "Courtesy of *your* Idris. For a life extended but now gone." He drops the hair. It crumbles into nothing. There's a shimmer I can barely see.

There, but not there. It swirls above the stone.

"And the last piece . . ." Idris's black eye bores into me. "Is you."

"Me?" I startle, but at the same time, I can't help but move closer to the stone. It's like it's calling to me.

"I need that." He points at my forever bracelet.

"Why?" I quickly cover it with my sleeve.

"A promise broken, of course." He nods knowingly—his right eye is still recollecting. I wonder what he sees. "Forever interrupted. It's the last piece."

"For what?"

"My curse," he snaps testily.

"Why would I give you my bracelet to make a curse?"

"Because." He rolls his eyes, annoyed that he has to explain this. "It serves what we both want."

None of Idris's words make sense. I have no idea what he wants. But as worst-case scenarios shuffle like a slideshow in my mind, the pressure is pulsing, pulsing, pulsing in my chest. *Did I make a mistake?* Images of Arzu, unconscious in a hazy mist, flood my brain. My mom on the couch with my grandparents, holding my broken protection pin, forever waiting for her sunshine to return. The pressure is too much.

Can't breathe. Need air. I am drowning in the ocean of my worries, in the big gaping hole that's burrowed in my heart.

Dark energy bubbles in my veins—the unraveling is seeping out of my hands. *Red alert. Red alert.*

"Relax." Idris does something unexpected—he takes hold of my palms.

"Stop, I'm going to hurt you."

"No, you won't." Idris squeezes gently. "All you need to do is take a breath. *You* control the ocean inside. It doesn't control you."

How . . . does he know that?

"Control it, and you'll be fine."

I take one deep breath.

"Good."

And another. The pressure subsides, and the darkness goes away.

"Everything's gonna be okay, Noorzad" slips from his mouth.

I stare up at Idris—familiar but not—and wish so badly for my friend.

"You don't trust me. With my power, most don't," he says plainly, "but that's fine. I'm not asking for that. I forget that you don't see what I see." He doesn't let go of my hands. "So let me show you." Both of his eyes go blazing white, and the strangest thing happens.

The room shifts, and I feel myself fall into a river . . . of time. I'm in his head. The room is hazy—like I'm there but also somewhere else. "Is this . . . recollection?"

"I don't like letting people into my head, but since time is of the essence"—Idris appears suddenly, and he walks along the river of his mind with me—"let me show you my truth, and then I'll let you decide."

And with that, he grabs hold of my arm, and we jump into the river.

———◆———

We emerge in a memory.

At least, that's what I think it is. There's a blurred cast over the room, but I can tell we're in the Room of Revelations. Standing in front of the Arch of Oracles is a nervous Idris. Dark hair trimmed and as neat as a pin. Clothes clean but old. The only thing that feels familiar is the fact that his hands are covered in ink. He's holding a glowing orb in his hand.

The arch is illuminated, with bright words revealing:

In the realm unseen
There live among the in-between
Of dying day and triumphant night
Seven kings who reign in eternal life

But with all magic comes a price
In pieces, chained through mist as cold as ice

In roots, dreams of sons all come undone
In wait for the half-blood chosen one

"Father?" Idris calls out. "W-what does this mean?"

"Nothing good," a familiar voice growls. "And do not call me *Father*."

"In wait for the *half-blood* chosen one . . ." I gasp. "Wait, that's . . . Is that meant to be me?"

Then something odd happens. My prophecy floats in, to fill in the rest.

An endless age, a fate defied
Without its roots, all things shall die
But should the end come rear its head,
There will be more than kingdoms dead

"*They will be—the beginning of the end,*" I whisper. *Was Yaseen right?* "Are our prophecies linked?" Two halves of a whole? I run toward Idris when the words peel away from the arch and slip into the orb, but shadows cover the scene, and he is gone.

THE MEMORY CHANGES.

It is the middle of the night, and there are voices, too many voices, and Idris is walking quickly, covering his ears.

Can you believe it, a secret son and a prophecy?

The king must be mortified. Have you seen those eyes? I would have kept him hidden too.

And there's something more. I hear there's something not quite right . . . in that head of his.

Something that father of his should be afraid of.

Idris moves so fast, I can barely reach him. My footsteps ripple in the moment. "Wait up!"

But the scene shifts again, with Idris running and muttering, "I know his secret. He should be afraid." He turns the corner, just when shadows fall on him, and he screams a bloodcurdling scream.

A HAND YANKS ME OUT OF THE RIVER.

"That—was—horrible. . . ." I cough and sputter on my hands and knees. "I *never* want to do that again."

"You get used to it." Idris shrugs as he wades through the river again. He's scanning the depths for something else.

"You didn't tell me my prophecy completed yours." I shake water from my bangs and scramble to keep up with him. I don't want to get lost in his head. No thank you. "You didn't—"

"Mention that we found out the same secret?" Idris turns around and stares at me blankly. There is a flicker of that same ocean of sadness in his eyes, but when he blinks, it's replaced with anger and steel. "Mention that once they knew we knew they weren't true immortals, they decided to intervene to keep *their precious order?* Hoard all the life for themselves and let others who aren't like them suffer?"

So what Azar told me in my dream was true.

And because Idris is part human, of course he wouldn't agree with their nature-correcting-itself plan—not when the collateral could be someone he loves. It all clicks into place.

"You're trying to stop the kings. . . . That's why you want to do a curse," I say softly.

"Why *we* must do the curse," he corrects me. "Don't you see? The kings think they can bend fate to their wills, but destiny finds a way. They thought they interrupted my prophecy, but they can't see what I see—that all of this is meant to be—*we* are meant to do something about it!"

"But what will the curse do?"

"I'll show you." And again, Idris and I plunge into the river.

I am back in Long Island.

The sun twinkles in a cloudless sky, with rainbows splaying every which way across my aunt's house. It's springtime, just warm enough to not need a jacket. There's music coming from the backyard, and so many cars are parked in the driveway.

"Don't forget the hamburger buns. These burgers are

sizzling fast," my mom calls out from the backyard. Smoke wafts up from the grill she's cooking on—a big smile is plastered on her face.

"This is why you should bring a plate out to set them on when they're done," my grandmother complains as she rushes through the glass doors into the house. "Instead of making an old woman hurry," she grumbles.

"Could I have two patties on mine, please?" Arzu peeks her head out from a deep lawn chair she's sitting on. Her brother clears his throat in the seat next to her, and she makes a face at him. "Ugh, and I guess the same for Amir too."

I stand, shell-shocked. "Everything is—everyone's—" *Safe*. I take a tentative step, too afraid to move in case I blink and miss them. My heart is pounding in my chest, and all my mind is telling me to do is *run to them now!* "Is it real?" I ask Idris when he appears next to me.

"It can be," he says back. "But only if you're ready to change the world with me."

The forever bracelet. I fiddle with it on my wrist. "But what would the curse do to . . . our dads?" My eyes water because this vision is an absolute dream.

"Make them what they should have been all along," Idris answers. "Mortal."

Well, that doesn't seem *too* bad. . . .

"Farrah, there you are," Madar calls out to me. She's waving a metal spatula. "I've got your burger ready to go. Come on, bring your friend too. There's plenty to go around."

"Yeah, stop hogging all the time with *my* best friend." Arzu jumps out of her seat and races toward me. She throws her arm protectively over my shoulders and playfully glares at Idris. "Though I have to say, your hair is much better this way."

"Thanks." He smiles awkwardly.

"I'm sure Farrah loves the new look too." Arzu winks, and my cheeks flush in embarrassment. "I'm just teasing, and anyway—" Suddenly, the ground shakes violently. Arzu and I topple over onto the grass. "What was *that*?"

"There's not much time left, Farrah," Idris whispers, helping me up. "It's now or never."

"Time for what?" Arzu brushes grass off her jeans. "Oh no, stained? I just got these pants."

"You know you're my best friend in the whole world, right?" I say abruptly, trying to fight back tears. Because I don't want to leave, but the scene is fading again. I look at my mom. "And you know I'd do absolutely anything for you too, Madar." Even if she puts a little too much weight on my shoulders. "I would do anything—" *Including curse a realm.*

Arzu's eyebrows scrunch up. "Why are you being so weird?"

"We're out of time," Idris whispers in my ear, and as quickly as we arrived, we are yanked out of the river of recollection and back into the nightmare realm.

A WAKING SOUL THAT DOES NOT BELONG. THE ALARMS ARE blaring so loud, it's bursting my head in two. *A waking soul that does not belong.*

King Maymun's castle keeps shaking as the snake below is fighting whoever is trying to reach us in the consciousness.

"Well?" Idris extends his hand. The stone in front of us is pulsing gray. "Are you ready to do the impossible? Are you ready to change the world?"

I hesitate when my dad's words come back to me. *There are worse fates for all of us if you try to get in our way.* But I can't think of anything worse than what I saw in my nightmare.

My whole life, my dad filled my head with impossible things—like phoenixes and faeries and dragons and jinn. He made me think if I was invincible—the smartest, fastest, strongest—nothing could touch me. Not the bruised part of my heart that was poked and prodded on every birthday. Not the endless weight of my mom's sadness and disappointment at putting her life on hold for me. Not the divide between us and my mom's family. Not *the rules* and *you know how it is* and *one day when you're older, you'll understand.*

He used to make me think if I was good, I could change my fate.

If I was good, I could prove I was worthy of his love, time, and attention.

If I was good, I could fill the boxes full of tough emotions and pack them away.

If I was good, I could be *loved.*

If I was good, I could be *seen.*

If I was good, I could *belong.*

If I was good—

If I was—

If I—

If—

Now as I fiddle with my forever bracelet, I think there's something nice about erasing all of that. Unraveling the *if* from its DNA and letting it blow away into the wind as dust—insignificant and irrelevant dust.

I *was* good. My father was just too blind to see it. But he'll see this—I'll make sure of it.

"Let's change the world." I rip the bracelet off and hand it to Idris.

You've finally embraced your truth, little one.

Welcome to freedom.

"You have to do it." Idris shakes his head and gives it back to me. "A promise broken. Forever interrupted. You have to unravel it into the stone. It'll filter through the consciousness and send the curse right to the kings through these vines."

Holding my bracelet, I blink at the golden butterfly, and slowly, I let the ocean of pressure in and feel the weight of it. Feel the weight of what this bracelet means to me. I glance at Idris. "This curse will only go to the kings?"

Idris nods.

"Okay." I let the word rush from my lips. Gripping my

bracelet, I take a second to say goodbye to the girl I was when Arzu first gave it to me—all that weight, all that pressure. And then I unravel it. From my fingers, my power erupts, wrapping its energy around the delicate golden links, and breaks them one by one—until the bracelet is nothing but dust. "To a new beginning," I whisper as it is absorbed by the stone. "To a new me." It pulses a deep scarlet and travels up the seven vines, changing their vibrant colors to one burning red.

Idris looks at me and agrees. "A new beginning indeed."

I close my eyes because I can see it now—that bright new world where I can be me, without any illusions or perfume.

I can see that sunny afternoon. My mom, grilling and happy. Arzu, bickering with her brother and waiting to tell me every detail. My academy jacket slung over my shoulder, filled with notes from Yaseen and Sufia, updating me on the new and improved City of Jewels—healthy and whole and thriving. The living sanctuary no longer in trouble. All seven realms fully in balance. The kings forced to be just like everyone else—mortal and limited.

And maybe, without all that infinite lifespan, a little more human, a little more understanding.

I hold on to that image. My home, where I don't have to choose anymore.

Where I'm accepted as both human and jinn.

My home, which is perfect and safe and alive.

"Ready to get out of here?" Idris interrupts my thoughts.

I open my eyes and smile.

Because Professor Lilac was right.

My prophecy is going to change the world.

And I can't wait to get out of here and see it.

ACKNOWLEDGMENTS

It's a dream come true to have another installment of Farrah's story out in the world. Sometimes, I have to pinch myself to make sure it's real, and I feel so blessed and thankful to the team behind the making of Farrah Noorzad.

Special thanks to my agent, Elana Roth Parker, who has championed me and my career since 2017. Thank you for being there for me during an especially tough year. Second book syndrome is real, and I wouldn't have made it to the finish line without your support and check-ins.

To super editor duo Liesa Abrams and Emily Shapiro, I am so thankful for your patience and grace through the editorial process on this one. In so many ways, this was a book of firsts—first sequel, first year following a slew of personal losses, first year figuring out a new normal—and I am so lucky to have had an editorial team that worked with me through surviving the nightmare of so many firsts.

To the incredible team at Labyrinth Road and RHCB—Katrina Damkoehler, Rebecca Vitkus, Clare Perret, Michelle Canoni, Natalia Dextre, Catherine O'Mara, Michelle Campbell, and Sarah Lawrenson—thank you for all you do in creating books for young people. Each book is a light in the dark, and I am so grateful to be a part of RHCB's legacy.

As always, thank you to my mother and my brother for your love and support.

And lastly, thank you, dear reader, for your continued support of Farrah and the crew! I wouldn't be able to do what I do without you, so thank you for joining the ride. It's been the joy of my life writing this series for you.

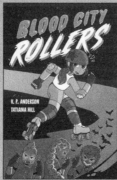

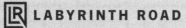